Breaking Möbius

T.R. Horne

YOSHIMA BOOKS

T.R. Horne

Printed in the United States of America

First Printing, 2013

ISBN-13: 978-0-9911063-0-1

ISBN-10: 0-9911063-0-X

Ordering Information:

Quantity sales. Special discounts are available on quantity purchases by corporations, associations, and others. For details, inquire at the website below.

Yoshima Books

www.trhorne.com

Book Design by Yoshima Books

Cover Design by Jelena Cedic

T.R. Horne

For my Sweetie Pie for giving me inspiration to do great things with my life.

Breaking Möbius

A Möbius strip is similar to life as it has only one surface - one boundary, but to break it is to free yourself from a never-ending cycle.

∞

The Bond

∞

Mali Struthers

∞

I've never been the type of girl to really miss home. As a small child, I never ran into my mom's arms after a weekend away or scrambled to hang on my dad's leg when he returned from working at the shipyard. Our tiny home looked as though it would crumble if leaned against, with its weather-beaten shingles lifting at the edges. It was a sad structure that looked on the outside how the occupants felt on the inside. The inside of our home was constantly filled with yelling, loud slaps and tears, so as a child I figured there wasn't much to miss. The Greyhound bus was filled with coughing old people and whining babies, reminding me that home was fading farther into the distance, like the taillights on a car. Leaving this town gave me a faint sense of sadness. I was leaving all I ever knew.

I'd developed a love of dancing with a group of young, talentless girls thrown together on the weekends by parents that cared about tutus and ballet slippers more than their daughters' dancing skills. I stayed away from home by staying at school when the dance studio was closed to stragglers. I didn't want to alert anyone to my alcoholic dad so eventually I stopped hiding out at school and tried to stay in the local library, pretending to read, when in actuality I was just enjoying the quiet. My time spent at home was filled with memories of my mother's battered face usually hidden behind caked-on makeup. She excused broken bones as "accidents" to those who cared enough to ask. I stayed quiet, fearful that the occasional slaps across the face from my father would eventually turn into brutal punches like hers had. The dance studio was a place where I could transform into something beautiful and graceful, a place to forget the pain waiting for me at home. Now when I think of home, I think of dance, not my dysfunctional gift from God called a family.

I cried tears of freedom when I graduated from high school and Mrs. Tomball, my dance instructor, told me to "go out into the world and do something great." I felt the fear of failure cave in on me when she spoke those words. The potholed streets of Bremerton and the green vines that stretched across our bungalow were all I'd ever known. Yet I didn't cry when I left my mother standing in the bus terminal, tears dripping down her sagging eyes with years of abuse, making the skin loose and darkened. Her pathetic eyes screamed *Don't leave me behind*. I had the courage to leave even if she hadn't in her eighteen years of marriage to a man overcome by evil. I hated goodbyes as much as homecomings so Mom wasn't surprised when I kept the goodbye short before getting on the bus.

"Be safe, Mom," I'd said as I straightened the thin sweater on her shoulder.

It was August in Washington but sweaters hid her scars all year round.

"I will, Mali. Will you?" She said my name with her Spanish accent, visually criticizing my outfit.

I wore tattered jeans with holes in both knees and a white V-neck T-shirt that had *Leave Me Alone* scrolled in gold script across the chest. My wild, curly hair licked toward the sky as if to taste the mist carried by the morning breeze. I guessed my mother took my T-shirt as a warning because she didn't comment on my clothes as she normally would have.

"I will, Mom. I'll call you when I get settled."

I could feel her chunky arms squeezing my ribs and tried to wrest free of her grip.

"Okay, Mom. I'll see you later."

I pulled her arms away and gripped her warm hands in front of us.

"Love you, Mali."

"I know."

I backed away so she wouldn't hug me again. She'd try to stuff me in her gray Corolla and speed back home if I waited any longer. I'd made it to the door of the bus before I faintly heard, "Please don't go…"

I raced up the steep bus steps before she could start her crying antics. My mother badgered me with months of discussions-turned-begging sessions to stay with her in Bremerton after finding out I was going away to college. I knew the real reason she didn't want me to go—she didn't want to be alone with Dad. Hell, no one wanted to be alone with Dad. I wasn't going to pass up my big chance to finally get away from his manipulation and abuse. If she'd been strong enough to leave on her own a lot earlier it would've saved us both some heartache and headaches.

The early morning dew had just settled on the grass surrounding the bus station and a young, skinny girl with thin bleached-blond hair kissed her boyfriend at the door to the bus. The kiss seemed to get deeper and longer as we waited patiently to pull out of the terminal on time. The bus driver, impatient with the minutes ticking by, began closing the door to rush them from their disgusting tongue kiss. Luckily, his technique worked and we were one step closer to leaving Bremerton in a haze of engine exhaust. After everyone, including bleached-blonde's boy toy, had taken their seats, the bus rumbled to a start. Outside the window, the sun was just rising over the tops of the tallest buildings in downtown Bremerton. I watched my mom's lip quiver gently as she pushed her mess of loose curls from her wet eyes and pulled her sweater tight around her. I sunk lower in my seat, hiding from her teary eyes.

My mother was a strong Mexican woman before my dad met her in Texas while on military assignment to Fort Hood. She'd worked in my grandpa's grocery store and provided for herself and her little sister, Dalia, before Dad completely swept her off her feet and carried her on exciting excursions around the world. Not too long after their shotgun marriage, my mother became pregnant with me. That's when things changed. I have very little memory of all the happy pictures she'd show me in our photo album. Pictures of me with my dad, minus the potbelly overlapping his dirty workpants and cottony salt-and-pepper hair, smiling down at my tiny body against his chest. Pictures of me kissing my mom's cheek while she laughed playfully at the beach. Too bad the world I lived in was nothing like those pictures. My mom had so much life in her big, brown eyes in those photographs. The light faded into a dull lifelessness when my dad deployed to war and returned a year later a different man. A man full of anger and aggression emerged overnight. To ease his transition, he found the sweet whispers of escape at the bottom of a liquor bottle. To this day, as she stood swaying softly on the sidewalk, Mom had never given up hope that the man she married would return one day and sweep her off her feet again. She was a fool to believe after so long.

My mother stared at me through the bus window with those eerie, dark eyes without breaking her gaze. I wondered if she was daydreaming or if she was trying to send me a telepathic message. If she had that power, I would have declined delivery. I already knew everything she wanted to say. All the apologies and promises of change couldn't make me stay home. I was ready to leave behind the fear of my father and find my own happiness. The bus grumbled passed her as she stood on the sidewalk with other people waving their loved ones away. She raised a single hand as the bus floated by. I put my hand to the window and waved one last goodbye.

The bus rounded the corner onto 11th Street and straightened to merge onto Route 310. Traffic started to collapse around the oversized bus as we pushed toward the highway. I looked out at the big, blue star of Doobey's restaurant slowly rotating high on its axle. Bremerton, Washington, was a beautiful city but Doobey's made it truly lovely. Doobey's was the home of the original hot chili dog. It was always fun to sit in a corner and watch adults try to tackle the hottest hot dog this side of the Mason-Dixon line. No one ever made it past the halfway point of the foot-long dog. They usually just ended up sucking down ice-cold milk and grabbing cheap napkins to dab at the constant flow of snot and tears.

My one true friend was and still is Jacinta Mack, even though she stopped speaking to me. Jacinta was a year ahead in school and had chosen to go a few states over to a school in Idaho to follow her high school boyfriend. She ended up dating a too-tall-for-her-tiny-frame, boyish Shannon Miller her last year of high school. Ironically, he happened to be Washington's best basketball player over the past ten years. I didn't think that was saying much, since his stats were only average when compared to players around the nation. Even still, he received a full scholarship to a pretty decent university and was officially treated like utter royalty around Bremerton from the time he signed his letter of intent. Shannon Miller was not drop-dead gorgeous by any means. On the contrary, he was oddly shaped with long arms and legs that made up his six-seven frame and a huge smile like a three-year-old. Even with all his oddities, he'd happened to bag my diamond of a friend, Jacinta. I never understood what Mack saw in him since he couldn't carry on a grown-up conversation, much less satisfy the romantic side of their relationship. I snickered to myself, remembering Jacinta's story of their first kiss. She was deflated of enthusiasm as she explained how awkward and weird it felt when they were alone. She figured she'd lead the hunt by grabbing his face and planting a passionate kiss on him. After forcing his placid tongue from her mouth after one too many attempts, she figured she'd be patient in the romance department. After that kiss, he'd proclaimed to his friends she was his girlfriend and, like a love story made for television, they fell into the sappiest puppy-dog love ever.

Mack and I were slowly fading away the longer she stayed out of Bremerton and remained tucked under Shannon's looming success. Jacinta Mack loved the attention she received in college for being with Shannon. All the girls envied her, some tried to befriend her and all the while she maintained her front-row seat at all his games. Within weeks of the start of basketball season, all her phone calls were about Shannon's success and Shannon's television clips. I was at my wit's end hearing about Shannon and his continued success in basketball, and I told Mack, in no uncertain terms, that she needed to get her own life.

"All you ever talk about is Shannon. Geez, Mack," I said when she had taken a breath between stories.

"No, I don't. I talk about school all the time." I could tell she was taken off guard.

"I can't even tell you what classes you're taking or what your major is. But guess what? I can tell you Shannon's stats for the last five games!" I tried to squelch my irritation.

"Well, if you don't want to listen to what's going on in my relationship or with me at school then maybe you should stop calling and asking!" Mack was trying to contain her anger but it was spilling over like hot lava.

"I didn't call you." It cut like a knife.

The phone fell silent but I could still hear Mack breathing deeply, trying to calm down. I could envision her round eyes red with anger.

"Well, in that case," she started slowly, "forget I ever called you. I have homework to do for *biology* class since I'm a *biology major…*" Click.

The phone went dead.

That was three weeks ago and she hadn't returned any of my calls or messages. Why did I even bother? I should have just listened to her infinite stories of Shannon's success and still had my best friend. On her voice mail, I promised her that I'd call her again when I got to Atlanta University.

I'd chosen the farthest school from my family. I'd studied dance in a small studio next to the local pottery store but I yearned to learn on a much higher level than Bremerton could offer. I envisioned myself on the big stage one day, maybe Broadway or the Las Vegas strip leaping and spinning through contemporary choreography.

Atlanta, Georgia, was the first, and only, choice since my parents' lack of money couldn't get me into the more prestigious dance schools. Atlanta was becoming the hip-hop music, music video and production studio mecca. I'd work my way up the chain. I'd have opportunities to audition, work on my craft and start a new life in Atlanta. It didn't hurt that Atlanta University offered me a dance scholarship to study under famed dancer, director and choreographer Rochelle Della-Rose. The scholarship was my only chance to go to college since my dad made it very clear that he wasn't paying for school so I could "waste his money partying all the damn time." I wasn't completely sure I even knew how to have a good time. I never attended homecoming or the prom in high school, so I wasn't sure why he thought I was so hell-bent on partying. Of course, I'd never tell him that. I wasn't about to poke that angry bull.

Needless to say, I was excited to leave the bleakness of Washington and enter a new world in sunny Atlanta, Georgia. The bus reached its full cruising speed on the interstate. I kicked off my shoes, leaned my head against the cool glass of the bus window and slid on my headphones. Soon, Adele's throaty voice streamed through the earbuds, made my eyes softly close and the constant rhythm of the bus soothed me into daydreams. Atlanta University seemed like a place where all my dreams could come true. A place where I could be whoever I wanted to be. I had three days on this Greyhound bus to figure out who I wanted to be and how I was going to start fresh.

Justice Bradford

∞

I had to be the luckiest guy on Earth. I was handsome, muscular and a star athlete. Not to mention, the finest girl at Atlanta University was my woman. I glanced at her naked back partially hidden by the sheets and touched her black hair that fell in soft waves against the pillowcase. I could smell the sweet scent of jasmine on her skin. I shook my head, knowing I'd smell that scent for days in my apartment. I had fallen in love with Nicole Bunn in high school. She had my heart the day she strutted into geometry class like a celebrity diva in a skintight miniskirt, black leggings and leather boots that tied up to her knees. She clutched her textbook over breasts that poked through the stretchy pink shirt and made my young loins squirm in my seat. Her face was like an angel with big, round hazel eyes and pouty, full lips. I swear I sat there staring at the back of her head as she sat in front of me, memorizing each strand of her long hair as she flipped it from one shoulder to the other. I was in awe that a goddess was sitting so close to me. Close enough to touch. I smelled the same sweet scent of jasmine and vanilla wafting from her hair back then. By the end of class, I had already thought of a strategy to get Nicole to be my girlfriend. That was nearly six years ago.

After using the bathroom, I slid between the sheets with Nicole and nudged myself closer to her firm bottom. It was only 5:23 a.m., so we had a few hours before I needed to be at weight training and she had to be in the studio. I inhaled the scent of her hair and wrapped my chiseled arms around her modest waist. She pushed her bottom closer until every inch of her body, from her feet to her shoulders, molded into me. I was still infatuated with this woman after six years.

Nicole and I stayed together through junior and senior years of high school. It wasn't easy, though. Our senior year was full of arguments about our relationship and whether we would stay together while we were in college. Nicole had her sights set on acting in New York while I was going to play football on a full scholarship at Atlanta University. My mother sat me down after I accepted my football scholarship to AU to talk to me about Nicole.

"You should be free for a while, Justice," she said as she placed her tiny hand on my shoulder. We were huddled closely in the formal living room of our home in Florida.

"Mom, I'm in love with Nicole. I don't want to be free," I reasoned.

She nodded her head slightly before patting my knee. "You are becoming a man now. You'll have to learn your own lessons about life and real love."

At the time, I was sure she was scared I'd get Nicole pregnant if we didn't have her watchful eye on us while at school. But now, I think she just wanted to make sure I was truly happy. She wasn't a huge fan of Nicole and our relationship but I figured she was being a normal protective mom. No mother wanted to see their son cherish another woman and leave home, I suppose. I tried to explain to her that Nicole was focused beyond any female I'd ever known. She was in modeling campaigns almost every weekend and in acting classes after school on weekdays. So I rarely had the chance to fully indulge physically with Nicole unless it was sneaking into her parents' shed late at night for a quickie. Momma didn't raise no fool, so we always used protection.

Still, the biggest issue was whether splitting up during the summer before freshman year of college was the right thing to do.

Nicole was accepted to a school in New York to pursue acting and since she was adopted, she received a special grant for college. She'd saved all her money from her modeling campaigns to help with the tuition. Her adoptive parents were gracious enough to fill out the state and financial aid forms which ensured she could afford to go to NYU under the minority student achievement program. Under the watchful eye of onlookers, I was happy she was going to live her dream, but internally, I was broken up over possibly losing the only girl I'd ever loved. After realizing my future was indeed leading me to Atlanta University, she surprised me and asked to meet me at her parents' shed to talk. I went to the shed, somber, knowing on the inside that it was the end of our relationship.

"Come on in."

She held the shed door open, just enough for me to squeeze through. The door clapped the seams of the shed as she sat on the front of the old, rusted-out Buick that hadn't moved in years.

"How are you?" I quizzed, trying to gauge her aura.

"I'm good."

"Well, you said you needed to talk. I'm here."

I scooted next to her, covering the headlight of the old car.

"Justice, do you really, really love me?" she said in a whisper.

"Of course I do. Why would you ask that?"

"Because I want to tell you something. Something I've been scared to tell you for a long time."

She was twisting the hem of her tank top, ringing it like a rag.

"Why are you scared? You can tell me anything."

"Justice, you don't understand how hard it is to…" she swallowed, "…be vulnerable."

I wrapped my arm around her rigid shoulder. I couldn't stand her being scared. "You know you can tell me anything, Nicole. I'll understand."

She began slowly. "You know about my mom and dad passing away. You know that I don't have anyone. So it makes it hard to trust."

"Nicole, you can trust me. I'd never…" She pushed her finger to my lips.

It was the first time I'd seen her eyes look like porcelain buttons as she struggled to keep tears from escaping.

"I want to say that I trust you, Justice." She released her finger from my lips. "And I love you."

I couldn't quite hear the words clearly. I'd waited almost two years to hear an emotion other than sadness or anger from Nicole. I scooped her in my arms and planted kisses from her nose to her lips until she breathily said, "And there is one more thing."

I held her close, telling myself I'd never let her go. If we had to drive to see each other once a month to make it work, I'd do it. I wanted to be with Nicole forever.

"What more could you tell me? I think that's the best news I could've ever heard." I smiled.

She reached in her denim shorts pocket and pulled out a wrinkly folded paper. She handed it to me demurely, a smile spreading across her face.

"'Atlanta University would like to congratulate you, Nicole Bunn, on being accepted to our prestigious university…'" I read aloud. Before I could finish the sentence, Nicole leaped onto me like a lion seizing its prey, pinning me under her weight. We tumbled atop the old Buick laughing at the good news. That crumpled letter was the start of our future together.

Soon after we met in the shed that night, her family bid her farewell at the front stoop of my house while my parents loaded a rental van with both our belongings and drove the seven hours to Atlanta. Nicole and I trailed them in my car, talking excitedly about our future plans at AU. Ever since arriving at AU together, it confirmed in my mind that she was the perfect woman for me and I was going to marry her when the time came.

It didn't take us long to be noticed on campus with her beauty and my skills on the gridiron, and in response, the campus buzzed with the news that we were the couple to envy. We had it all. My football career was going to take off and Nicole was ready to conquer Atlanta. Nicole changed her future to be with me, gave up on her dream of acting in New York to journey with me to the NFL. And by staying with me, I was going to make sure she had a great future ahead of her.

All the money, the cars and the clothes her heart could desire I would provide for her when I got signed to an NFL team. Nicole was the perfect arm candy for a professional athlete, with a small waist, thick hips and perky, round booty that made every man on campus stop and stare. So it was no secret that I was totally whipped. Hook, line and sinker.

Nicole looked like a lioness stalking across campus with her four-inch heels. I used to think, *Damn, don't her feet hurt in those things?* But I realized she was beyond a perfectionist. She would change five times, each outfit better than the one before, until she found the perfect look. She could hold her own alongside the women on television or on magazine covers. She was the total package and that's why I supported her in everything she did…except music video modeling.

Since Nicole's second semester at AU, she's received more attention from the entertainment industry to shoot music videos through a well-known talent agency, Dunkin Studios. Personally, I couldn't stand the way she looked in those videos and even worse, the way my teammates looked at her when we were on campus. I remembered seeing her first video hit MTV's Top 10 playlist. She gyrated in a bikini around a pool as groups of men stared at her body and pointed at her booty as it swirled in tight circles to the music. I felt the bile rise to my throat as I watched her be degraded on national television. Since then, I blocked MTV and BET on my television. The less I saw, the better I felt.

I fully understand what she does in the videos is just acting but my pride gets in the way sometimes. I try not to be jealous but there's a limit to how supportive I can be when my girl is half-naked, gyrating on some thuggish rapper and his entourage. I wonder if the tables were turned if Nicole could handle seeing me romance another girl. Being swarmed by groupies after the games and in the club tests my focus but I make sure my image is never tainted by a slipup. The last thing I need is to be taking a damn paternity test. My love for Nicole keeps me out of trouble and I've never stepped out on my lady. Not once in five years (the first year was a tough transition). I was still young and dumb, ready to smash any girl that would smile at me when I was in high school. Now, I'm a senior in college and as soon as I make it in the league, I have no doubt that Nicole will be my wife. All I know is Nicole better be just as loyal around those thirsty rappers as I am around these groupies.

A part of me wants to tell her to stop dancing in music videos but the other side says she deserves to make a living too. I'm not making any checks from football yet so technically, she's holding her own. I have to respect her hustle since I'm living off my meager monthly allowance. Her video modeling was partly my motivation for working so hard in football. I didn't want my woman to have to sell herself out to get a few bucks in the industry. She was smart enough to produce her own videos, not dance in them.

The clock buzzed loudly in the stuffy bedroom. I woke startled. I hadn't realized I'd dozed off. Nicole was already in the bathroom brushing her teeth, butt naked. I rolled over in the bed and watched her bend low to spit in the sink, showing the depths of her round behind as she did. A chill ran down my spine. Nicole still makes me tingle to my core when I look at her. She looked in the mirror above the sink and saw me staring at her from the bed. She winked and flashed a smile before flicking off the bathroom light and lying on top of me.

"What're you looking at?" she said, playfully tickling my sides.

"The most beautiful woman in the world," I said as I wrestled her hands away from my tender parts.

"You just got some last night. So I wasn't expecting any compliments until maybe this evening at the earliest." She laughed as I spun her to the bed and pushed my body weight on top of her.

"So you trying to say you don't accept my compliment?"

"No. I don't accept it. I think you're just telling me that so you can have your way with me." She grinned seductively.

"Well then…" I slid down to her bald mound of flesh and kissed it softly, "…I guess I have to prove it."

Nicole moaned as I searched for the pulse of her clitoris. She arched her back to lead the way. The vibrations of my tongue against her silky lips made her body shudder and grind against my face. Her button exposed itself as I lapped like a wild animal in the waters of her canal. I could feel her hands clench the sheets in ecstasy as I gripped her waist and moved her against my rhythmic circles. I ached to feel her warmth surround me, so I entered her juicy center and hardened even more as she rolled her hips to my music.

Her breathy grunts filled the room and forced me to go longer, harder than I intended. Our bodies danced in harmony as the sun poked through the blinds and splayed lines across her bouncing breasts. I flipped her on her side and watched the ebb and flow of her skin pound against mine. I fought the urge to come as she tossed her ebony hair to the side and the silhouette of her face in the sunlight looked heavenly. I felt the needles start to prickle from the backs of my ankles, rise up my hamstrings and surround my pelvis as she slammed harder and harder into me. With a fist full of her hair, I pulled away just in time to spill the contents of my love onto the sheets. She lay haphazard on the bed breathing deeply as the comforter lay in the middle of the bedroom and the pillows had vanished.

"So are you the most beautiful woman in the world?" I slapped her rear end playfully.

"Yes." She sighed, spent.

I started our shower running and brushed my teeth while it warmed. Nicole grabbed a banana from the kitchen and bit off the tip as she laid her clothes across the bed neatly. She tiptoed into the shower and washed quickly as I rinsed my mouth and smoothed my close-cropped waves in the mirror. There was enough room for only one in my tiny shower so we timed our exchange perfectly. I knew she'd be dressed by the time I finished showering and we'd be out the house in less than thirty minutes. Needless to say, today was no different than any other day. I dropped Nicole off at Dunkin Studios with ten minutes to spare. I breezed through weight training and headed to the Union in the center of campus. The Union was the nucleus of the campus since every student passed through its walls from orientation to graduation. Classes were set to start in a few days and the freshmen were already trolling around campus, looking in every corner for something new and exciting about Atlanta University. After being here three years, I knew every crack, crevice and hidden gem at Atlanta University. Nothing could surprise me about this place.

Nicole Bunn

∞

"*Dayum*! I look good!" I said as I looked in the mirror at Toni's latest creation.

Toni is an international makeup artist with the personality (and attitude) to match his worldwide status. I was lucky to have Toni as a friend because he was hard to catch up with in this industry. The man knew how to work magic on a face like no one's business. I palmed the mirror and stared closely at my hazel eyes traced with dark green eyeliner and flecked with gold in the crease. He had my lips bursting in bright red shiny gloss. I was as flawless as Poison Ivy from the movie *Batman* but a whole helluva lot sexier!

"I know you look good, Trick. That's why I make the big bucks." Toni was so flamboyant with his pink silk scarf tied tightly around his close-cropped hair making a tiny bow in the front.

He exuded confidence as he strutted to the makeup bin and extracted a brow brush and tweezers.

"Now let me get those hairy eyebrows of yours."

Toni was a good friend in a business where friends are a dime a dozen. We'd gotten closer while on the video shoots for my mentor and director, Will Dunkin. I wondered if Will Dunkin worked with Toni so often because he gave him exactly what he wanted on set, including all the sass and backtalk he could take.

"So what they got you doing today on the set?" Toni asked between painful tweezing and pushing my head back with his middle finger so he could pull the stubborn hairs.

"I'm working with Webby and DJ Cringe on set today. They got me doing main chick again," I said proudly. Being the main chick meant that you were the most talented, beautiful and highly rated girl in the music video game and usually led to more money. Main chicks got about ten to fifteen shots per video while dancers in the background were never directly zoomed in on.

"Webby?! Baby, he is so damn fine! I swear, if he was drunk and I had a chance…I'd turn him to the dark side." Toni said, glancing at me under his long, mascara-laden eyelashes with a devious grin.

"You are so silly! Yeah, he's a little cute." I laughed at Toni's raunchy humor.

"Girl, that man ain't *cute*…he's F-I-N-E. Tall, dark and handsome, plus he look like he can lay it down!" Toni stamped his foot on the ground three times to emphasize how Webby could *lay it down*. "All them doggone tattoos means he like pain." Toni stopped plucking and looked to the ceiling dramatically. "And ain't nothing wrong with a little pain!" he finished with a shoulder shrug.

Toni was so nasty. He talked about rappers like they were a buffet meal, open for him to choose which meat he preferred. Usually, it was dark meat he fancied. Toni even talked about the female models that could turn him straight, me included. I shook my head at the thought.

Webby was the hottest rapper out on the mainstream Billboard charts with his song "Beat up the Beat." He'd been in the rap game for about six years now, which is a lifetime in this industry. Unlike most of his counterparts, he'd managed to stay out of jail. I vaguely remembered rumors of assault and blackmail of an ex-girlfriend and his manager but that was swept under the rug within weeks. Not really sure how it ended but I'm guessing it went pretty well since he's not in a black-and-white jumpsuit rapping for the inmates downtown.

"Toni, when are you going to quit daydreaming about these folks and just ask one of them out?" I wondered aloud.

"Girl, I got a man. He's still on the down low. He ain't ready to be out yet," Toni said quietly, almost in a whisper.

"Oh. I didn't know. I thought…"

"You thought because I have a man that I gave away my damn eyeballs? All of a sudden I stop seeing people that look good enough to eat for breakfast?" Toni finished my sentence and plopped a hand on his narrow hip. We both broke out in laughter. Toni was a handful but he also had wisdom tucked in his humor. Toni helped me through some tumultuous times with my relationship woes. Justice and I have had a strong bond since high school and I try my best to be there for him since he's going to the NFL draft next year. He hates that I dance in music videos and makes sure I hear about it every opportunity he gets. In turn, I kindly tell him music videos are making me mainstream and paying my way through college. That usually backs him off for a while since he realizes being broke means you forfeit your opinion on all money-making decisions. Until he makes enough money to give me the lifestyle I deserve, nothing he says will have me quit making this easy cash.

"Five minutes, Nicole! We need you!" the production assistant yelled from outside the makeup room door.

"Okay! Damn!" Toni yelled back while rolling his eyes and smacking his lips loudly.

He hated being rushed. Even with the rush, he managed to get me out of the chair looking the part of a mainstream video vixen. I air-kissed Toni as I sashayed out the door.

Coming out to the set, I could see Webby and DJ Cringe sitting in director-style chairs facing the white backdrop.

"There she is!" Will Dunkin announced as I sauntered over. He flashed Webby and DJ Cringe a crooked smile.

I stood politely next to Will as Webby eyed my curves and DJ Cringe tried to contain his reaction by pulling his hat down low over his eyes.

"Nicole Bunn, right?" Webby was the first to put his hand out. That was a nice gesture.

"Yes. I'm Nicole. You must be Webby," I said, shaking his hand firmly. "And you must be DJ Cringe." DJ Cringe didn't take my outstretched hand, so I awkwardly retracted it while I swallowed the urge to snatch off his ball cap and crush it with my stilettos. DJ Cringe shifted away from me and typed on his cell phone as if I wasn't standing there. I must not have hidden my foul facial expression because Webby chimed in enthusiastically, "Don't worry about Cringe. Let me show you the set."

Webby was about six-two, with unblemished cocoa-brown skin and extraordinarily sparkling white teeth. He sported a gold Adidas track jacket that covered his wide shoulders. His black Levi jeans stretched across his thin legs down to black-and-gold Adidas high-tops. My eyes followed his every move as he pointed out the different sets we'd use for the shoot. Damn, he was fly. He had on all the jewelry expected of a rapper of his caliber. Three gold chains hung from his neck—one with a cross, another a dog tag with a name on it that I couldn't read from this angle, and the last one was a diamond-encrusted pistol. I eyed his wrist as he pointed at the lighting and sound bars that hung from the ceiling and his watch sparkled with diamonds.

"Nicole?" He interrupted my ogling.

"Oh, hmm?"

"I asked if you have a side you want to stand on that's better for you." He looked at me inquisitively.

"Oh! My right side toward the camera would be best. I have a dimple on that side." I smiled to show proof. He smiled back.

"By the way, you are incredibly beautiful...but you probably already know that. I'm sure you hear that all the time," he said, shaking his head as if he regretted saying it.

"No matter how many times you hear it, it still makes you feel good."

"You were on the cover of *Image* magazine a few months ago, huh?" He changed the subject easily.

"I was. Do you make it a habit of picking up women's magazines on a regular basis?" I joked.

"Only when someone as beautiful as you is on the cover. Which means I've done it only once...a few months ago."

He let the comment linger as he searched my eyes for a reaction. I didn't give him what he wanted.

"I bet you have lines like these for every model in your videos."

I should have just accepted the compliment but I couldn't stop the words from coming out of my mouth.

"Nah. It's not a line. I'm single but I don't compliment every woman I meet." He winked. "I'm picky. And I don't like playing games. When I see something I want...I go get it," he added as his brown eyes pierced into mine.

"Umm...what's the deal with DJ Cringe? He doesn't like me?" I tried to sound like my feelings were hurt. In actuality, I needed to change the subject…immediately. Webby's flirting was making me overheat inside my skimpy gold outfit.

"Cringe's wife showed up on the set with her friends. He's trying to be on his best behavior, so to speak." He chuckled and shook his head. "Trust me, there's nothing wrong with you in any way."

Webby sensed my discomfort at his intense stare and relented. This man certainly had a way with the ladies. I averted my eyes from Webby's sparkling smile to my sparkling gold heels as we continued walking. *Lord, let me not stare at this fine-ass man for too long…*

As if hearing my plea, Will Dunkin blew the set horn for all actors, models and musicians to come to the first call. As I walked to my spot and watched throngs of people shuffle to their areas in front of the backdrop, I mentally replayed my conversation with Webby. He seemed to be more mature than the other rappers I'd met in the industry. Maybe it was because he was almost ten years my senior but I ventured to believe he was a true gentleman. I wasn't sure if he was playing the Mr. Nice Guy role to get a chance with me but I liked that he made me feel like I was the prize. Most rappers that trailed through Dunkin Studios acted like I'd be lucky to be with them. It felt different with Webby.

Thinking of Webby made me think of DJ Cringe's lackluster first impression. As I stood on set, ready for the first take, I found DJ Cringe still sitting behind the camera next to the director's chair. He was throwing multiple glances toward the corner of the warehouse so I followed his gaze curiously. In the corner, with her friends cackling behind her like wild hyenas, was his wife. She was clearly an ex-video girl which was evident in her long extensions, thick makeup and ultra-tanned appearance. Her trashy aura was a dead giveaway even if I didn't catch her staring back at him like a pampered diva, watching Cringe's every move like a hawk. She still wore the raunchy clothes DJ Cringe had

probably found her in. Her over-average height didn't help mask
her super-short, hot-pink spandex dress that pushed her double-D
breasts into the base of her neck. Her spandex dress crept up the
front of her thighs. She pulled the hem down inconspicuously to
ensure she didn't showcase her goodies to the entire staff. I shook
my head in disgust, she looked thirsty enough for the spotlight to
run on set in those five-inch heels and start booty-popping for the
camera crew.

The one thing I couldn't miss under the glare of the lights
was the bling on her finger. Her wedding ring was like a lighthouse
beacon in the middle of a foggy lake. It sparkled in the darkest
corner of the warehouse, so much so that without squinting I could
make out the cut, color and clarity from where I was standing. I
sighed and focused on the team scrambling to measure actor
placement on the set. It irked me to see millionaire wives on set
with Prada and Gucci purses hanging from their manicured hands
and Manolos that had only scratched the pavement once. They
lived the best lives, full of shopping and rubbing shoulders with
other rich and famous people, while I made their men look good.
They lived the dream while I acted it out in music videos. If that
woman in the hot-pink tube top masquerading as a dress could live
a millionaire's life then what was I doing wrong? I inadvertently
glanced at Webby smiling at me from across the set as the lighting
team inched fluorescent lighting bars toward his face. *My time is
coming,* I thought. *Justice is going to make it to the NFL and soon I'll be
one of those wives.* Or maybe there was something new budding on
the horizon?

Mali

∞

Atlanta University looked like it could swallow me whole. The campus sprawled across the entire western edge of the city. Students hustled around campus, laughing with their families while they carried large boxes into the dormitories. I overheard girls chattering excitedly about the welcoming party tonight at the Student Union ballroom. Boys dressed in sagging jeans walked around with their buddies in tow, looking at every girl that passed like dogs in heat. By the look of the pack, it would only be a second before they started humping someone's leg.

The campus was bursting with excitement as I toted my bags from the bus station drop, about a half block from the front gate of Atlanta University, then on to Cramer Hall, my dormitory. Cramer Hall loomed high and stately in the bright daylight. It was a large, five-story redbrick building with ornate white detailing at the roof corners that reminded me of the dormitories I'd seen in movies. The windows opened outward on the first and second floor. Students happily leaned out to pass bulky furniture that couldn't fit through the doors. The upper three levels had windows framed with thick white borders, and ivy vines snaking the roofline gave the aging building a regal appeal. Multicolored, glittery welcome banners swayed in the afternoon breeze atop the massive entry, flapping softly against the red bricks. Students walked in every direction, covering every inch of grass with bright-colored folding chairs, plastic bins with their drawers filled to capacity, oversized stereo systems and boxes simply labeled "clothes" in permanent marker. I weaved my way through the housing madness to find the wooden double doors marking the entrance to Cramer Hall.

I bumped into two girls in the hallway as I carried my mismatched suitcases to the third floor. They smiled at my apologetic expression and zoomed toward the front lawn, chatting excitedly. My room number was 306 and I was grateful to be on the third floor after tackling three flights of stairs with bags that looked as if they were going to split at the seams. Apparently, Cramer Hall was too old for an elevator as I wheezed on the third-floor landing. *That's just great,* I thought to myself as I reached room 306. The door was cracked open and I pushed through, banging my heavy suitcases on the wooden floor. I was exhausted and found that leaning on the door was a perfect resting place.

"Oh! Hello!" said a girl with black-rimmed glasses propped on her nose.

She had spun around at the sound of my loud entry, along with a short and stubby lady who resembled Ricki Lake. Two men, one in his mid-twenties and the other older, stood nearby dressed in T-shirts and jeans. I straightened stiffly against the door frame at the sight of four startled faces staring back at me.

"I'm sorry. I didn't mean to come in like that. It's just that these bags…" Before I could finish my sentence the mid-twenties man crossed the room, picked up my run-down suitcases and placed them near what I assumed was my bed.

"Thank you," I muttered.

"Oh, you didn't scare us, sweetheart! We've been waiting to meet you since this morning. I'm Marney Cole. That's Craig, my son." She pointed at the man who'd carried my suitcases. "And my husband, Jake." She motioned toward the older gentleman who gave a weak military salute.

The girl with the glasses chimed in enthusiastically, "And I'm Carey Cole, your new roomie."

"I'm Mali Struthers. Nice to meet you all," I said while inching from the doorway to the empty bed across the room. My feet were starting to ache from the walk.

"Where's your family? Are they coming up?" Marney asked, quickly glancing at the door. Anyone could tell she was a talker. Even with her thick Southern drawl, she could speak faster than a car salesman on a Saturday morning.

"Uh, no. I took the bus from Washington," I said matter-of-factly. Marney's green eyes grew large at the thought of me traveling alone such a far distance. Her husband stopped fidgeting with Carey's closet organizer and looked over his shoulder in amazement. Craig leaned against Carey's bed looking at the floor. The silence grew thick enough to slice with a knife.

"Well, then it's settled! We'll help you move your stuff in and as repayment for our services, you can go to dinner with us before we head back to Mississippi," Marney proclaimed in a loud voice, breaking the silence. I didn't have reason to object, so I smiled instead.

"Sure. Why not?" I tried to sound excited but it fell flat.

Craig looked up bashfully and ran his hand through his long brown hair that fell to the base of his neck. How could I refuse this perfect family?

After warning them that I didn't have much to unpack, they removed two of Carey's racks in her closet and added them to my empty cave of a closet. Was this what people called Southern hospitality? I was starting to think I had stepped into *The Twilight Zone* and any minute they would all turn into zombies and attempt to bite me.

Carey, Marney and I chatted pleasantly as Carey put up some photos of her high school friends, giving the room some much-needed personality. I slid two pictures out of my suitcase as we talked. I had stolen them from my mom's picture album in a box under her bed.

"Is that your friend from home?" Carey pointed at the picture in my hand. The picture was of Mack and me after a halftime dance at our high school.

"Yep. Her name is Jacinta Mack. But I call her Mack," I answered.

"She's pretty. What's the other picture?"

"My mom," I whispered.

The picture was of me as a toddler. My mom's dark hair fanned into the wind as my floppy pink hat flipped back, exposing my forehead. It was our favorite photo of us together.

"You two look so much alike...except her hair isn't as curly."

"That's what people say all the time. We may look alike but trust me, we are so different."

I stared at the photo as Carey strolled to her side of the room and busied herself with taping another poster to the wall. Mom would miss this photo but I needed it more than she did right now. I needed to remember her the way she was in this photo, not her crumpled, defeated spirit at the bus terminal or her fearfulness throughout the muted years of my childhood.

This picture was the only way I could muster enough strength to call her and relive the horrors of my father's brutality. If I could run farther away, to the edge of the earth to escape the memories of my dad pounding his fist into her head, then I would. I feared one day she'd be gone or, worse, I'd find that my dad's alcoholism and depression were hereditary. I tormented myself waiting for the call to hear that he had finally ended her misery and killed her in one of his drunken rages. I shook with the thought as I ran my fingers over the photos. The only two people in my life that ever loved me were in these pictures.

I felt Craig's intrusive gaze on me. I tried to mask the hurt in my eyes, but just as quickly he turned his back to look out the window at the students scuttling about like little ants on the lawn. I carefully taped the photos to the wall above my nightstand, feeling alone for the first time without my mother.

Decorating the room took longer than expected. The sun was creeping toward the horizon and the front lawn of Cramer Hall was dormant after the morning's excitement. The halls still echoed with the babble of friends and family but the constant noise outside our door had quieted over the past few hours. I glanced at Carey's side of the room and assessed my own barren space. Carey's area was a hodgepodge of color and resembled her quirky personality, complete with boy bands. My side of the room was dark and dim since I hadn't thought to bring a lamp. I had my two pictures taped to the wall and my bed cover from home. It was soft, warm and still held the scent of my room.

Carey floated from her closet to her nightstand, placing things here and there around the space. She was a short, petite girl with her brown hair cut into a short bob that hung longer on the right side, stopping at her jawline. She had on slightly baggy jeans rolled at the bottom, a loose-fitting shirt that periodically fell from her bony shoulder and black-rimmed glasses that made her look studious and less childlike. Carey's face was quite pretty beneath the glasses, with a strong nose and naturally rosy thin lips. She carried an effortless sex appeal in her bohemian, comfortable style as she walked around the room, sliding the shoulder of her shirt up without thought. I lay on my bed, looking at how easily her family got along in the small space. My father couldn't be in a house with me and my mother without someone being belittled or threatened.

I played with the thought of what life would've been like as a Cole kid. I wondered if opportunities would have unfolded for me if I'd had a dad like Jake who hugged his daughter and a mom that spoke her mind.

"I think we're done." Craig patted his stomach and looked at Marney for agreement. "Ma, I'm starving."

"Yeah, Marney, let's get some grub," Jake agreed with his son without looking up from the television.

Carey's dad had resigned himself to becoming a petrified log across Carey's bed, watching the television he'd installed. Marney was still fussing in Carey's closet as she tried to organize piles of cotton shirts that stacked from floor to ceiling.

She sighed, giving the closet a look of defeat. "Alright, let's go eat, folks."

Marney gave one more disapproving look at Carey's closet and shut the door without a second thought.

We piled into Jake's red, four-door Dodge and felt the truck surge forward and out into the busy streets of downtown Atlanta. I felt strange being nuzzled between Carey and Craig as they both looked out the window at the city, not wanting to miss anything. Craig was a bit taller than I originally thought as his knees pressed into the back of Jake's seat. He was clearly uncomfortable in the seating arrangement, as he shifted his legs to gain a few inches of space. Even though I was slim and only five-seven, I still felt the constraints of the pickup truck. I wondered how they had made the trip from Mississippi in here without a brawl breaking out over leg space.

After a few turns, we pulled into the large parking garage of a restaurant with a red neon *V* shining into the dusky night. The restaurant was a blast from the past. Servers with red-and-white sailor-style hats swiveled through rows of stainless-steel chairs in

1950s-style decor. They all yelled in unison as we stepped inside the entry way, "Welcome to the Varsity!"

The food smelled deliciously greasy. Smoke curled toward the ceiling in the open chef's station but the smell resonated of seasoned hamburgers and French fries. Varsity reminded me of Doobey's back in Bremerton with its hometown feel, even though it was three times the size of Doobey's. We ordered our food and toted our heart attack meals to a table near a window facing North Ave. Craig sat near the window across from me to watch the city pass by and Carey scooted in on my left.

After everyone had settled into their seats, Marney announced, "Please bow your head in thanks."

Everyone at the table lowered their heads while she blessed the food with a prayer. *Yep, I'm in* The Twilight Zone. I stared at the steam of my cheeseburger and quickly glanced to each person as she continued her prayer.

"Thank you, oh Lord, for the food we are about to eat. We pray that it shall nourish our bodies…"

I'd never been raised to praise anyone, let alone an entity I couldn't see or feel. Sitting at the table with complete strangers and bowing to the unknown was awkward enough to make me want to run out of the restaurant and foot it back home. The closest I got to religion was participating in the pledge of allegiance at school and that was only because it was mandatory. There couldn't be a God because he'd have surely given me a nonalcoholic, nonabusive father and a stronger mother. What had I done to be stuck with a dysfunctional home life?

I had only this one chance to make it in this world and never would I live under my father's roof again. There was no one there to save me from my father—not even my mother. I was the only one with the courage to get out of his house…and get him out of my life.

Marney ended her lengthy prayer and the Cole family said "Amen" in unison. I guess that meant it was time to eat since Craig demolished his chili dog without restraint.

"Mali, are you going to the welcome party on Saturday?" Carey asked eagerly while taking a large bite of dripping hot wings. Craig looked up from his second hot dog, his brown eyes searching my face until he realized he was staring and focused on taking another monster bite of his hot dog.

"I'm not really much of a partier. I was thinking of just chilling out in the room, maybe read a book or something," I said after swallowing the first bite of cheeseburger. It was as delicious as it looked.

"Awww, come on, Mali! Don't be boring. You've got to go with me! I don't know anyone but you."

Carey had inched closer and if I didn't oblige, this girl was going to be sitting on my lap.

"Fine! I'll go with you," I said with a smirk between bites. "But you owe me."

I thought I saw Craig smile when I said that but as quickly as I saw it, it was gone.

Over dinner, I found out through Marney's constant ranting that Craig was twenty years old and a junior at Atlanta University. Of course, Marney added that he was the reason his sister chose the school. Craig sipped his Coke and acted uninterested in the conversation. Marney gushed that Carey was studying premedical courses to be a neurosurgeon and Craig was starting his major courses in political science with an international business minor. The pride in her eyes was contagious as Jake finally looked at both his kids and smiled unintentionally. Craig managed to glance back and forth between his empty plate and the parking lot outside as Marney smiled from Jake to Craig. Obviously, Craig was bored with our conversation and had succeeded in tuning us out completely. I couldn't believe both Marney and Jake had been so lucky to have not one but two smart kids. They made my dance and theater major seem like I was playing dress-up in my bedroom and reciting lines of Shakespeare to my mirror. Carey and Craig were getting ready for the real world, and I was still living in a fantasy world. I pushed the thought away, realizing that was my father's manipulative seed he had planted in my head. I would never be good enough or smart enough to please him.

After dinner was devoured and the plates were all but licked clean, we sat lazily in our padded steel chairs, rubbing our bulging bellies. Marney leaned her elbows on the table and plopped her pudgy face in her palms.

"I'm gonna miss you guys so much." Her eyes watered as she searched for the used napkin near her plate.

"Mooooommmmm…" Carey rolled her eyes, exasperated.

"I know, I know. I said I wasn't gonna cry again, but…" She wiped the tears before they could smudge her makeup, "…I'm so proud of you both. I know you'll do great things."

"Craig, you look out for these young ladies. You know our expectations of the type of man you should be." Jake finally broke his silence. "Watch out for your sister…and Mali."

I cowered at the sound of my name. I didn't see myself as having to be looked after but it felt good that, for once, someone cared that I was safe. My mother was usually too busy worrying about her own safety to really care about mine.

Craig finally turned from the window and with an alertness in his eyes that I hadn't seen before, answered, "Yes, sir. I will."

It was a strange feeling that came over the family from Jake's words. I wasn't sure what he meant by "the type of man"

Craig should be. Everyone at the table seemed to understand Jake, except me. I shrugged away the intensity of the moment and smiled at Jake in response to his attempt to show me he cared. The awkwardness of the moment was stifled as we gathered our trash and empty plates and piled back into Jake's cramped Dodge. The family talked among themselves happily as I sat nudged between Carey and Craig again. I felt like I belonged when I was with this family.

The laughter between Marney and Carey filled the cab of the truck as we rounded the dark corners of downtown Atlanta. Jake even managed to snicker under his breath at Marney and Carey's comedic relief. They had a very different relationship than me and my mother. They were so carefree while I worried about my mother's safety, hourly, in most cases. Marney was so in control of all situations; meanwhile, my mother seemed to be victimized by almost anything. Marney was the enforcer and the nurturer all in the same evening. I was secretly questioning if she was bipolar. Even still, no one questioned Marney's decisions and Jake stood behind her wishes. I'd never seen that strength in a woman or that kind of emotional support from a man. My mother could never stand up to my father and he, undoubtedly, would never allow her to speak outwardly if it didn't suit him. I was amazed at how the Coles found a way to organize their family in a way that allowed everyone to feel valued and important. On the contrary, the only important person in my family was my father. My mother and I were mere slaves to his alcoholism and anger. I snapped out of my thoughts as Jake pulled the Dodge into a parking space outside Cramer Hall. We piled out silently. All of us knew it was time to say goodbye for good.

"I appreciate everything you did in the dorm. It looks beautiful." I seized the moment of silence to say goodbye. "Thank you for dinner too."

Marney threw her soft arms around my neck and pulled me to her supple body before I could finish. I formed to her like

Play-Doh and sunk into the hug. I felt like I could hug her forever. Her perfume was like a floral shop, a blended sweetness of various flowers. She released me and touched her palm softly to my cheek.

"Bye, Mali. We'll see you soon." She winked and stepped aside.

Jake gave me a stiff pat on the back before saying, "Come visit us in Mississippi when Carey and Craig come home. You're always welcome."

I waved to Craig and walked back to the dorm. Before I entered the wooden doors, I turned for one last glance to find Carey and Marney crying in each other's arms. Jake and Craig stood nearby and shook hands like two rangers in an old Western movie. Jake concluded his goodbye with a prideful smirk and a nod of approval.

Justice

∞

The excitement from freshmen moving into the dorms made it directly to the football team's locker room. More importantly, the football players had already scoped out the freshmen girls and were itching to meet them at the welcome party. Now me, on the other hand, I was chilling. The excitement of freshmen stopped being an issue after the first year I was here. It always ended the same way. The football team would run through all the cute girls (and some not-so-cute ones) in the first six months, passing them from teammate to teammate until the last six months. Then they'd try to get rid of those crazy broads. I had no worries in the world. Nicole called me an hour ago and said she was on her way over to my apartment after wrapping up her video shoot. So I knew we were going to hit up this welcome party like the true superstars we were and then bounce back to my place for a nightcap.

I took a quick shower then slathered baby oil on my body like I was on the cover of *Men's Fitness* magazine. I looked in the mirror at my caramel-brown skin, muscular and chiseled through years of running, weight lifting and fighting 250-pound men on the football field. As a starting receiver on the team, I'm watched like a hawk on the field. It's up to me to make the touchdowns that count, catch the passes that no one thinks I can and be the face of our school's athletic program. It didn't hurt that the face of AU was so damn good-looking. Coach knew it was me that put the butts in the seats on game day. He heard the chants ring loud around the entire stadium—"JB! JB! JB!"—just like I could hear them on the field. There was a time when the chants used to distract me, but now they give me fuel. I'm unstoppable when I hear my name roaring across the stands as the band plays our song.

Needless to say, my time here at AU is filled with perks. Besides the fact that all my teachers want autographed balls and jerseys for their families in exchange for lenient grading, being a star athlete makes my job as a student much easier. I'm invited to all the parties, even getting paid under the table by promoters to show up. Promoters know that if I show up to the party, all the females were going to come dashing through the door like they were on the track team trying to place in the Olympics. I couldn't help it. Even the guys on the team look up to me as a mentor. If I said a party was hot, then it was, no doubt, filled to capacity with football players and fame whores trying to get a chance at a future baller. Not to mention that my girlfriend is hot in the music video industry, so they're paying both of us to show up to parties together. It was all about keeping up the image. My image was the reason scouts were beating down my door offering me and my family everything under the sun. Cars, vacations and jewelry were at my disposal. Whatever I wanted, they offered. I wasn't a fool, though. I never took a gift, not a dime, from a scout or agent. I wasn't trying to ground my career before it even had a chance to take flight. I stared at my reflection in the mirror and flexed my chest. NFL scouts know I have the juice that the public is thirsty for and for them, my playing skills are just the icing on the sweet-ass cake I'm serving up.

I shook my head at how good life was as I pulled on black, European-cut boxer briefs that accentuated my six-pack abs and thick, muscular legs. My body was still sore from football practice but the results of a great workout were apparent in my bulging chest and biceps. I admired my physique in the mirror. I'd gotten my slanted, Asian eyes and smooth skin from my mother. She was a Japanese lady with a whole lot of sass packed in a pint-size body. My father, a strong black man, gave me the perfect athletic build, from the broad shoulders to the square jawline. Most people thought I resembled my dad except for the eyes and height. He had stretched to six-six and played professional basketball for two years in Miami where he met my mother on vacation during spring break. I can thank my five-two mother for stunting my height potential. I always teased her that she ended my dreams of being a basketball star, so I had to settle for football. She usually slapped me on the arm when I said that. I laughed aloud at the thought of her tiny hands trying to do damage to a body that gets hit by aggressive grown men daily.

I pushed Play on the stereo in the living room to start up some slow jams to get my mind right. Sade's "Soldier of Love" whispered from the speakers and filled the living room with a relaxing vibe. After knocking out 100 push-ups in the center of the living room, I collapsed on the carpet, thinking about what I was going to do to Nicole when she made it over here. Nicole and I had an unspeakable chemistry. She was fiery in and out of the bedroom. I never had to wonder if Nicole knew how to please her man. She was always willing to try whatever I wanted and usually, she ended up liking it more than I would. I smirked, thinking about the raunchy wigs and outfits she'd buy and show up at my apartment acting like another woman. I must admit it was definitely entertaining on those nights.

I imagined that I could smell her sweet perfume as I pulled out her plump breasts and teased her nipples with my tongue. My package bounced to life inside my boxer briefs as I drifted deeper into the dream.

I almost missed the soft knock on the door because I'd dozed off for what felt like a brief second. I glanced at the wall clock and noticed it was already nine. I snuck a look in the mirror by the door, pulled free a tuft of carpet lint and pulled open the front door. Nicole was standing in the muggy night air dressed in a short yellow dress that clung to her curves in all the right ways. I could smell the scent of her freshly showered skin as she walked in, slowly eyeing my half-naked body. Her hazel eyes scanned every inch and stopped at the bulge in my boxer briefs. Her tall, tan high heels almost made her taller than my six-three frame. She had her dark hair pulled up in a tight, neat bun with a star-shaped diamond pin on the side. I was aching to pull it free so her hair could fall wild around her beautiful eyes. I wanted to feel her hair in my hands, smell the jasmine. That smell always brought me back to high school. Always reminded me she was my first love.

"You waiting up for me?" she said silkily.

"Me? Wait for you? Nooooo…" I shook my head dramatically.

Nicole stepped over the threshold. "Well, that's a shame."

Nicole threw her purse to the floor and slammed me against the front door, pushing it shut loudly. The walls shook under her pressure as she ground her soft curves into my hard muscles. Her hands roamed my body like she was looking for a spot on a map. She teased and scratched, licked my neck then nibbled it hard enough to let me know she meant business. I loved when Nicole got this intense. I grabbed her hands and held them behind her back, spinning her to the door and pinning her down to taste her mouth. Her minty lips tingled against mine as I sucked and bit her plump bottom lip. She moaned in anticipation of my tongue. I could feel my body reacting to her heavy breathing. Her body begged me to touch her as she bent like a bow toward me, her hands still tightly pressed behind her. She growled against my lips as she realized she was not in charge of this altercation. I released her hands and cupped her large buttocks that overflowed in my big palms. Her lips found mine as she wrapped her legs tightly around my waist and with her dress pushed to her midsection, she grinded into my stiff member. I could feel the vibrating heat from her pulsating groin. She groaned and pleaded for more as I wound my hips in small circles while holding her up against the door. I could smell the sweetness of her essence fill the room with a radiance that permeated through my boxers and coaxed me to go further. Carrying her soft, firm body to the couch, I slammed her down roughly and pulled her yellow dress high above her head, exposing her stark nakedness. No panties? I shook my head in wonder. I *really* loved this girl. Her walls collapsed around me as I entered her roughly. She gasped into my neck, sending a prickle down my spine as she dug her nails into the muscles of my back. I winced under the feeling of her sharp nails but kept pushing deeper into her wetness until I heard her guttural moans ring out in the living room. The couch squeaked loudly as she swirled her hips to the rhythm, softly then more hungrily. She thrashed against me as I pounded her wet mound until I could feel her deepest depths. Her waters dripped around me and melted like hot butter on a warm roll. I stared at this beautiful being beneath me as she grunted, dug her nails into my buttocks and pulled me deeper into her. Her half-closed eyes fluttered with each thrust and her lips pouted with pink juiciness. I could feel her body tightening around me. It was a feeling I'd known since high school. Her face contorted in pleasure as she reached her peak and screamed into my neck, "I'm coming!" Her body convulsed and jerked against me as little throaty moans of pleasure escaped her lips. I followed soon after, no longer able to withstand her sweet nectar, and collapsed on her ample breasts, breathless.

"Now the party can start," I commanded.

The welcome party was in full effect when Nicole and I parked her red, convertible BMW at the Union. The sounds from the bar poured out into the parking lot as people bobbed their heads to the music as they waited in line. Girls were out in their finest attire, strutting like tonight was the only reason they came to college. I saw a couple old faces in the crowd as we walked up to the front entrance. My best friend, Big Deuce, was already on the prowl. He winked and turned back to the group of girls to continue his coercion. He'd scouted three girls in line and was making great strides at getting the light-skinned one to bite the bait. She snickered shyly and looked from her friends back to Big Deuce. He would be telling them the same story he told a group of girls last year around this time, most likely. It was the start of a new year but sometimes old tricks worked better on new fools.

"There goes Deuce again," Nicole said, shaking her head in disdain. "Will he ever grow up?"

"Probably not. It seems to work on these girls every year…so why would he stop?" I shrugged.

"Ugh…he's so gross. How could you even be friends with him?"

"He's not trying to get in my pants…so we're cool." I laughed.

I grabbed Nicole's hand firmly and laced it under my arm as we approached the Union entryway. It was like Moses parting the Red Sea as people moved to the side of the entrance to watch us walk through. Girls whispered to their friends with wide-eyed amazement then quickly collapsed into lustful stares and suppressed giggles. The men's eyes roved over Nicole in her yellow dress as she sashayed through the glass doors and into the thick of the party.

Inside, the spot was jumping. The DJ had the most popular jams pumping through loudspeakers flanking the stage. Girls danced onstage as the men stooped to catch a glimpse up the girl's skirts at their precious secrets.

The Union was a futuristic jungle with fake tropical trees and sweeping leaves in the dimly lit ballroom. Blue-green lights bounced off the walls from light boxes affixed to the DJ stand and splayed across the dance floor in quick moving lines. The darting lights played laser tag on the dance floor, zipping through balloons of every color and people leaning on walls. People hovered around the glass bar situated in the center of the room with long, cylindrical vases filled with blue water and bright green apples. The dry bar served soda and water to the awaiting crowd that gossiped about everyone that walked through the doors. The university was tense about drinking after a student was killed by an underage drunk driver last year. That event plastered the university all over the front page of the national news. No one had stopped the students from getting drunk before the party even started, though. Young men leaned lazily against the wall as lasers bounced off their foreheads while they hung on to the last bit of sobriety they had left. Teenage females hung to their girlfriends' shoulders, some laughing uncontrollably while others just drooled and collapsed onto cushiony stools tucked away in the corners of the room.

Nicole saw her friend Lisa across the room and waved eagerly.

"I'll see you in a bit." She kissed me on the cheek before disappearing into the crowd.

Before I could get a breath, Big Deuce ambled over with his wide body filling any gaps in the crowd. He looked like the kind of guy you wouldn't want to see alone in a dark alley. His six-one height didn't balance out his wide body at over 250 pounds. He was a brother that loved only light-skinned or white women even though he was dark-skinned. He'd never try to talk to a female that was even a shade darker than Halle Berry. I could tell by the big, childish grin on his face that he'd found his first victim of the year.

"Yo! What's up, man?! Isn't this party crazier than last year?" Big Deuce had a husky voice, so hearing him strain to yell over the music sounded painful.

"Man, these hoes are ridiculous!"

I scanned the crowd and caught three girls near the bar checking me out. One girl I knew from the gym, so I waved.

"Dude, those girls I was talking to outside," Big Deuce pointed his finger in my face, "they only want to come to the after party if you fall through the spot." Big Deuce was the kind of friend that always tried to keep you in trouble but always got you out of it without a bump, scrape or bruise. I trusted Deuce but I knew he was trying to get as many girls to sleep with him before the rest of the team had their chance. It was a race to the finish every year with these guys. No one wants sloppy seconds, not even whore-mongering football players.

I brushed his finger out of my face and said, "Deuce, you know I don't get down with these young girls. You better leave them alone before one of their daddies come up here with a shotgun. Or worse, you end up being someone's daddy." Big Deuce smirked and turned up his lips as if to say, *Yeah, right.*

"Brah, trust me. These girls at the party are ready to go." Big Deuce led the way to the second-floor balcony as he rationalized my cameo appearance.

"Man, you better be wrapping it up. Every girl ain't clean. You remember that itchy shit you had last year? You lucky that shit was curable," I warned.

Big Deuce waved my words away like a gnat was in the air.

"Dude, I'm good. Leave my dick to me. I learned my lesson." He tried to look sincere. "But seriously, I already chose one for you. If you don't like her, I'll even let you get the light-skinned one! And you know I like 'em light and not so bright." Big Deuce tried to look serious before bursting into laughter. I laughed but I couldn't believe my best friend was bargaining with me over women like he was running a brothel in his apartment. I couldn't expect more than that from Deuce—he was a twenty-one-year-old with a fifteen-year-old's sex drive. We finally reached the balcony patio and walked into the muggy night air. The balcony was the designated smoking area but it was quiet and had the best view of the campus.

"Deuce, I'm not coming through, man."

I wasn't going to turn down mine and Nicole's second act to kick it with Deuce and a few random chicks.

"Why don't you just lie and tell them I'm coming? When they show up, tell 'em if they leave they might miss me."

I saw the lightbulb turn on in his head. I might just be off the hook.

"Alright, you know I'll do whatever it takes." He shrugged his shoulders. "I didn't want to give you the yellow bone anyway," he said jokingly and disappeared into the Union without looking back.

Big Deuce was born Deuce McMann to a mother who passed away while giving birth to him, leaving him to be raised by his skirt-chasing father—which may have been the reason he lived so recklessly, never committing to anything other than his own happiness. He'd come into the world alone.

Deuce was loved by everyone except the young girls he conquered then discarded like played-out CDs or old shoes that no longer fit. So it was no surprise to see him dodging girls after class or sneaking girls into the back gate during the games. We all knew it was Deuce just being Deuce. His humor usually got him into altercations then almost as slick as a snake, he'd get himself out. I had to admit, he had a true talent at getting his way.

I really didn't want to head back into the party. I eyed a blond couple huddled in the corner of the balcony on a concrete bench sharing a cigarette and talking quietly. I eased to the opposite side of the balcony to escape the cigarette smoke and looked out over the parking lot. I spotted Nicole's red BMW nestled between a gray Oldsmobile and yellow VW Beetle. Stepping out of the VW Beetle was a woman with wild, curly hair swinging in the night air. A teal, floor-length sundress hugged her small breasts and tiny waistline. My mouth watered at the sight of her. She turned to grab something from the passenger seat of the VW and her exposed, tan back glistened in the street light. She emerged with a purse and tucked it under her arm before sashaying across the parking lot. I didn't blink until my eyes watered, scared that I was dreaming and she'd be gone. Nope. She was still there, except now I noticed a petite girl in black glasses keeping in step with her. Her stride was smooth, fluid and confident as the people hanging out at the entrance to the Union turned to look at her as she approached. The girl in the teal dress seemed oblivious to their gawking mouths and loud whispers of "Who is that?" Her skin was radiant in the moonlight, almost glowing as she listened intently to the girl in glasses and smiled every now and then in response. She floated to the front door of the Union and quickly disappeared from my view.

Nicole

∞

This party is so lame. I mean, how many freshmen can you see without feeling like you're back in high school? I need to make a note to myself not to come to any campus parties this year. I'm getting way too old, at twenty-one, to be anyplace with a dry bar. Lisa and I perused the ballroom from the base of the stairs perched on the wooden banister. I eyed a short, dark-skinned guy with a huge gap in the front of his smile staring from the stage. I rolled my eyes in disgust and settled on watching the dancers roll and twist to the blaring music.

"These guys look absolutely disgusting with their pants hanging all low on their behinds. At least if you're going to show it, don't wear cheap underwear." I eyed the boys prowling the party.

"I know, right? When did that become the style?" Lisa said, shaking her head.

The DJ's voice broke through the beat and announced that he had the latest hit from Webby. I smiled thinking of Webby and me at the studio. The dance floor went wild with hoots and yells as the opening beat started. Thank God! The party was alive again. Two guys walked past, heading up the stairs, both staring and licking their lips like they'd ever have a chance. I turned my back before they could even attempt to start a conversation with me. Why do the ugliest guys have the balls to come up to the prettiest girl in the room? At some point, I get tired of people gawking and just want to find a corner and hide. So that's exactly what I did with Lisa by the stairs. Lisa was standing behind me looking out onto the dance floor, swaying to Webby's hot track.

Lisa had been dating Jack Campbell, one of Justice's teammates and a supreme douche bag. She's always there to listen when I'm having relationship trouble but she's definitely not one to take advice from. Jack blatantly cheats on her with these sleazebags on campus and she still takes him back every couple of months. We both know the script. He'll apologize, cry and tell her he needs her, loves her. *Blah, blah, blah.* Then he'll come over to her apartment late at night with tears in his eyes, beat her back out with a little rough sex, then she'll be calling me saying, "Girl, we're back together!" It used to baffle me how she could forget and forgive so easily. Now, I don't answer my phone for a few days after they break up—that way I miss all the crying and sexing and start off at the "we're together" part. It saves me valuable time giving her my good advice. Doesn't she know my advice ain't cheap?

I don't have that same forgiveness in my genes like Lisa, apparently. If I ever found out Justice was cheating, he'd be running from a Louisville Slugger, not asking for forgiveness. You would think Lisa wasn't eye-catching by the way she lets Jack use her heart as a doormat but she's actually quite attractive for a basketball player. She sports an unsightly pixie haircut, which I never understood since she's already tall. Can someone say Neanderthal? I'd hate to be six-one like her but at least she has a nice, lean body and deep dimples. Now that I think about it, there are probably slim pickings for men interested in a six-one girl rocking a pixie cut. So her best bet might actually be to stay with cheating-ass Jack. At least he might go to the league and make some damn money. Ain't nothing worse than being six-one, broke and in the market for a man. I shook my head at the thought. Poor Lisa.

Other than Lisa, I've learned not to trust any of these tricks at AU. They only want to be your friend so they can steal your shine or steal your man. Needless to say, no one at this party could even come close to getting either one from me. My shine was too bright and my man was too pussy whipped. Thinking of my pussy made me scan the crowd for Justice but I didn't see him in the ballroom. He was probably with Big Deuce somewhere. I dreaded the thought of both of them together in a crowd of thirsty groupies. Big Deuce was trouble with a capital, bold, italicized *T*. It was something about him I couldn't stand and I was pretty sure he couldn't stand my ass, either. But in the big scheme of things, I'd always win when it came to Justice. So he tended to back off when I was around...as he should.

The crowd yelled from the dance floor for the DJ to play Webby's track one more time and sure enough he complied. The opening beat rumbled the walls to the ballroom and everyone threw their hands to the ceiling and yelled with glee. The girls were dropping it lower on the dance floor, hiking their skirts up while the guys were grabbing their knees trying to stay just as low. I forgot Lisa was standing next to me until her voice broke my concentration.

"Who is that?" Lisa said and dipped her head low.

I followed her stare to a beautiful girl swaying to the beat in the middle of the dance floor.

"Umm. I don't know." I tried to get a better look but a crowd was forming around her and her friend.

"You want to get a little closer?" Lisa quizzed without tearing her eyes from the crowd. I wanted to see who this girl was but I wasn't going to let another trick steal my shine.

"Nah. Probably just some freshman," I said in annoyance at Lisa's concentration on the girl.

"Oh. Okay." Lisa pouted like she was on punishment standing here with me.

"Where's Jack?" I said, trying to distract her.

"He's around here somewhere. Probably in that crowd over there." Lisa stood on her toes making a dramatic attempt at looking around the ballroom. "I think I'm going to go look for him. See you in a sec."

I watched Lisa wander off into the crowd and look over her shoulder at me only once before dipping into the thick mass of moving bodies. The bad part about being as tall as she was is that she could never hide in a room full of regular-size people. I saw her head bobbing through the crowd until she reached the opposite side of the floor. She was standing on the outskirts of the crowd, watching the girl from a distance. How dare she leave me standing here alone to go stalking some freshman. Who the hell was this new girl?

I was two seconds from stomping over to Lisa and coercing her to go outside with me for some air when out the corner of my eye, Justice emerged from the top of the stairs. He almost bumped my shoulder as he skipped down the stairs a little too quickly. He didn't even see me as he kept his eyes trained on the same crowd that had distracted Lisa. What the hell was going on? First my friend skips out on me. Then my man stumbles past without even recognizing me? Justice settled on the outskirts of the dance floor, his back to me, and jammed his hands into his jeans pockets. Big Deuce spotted him within seconds and clapped his arm around Justice's shoulder as they spoke closely, talking and staring at the girl in the center of the dance floor.

I eyed Big Deuce as he pointed out the girl in the teal dress as she moved like a hip-hop ballerina in the center of the room. Justice was unfazed as Big Deuce spoke but I did notice he was watching her a little too closely. I could see his eyes roaming over her body as she moved. The rambunctious crowd screamed "Oh!" over the contagious beat as she gracefully leaped and spun, her long dress flowing behind her like a cape. She made Webby's song seem like it was written for her. The girl in the teal dress hit every beat hard and twisted her tone, tanned body with control and power. Even the DJ seemed to prolong the song just to keep her going. I inched closer to get a better look. What I saw was shocking. The girl in the teal dress was beautiful. She looked Spanish except for her full, coily hair that rhythmically bounced as she dipped to the music. Her brown eyes were framed by dark, thick lashes that dusted her high cheekbones. She was deeply focused on her dance as her face shifted from smiles to intense concentration with each movement. The track finally faded into a slow song and the girl with the teal dress seemed to snap out of her trance as she looked at the crowd around her. Even Lisa had managed to work her way to the center of the circle, smiling. Onlookers gave the girl high fives and shouted "You go, girl!" as she hustled from the room and disappeared down a side hallway.

Everyone was murmuring about the girl in the teal dress. *What's her name? Where'd she come from? Was she a freshman?* Justice was standing with Big Deuce about five feet away. I struggled to hear the conversation without stepping too close. Lisa waved shyly in the distance. I rolled my eyes in response, still straining to listen in on Deuce. I was already in a sour mood and couldn't hear over the music so I aborted the mission and plodded over to Justice.

"Babe, let's roll." I interrupted Big Deuce midsentence without glancing his way. He pursed his lips like he had something to say but thought better of it.

"Alright, baby. I'm almost ready. I've gotta talk to Deuce about something real quick. Can you pick me up out front?" He leaned in to kiss me on the cheek. Deuce smirked and sipped soda from a red disposable cup.

"I guess so," I said through tight lips.

I wasn't about to walk out alone to a party I came to with my man. My anger was starting to boil over.

I smoothed out imaginary wrinkles in my dress and said, "I take it that Deuce is keeping you warm tonight?"

Deuce choked on his drink. Resting my hand on my hip, I waited for an answer even though I knew it was rhetorical.

"Man, I'll have to catch you in practice on Monday." Justice smirked and gave Big Deuce a quick handshake before putting his palm on the curve of my back and escorting me out of the ballroom.

"Damn, why you gotta be like that?" Deuce asked as we walked away. I turned and winked in response. Checkmate, motherfuckah.

The street outside the Union was packed with people waiting for rides. I tossed my purse into the backseat of my BMW, quickly slid inside and hit the button to close the top. Justice wedged his tall frame into the two-seater and the car shook as he slammed the door shut. The silence was broken by the quiet purr of the engine.

"What's wrong with you?" he asked, staring at me through slitted eyes.

Could it be that I'm mad because he just visually fucked some girl at the party like she was the greatest thing since sliced bread? Oh, or maybe it was because he damn near knocked me over trying to get to the dance floor to see her? Oh, no, that's not it. It has to be when he told me to get the car like I was one of his cronies. I fumed in the driver's seat without moving the car an inch.

"What's wrong with me? That's what you want to know? I should be asking your ass the same thing."

Justice laid his head back on the headrest, staring out the front window.

"What did I do now, Nicole? Just tell me and stop the dramatics." Justice had a way of diffusing the situation, but not this time.

"I saw you looking at that girl." I gripped the steering wheel tightly, trying to keep my voice calm.

"Everyone was looking at that girl dance." He pointed back to the ballroom entrance. "But the only person you see looking is me?" His furrowed eyebrows made his eyes look tired.

"I saw you standing there with Big Deuce. You know he's up to no damn good. You couldn't take your eyes off that girl. Not even long enough to see me." My voice rose an octave.

"So because Big Deuce is up to no good then that clearly means I'm up to no good?" he said sarcastically.

"Birds of a feather, right? I don't like the way you acted tonight. You didn't pay me any attention."

It came out like a whine instead of sassy, as I'd planned it in my head. I didn't wait for a response as I put the car in reverse and maneuvered through the students still convening behind an old pickup truck. The sound of the tires hitting the pavement filled the silence as Justice continued to look out the window without even glancing in my direction.

"You know I love you, right?" It seemed to come from another person. Justice's voice was distant even though he sat directly beside me in the small cabin.

"Yes," I said quietly.

I stopped at the red light adjacent to the West End Mall.

"Then what makes you think I would want someone else?"

He turned to me with his Asian-infused eyes. "You are the most beautiful woman I've ever laid eyes on. Tonight. Or any other night."

He pushed my hair behind my shoulder so he could see my face. The light turned green and I tried to focus on getting us to his apartment complex two blocks down. I could feel his eyes piercing into the side of my face. I felt silly for even thinking he was interested in that girl. When he had someone like me, why would he need anyone else, right?

I pulled into the dark parking lot next to his black Impala and turned to him in my seat.

"I don't want anything to come between us," I choked out.

I was overreacting earlier, letting my insecurity get the best of me.

"Nothing ever will," he whispered in the darkness of the car.

I felt his fingers on my chin as he pressed his soft lips to mine. We kissed tenderly and a crooked smile stretched across his face.

"You ready to wind down from this crazy night?"

"Hell yes."

I exhaled and grabbed the door handle. Before I could push open the door, Justice gripped my shoulder and pushed me back roughly into the driver's seat. He kissed me deeper and more passionately then I'd felt in years. My pussy jumped under the pressure of his soft lips. Within minutes, I managed to tackle two flights of stairs and stumble inside his apartment. My head was still swirling with unbearable visions of Justice leaving me for another girl. I hated feeling like there was someone out there better for him.

I had a good man and I'd do whatever it took to make sure he stayed under my spell.

Justice emerged from the bedroom with a bottle of oil and took my hand, leading me into his bedroom. A candle on the nightstand swirled shadows around the darkened room. As I lay naked across his bed, Justice massaged my body with jasmine oil and eased out the insecurity with his touch. He was passionate and firm as his hands ventured through every hill and valley of my body, stopping only to tease the curve of my back. He traveled lower and firmly pressed the tension from my thighs and planted a kiss on the firm meat of my behind. Justice made love to every inch of my body as if he was apologizing for all his mistakes with every stroke. And I forgave him with each earth-shattering return of his rhythm.

Mali

∞

I was so embarrassed. I couldn't believe that I let Carey talk me into going to the welcome party. She owed me big-time after I'd managed to make a fool of myself on the dance floor then topped it off by running to the bathroom like a scared twelve-year-old child at the end of the song. Carey chattered the whole way back to the dorm about how amazing it was that I could dance like that. To see a ballroom full of students staring at me with huge smiles on their faces was a little shocking. I couldn't remember how I started dancing. One minute I was laughing with Carey and the next I heard Webby's song on the loudspeakers and a feeling of freedom filled my body. Free was not exactly how I felt now. I was mortified at the thought of showing my face on campus Monday. Everyone would be gossiping about the girl who ran from the party like a dog with her tail between her legs. Just like my dad forecasted, I'd found a way to screw things up.

I stripped down in the dormitory shower stall and turned the knob as scalding-hot water sprayed out. I sat on the bench gathering my shampoo and body soap, waiting for the water to cool down.

"Mali?" Carey's voice came from the next stall. Ugh, I hope this didn't become a habit.

"Yeah. I'm here," I said, lathering the soap in my sponge.

"Oh, I didn't know if that was you."

"So did you enjoy yourself tonight?" I quizzed, even though she had chattered the entire ride about how much fun it was.

"Oh yeah!" she answered excitedly. "I can't believe how good you can dance. I wish I had some moves like that. I can barely take two steps without injuring someone." Carey chuckled at her own expense.

"I used to dance back home. I came to AU to learn a lot more. Bremerton was too small for what I want to do."

"Well, I can honestly say, you definitely found your calling," she said.

"Thanks. I really hope so."

"If it's something you love to do…then it's your calling. I've always known that I wanted to be a doctor. I love the thought of helping someone, figuring out problems."

"Not to mention you make a boatload of money doing it."

"That's true." We laughed together.

"Hopefully dancing can do the same thing for me…" I wondered aloud.

"You're gonna make a boatload of money too. With the way you dance, someone is gonna discover you. Just remember, I want front-row tickets. I ain't playing!"

I continued washing my wild hair as we giggled together. The scent of my creamy shampoo filled the small shower stall as I finally felt a sense of pride in choosing my major. Maybe I really was good at dancing. The music seemed to take over my body and the steps came to me like a dream. Atlanta University was going to be the start of something big. I could feel it.

After the shower, I padded to the chilly dorm room and wrapped my flimsy green robe tighter around my waist. I turned off the air conditioner and searched through the closet drawers that Marney had graciously organized. I stretched out across the bed in my Sunday best, worn gray sweatpants and a black tank top. My damp hair clung to the pillowcase as I stared at the popcorn ceiling, daydreaming about the welcome party. I didn't feel like sleeping, and talking to Carey about the party seemed like overkill so I slung my messenger bag across my chest, grabbed my flip-flops and eased the room to take a walk. I didn't know where I was going but being cooped up in the room with Carey for the night seemed like undue torture. I liked Carey but being with an Energizer bunny all day had tired me out.

The evening air refreshed me instantly. The night was still abuzz with excitement from the party. Two girls dressed in sparkly tops carried each other to the dorms across the grassy yard, laughing hysterically as they stumbled along. The welcome banners managed to tangle and snake around a tree branch as the strings hung like vines above the sidewalk. My wet curls licked the tops of my ears as I maneuvered down the well-lit sidewalk avoiding discarded beer cans and food wrappers. I heard laughter in the distance and spotted a group of guys standing outside Pizza Stop. Frat boys with Greek symbols splayed across their jackets stumbled around on the pavement as the others snickered at their obvious drunkenness. The guys whistled in cadence.

"Mmm… Is it cold out here?" one guy asked his friends as they erupted in laughter.

I followed their stares to my protruding nipples. In my haste, I'd forgotten to wear a bra. I shielded my tiny breasts and escaped into Pizza Stop. Luckily, Pizza Stop was nearly empty, sans a guy drooling on the table, passed out in the rear of the restaurant. I ordered a slice of cheese and a Coke and sat uncomfortably in the iron chairs to wait. Pizza Stop was a Venice knockoff café. The plastic, curling grapevines streaming from each corner of the ceiling and the fake wood-burning oven was a dead giveaway. I grabbed the pizza to go, hoping the guys outside had moved on. Their voices carried on the wind but it was a few blocks over.

I settled on a bench behind Clark E. Rice Complex, a sports complex built across five acres of land. It was built in remembrance of a legendary alumni that had gone on to play professional football, then lost a battle with lung cancer at the age of fifty-six. He had donated most of his life savings to the college, so the sports complex was renovated and expanded in his honor. At my age, fifty-six seemed like a lifetime away. My mother and father were slowly ticking past forty-one years of age. I gobbled the corner of the piping-hot pizza and drenched it with Coke. I wondered how my mother was doing after less than a week alone with my dad. I hadn't called her yet because I was hoping my silence wouldn't disturb things in the house. I'd tried my best to be unseen and unheard when my dad had come home. The house would fall silent when he was there, my mother usually busying herself in the kitchen or outside in her makeshift garden. I wondered if my dad rejoiced that I was finally gone and he could get back to living again. I looked off in the distance, hoping my mom was right that he'd find some type of happiness. The street was quiet and still.

Was I the problem? My mother told me I was an unplanned pregnancy when she described the first sign of change in my dad. She smiled as she told me how excited she was to tell my dad that she was pregnant and how he reacted by immediately asking his commanding officer for an assignment to Baghdad in the heart of war. Was the thought of having a baby so bad that my dad had to run toward grave danger? I had to stop blaming myself, that's what Mack always told me. She was right, but all I ever wanted was a normal family, a kind father. Was that too much to ask?

Only pizza crumbs lined the square box when I looked at my watch. It was 1:13 a.m. I downed the remaining Coke that had grown warm and found a trash bin on the walk back to Cramer Hall. When I slid into the dorm room, Carey was softly snoring under her black-and-white polka-dot blanket. I kicked my sandals into the closet and eased onto the bed.

My cell phone vibrated on the nightstand, throwing light into the darkness. Who would be calling me at this hour? It was a text message from a number I didn't recognize.

You shouldn't walk around alone at night. It's not safe.

My heart bumped against my chest. Was someone following me tonight? I sat up in the bed and looked out at the dark, empty campus below. No one was lurking in the darkness. There was no movement in the parking lot from what I could tell at this distance. Instinctively, I shut the blinds and stared at the text message. Who could this be? And why did they care whether I was alone or not? Obviously, they wanted me to know they saw me and I hadn't noticed them. My fingers shook as I texted the number.

Who is this?

Within seconds, a response:

A friend.

I breathed a sigh of relief. I tried to shake the eerie feeling that still lingered in my belly at the mysterious text. I was curious. So I pushed Call Sender and waited for someone to pick up. Before long, a smooth, deep voice answered in a hushed tone.

"So you got the courage to call?" His voice sounded soft as if he were whispering.

I couldn't place a face to the voice.

"I wouldn't call it 'courage,' per se. More curiosity than anything else."

"Well, do you know who I am?"

"No. Should I know who this is?" I questioned.

"Yes, you should. You should really take the time to get to know me better." He sounded self-assured. I was not as confident.

"Okay, I'll play your little game. Why should I take the time to know you? What makes you so special? And how did you get my number anyway?"

"You should get to know me because I'm a good guy. Your number was given to me by," he paused slightly, "a friend of yours."

"A friend, huh? I don't have many of those. So your game is going to come to an end sooner than you think." I giggled at the thought of possibly beating him at his own game.

"Well, isn't that a shame, Mali? The game is so fun." With that, the line went silent.

I stared at the phone for a second with an amused smirk. I must admit, the mysterious man was an interesting twist to my night. The sound of my name on his lips was comforting, reassuring. He didn't sound vindictive or psychotic in the least but neither did Ted Bundy or John Wayne Gacy, I reminded myself. I decided to tread lightly, keep the mystery alive but be cautious. I glanced at the clock and realized that the sun would be up in a few hours. So I stripped off my pants and pulled the covers to my chest.

Sleep invaded like a thief in the night. I dreamed that I was performing a live show on Broadway with Lucille Ball. Our names were in bright lights above the theater box office as people milled about buying their tickets for the nearly sold-out show. Backstage, Lucille was in her prime, beautifully draped in a black gown that highlighted her pale skin. Her lips were still drawn to their unique shape and slathered with dark red lipstick. Clad in a silver midthigh

cocktail dress, reminiscent of a 1960s showgirl, I shimmied to meet
Lucille center stage. We held hands as the thick velvet curtains
opened to a crowded auditorium that cheered and whistled loudly.
Lucille winked as we started the number with the crowd roaring
loudly over the music. I danced to all corners of the stage, keeping
in step with Lucille as we playfully kicked and spun in our comedic
act. The rollicking crowd kept the energy blazing onstage as Lucille
and I danced merrily under the spotlights. I searched the never-
ending faces in the crowd. There, in the front row, I could faintly
see my father's face, smiling proudly. I smiled back. Beside him sat
a dark figure, clapping his hands to the music. I strained to see who
he was. The harder I strained, the more he faded like smoke into
thin air. There was nothing left but the chair and my father. I felt
disappointed as I looked at the empty seat. Lonely.

Justice

∞

September opened with the first away game of the season. Fortunately, the game ended on a high note, for my statistics at least. I received nine touches for 186 yards and finished with two touchdowns, a great start to the season. The local radio stations buzzed about our 21-6 win while the fans calmed down with BBQ pits blazing and tailgaters celebrating. I heard the fans start their infamous chant, "JB! JB! JB!" as one run lasted thirty-seven yards while the other held tight at seventeen yards. Luckily, it was a televised game against the Rockets who plummeted in the third quarter and ended up stalling completely in the fourth quarter. NCAA Player of the Week whispers in the locker room after the game made me puff out my chest. With a title like that this early in the season, I'd be set for the draft.

I eyed Coach Dempsey strutting coolly around the locker room, pumped up from the win. He was built lean like a runner and his face forced wrinkles around his eyes and forehead when he spoke. He started his excitable speech as the team settled in front of their lockers to listen. Some men, half-dressed, nodded eagerly as he spoke. Big Deuce was standing with pride in nothing but his underwear and tank top next to Buddy, the defensive head coach. Deuce had made a good enough contribution to the win that he knew he was getting some good looks by scouts. The more televised wins we had, the greater the chance that our team stayed on the radar when draft season started.

I sat in front of my locker, pushing my foot through the leg of my sweatpants, as Coach Dempsey clapped me on my back appreciatively.

"JB, outstanding game today!" he said excitedly before gripping my shoulder. "You keep performing like that and you're guaranteed to take this program all the way to the championship." Coach Dempsey smiled his yellowing, toothy grin and palmed my head.

"Come talk to me after practice next week," he called over his shoulder as he headed toward Big Deuce and Buddy.

"I'll be there."

The coaching staff herded the team like cattle onto the oversized university football bus. The awaiting crowd outside the gates yelled our names as we filed onto the bus and found a seat. Coach Dempsey didn't take chances with opportunities for bad publicity, especially when we were on the public radar. I completely understood why as I looked out the window at the crowd surrounding the bus. Beautiful women with their breasts bulging from tight-fitting dresses of every color were sprinkled in the crowd. All of them stood gap-legged in four-inch heels, waving seductively at the bus. The temptation was strong at these away games. I shook my head at the sight. A voluptuous blonde stood on the sidewalk outside the gate and pulled down her red tube top, flashing our bus with extraordinarily beautiful double-D breasts as we departed the stadium. My mouth dropped open from the sheer glory of this bold woman.

Big Deuce snapped a picture with his smartphone and proclaimed, "Got another one!"

Everyone on the bus laughed at Big Deuce's constant ability to never miss a bare breast. He had an impressive collection of breasts on his phone, trophies after every win. Cars honked their horns in congratulations as the bus inched through the tight streets.

Our bus completed our parade through the city and merged on the interstate back to AU.

I hoped Nicole was in the mood to talk as I punched the number into the phone and waited for the sound of her voice.

"Hello?" Her voice didn't sound rushed. A good sign.

"Hey, baby. We're on the bus headed back. Did you see the game?"

"Uh. No, I didn't see the game. Lisa told me about it, though."

"Why weren't you watching? It was the first away game of the season." I tried to hide the hurt in my voice. "You missed one of my best games."

"Sorry, I just couldn't get to a television." Her voice trailed off. Nicole always had access to a television. "Nicole? Everything okay?"

"Oh, yeah. Everything's good. I'm just trying to let Toni do my makeup without moving."

"Oh. That's cool. You wanna celebrate when I get back? I've got some new plays I want to show you," I said with sultry sarcasm.

"Can't. Sorry. I've got a promo tonight at Club 126." She didn't seem the least bit sorry. Matter of fact, she seemed dismissive and it was stifling my mood.

"That's cool, Nicole. I see your little party is much more important than spending time with your man after one of the greatest games of his life," I said through clenched teeth since the players were all asleep on the bus. Nicole sighed heavily, as if I was a nuisance. It took everything in me to keep from reaching through the phone and strangling that pompous tone out her voice. I opted for the less violent route and just added, "Don't worry about it. I'll find someone else to hang out with," before pushing the End button on my cell phone. I felt awful for what I said as soon as I ended the call.

Nicole could be so selfish. If it wasn't about her career or her publicity she couldn't care less. I could count on one hand how many games she'd gone to my entire career at AU. I peered out the window at the darkening sky and remembered a time when we would sit outside on her front porch and talk about college. She used to be so easy to talk to but now, I had to be penciled in to her schedule. I was usually slotted thirty minutes before Toni and two days after promotions. I was getting tired of being my own support system.

Nicole

∞

Sometimes men could work your last nerve. Justice called about that dumbass game and ruined my high. He was a buzz kill when I wanted to have a little fun with my friends. I couldn't have fun with him clinging to my coattails all the doggone time. I was elated to finally get the call for promotions at Club 126, the hottest club in Atlanta. But Justice had managed to make me feel the tiniest bit of guilt because I wasn't sitting in front of the television, being lazy, for half the day. Couldn't he see I wasn't that type of girl? I could hardly stomach watching a game. I never understood what was going on and frankly, sweating in the heat with people in jerseys yelling at the top of their lungs didn't sound like a great weekend activity. Not to mention, Webby invited me to Club 126 himself via text message and I wasn't going to pass that up. I'd been thinking about him since we met on set. He'd been texting me for the past three weeks since the video shoot.

"Girl, was that JB on the phone?" Toni interrupted my thoughts about Webby.

"Yeah. That was JB, whining on the phone about the damn game." I rolled my eyes. Just talking about him made me irritated.

"Oh no! They lost?" Toni stuck out his bottom lip in a pout.

"No. They won. JB supposedly had the best game of his life," I said, mimicking Justice's tone on the phone.

"Well hell, what's he whining for then?" Toni flung his hands in the air and turned back to the makeup stand set up in my bedroom.

"He wants me to hang out with him tonight. And you know good and well that I'm not missing this party tonight," I said, looking at my perfectly shaped crimson nails.

"Ask him to go to Club 126, then everybody's happy," Toni said with his back still turned. Almost as if on cue, he turned to face me.

"Wait a minute, missy. Are you going up there to meet Webby?" His eyes were big with surprise, awaiting my answer.

"Why're you all up in my business, Toni? Damn!"

I walked into the closet and started sliding clothes off the rack with a bit more force than necessary.

"I'm up in your business because you're about to mess up! And I'm your friend, so I don't want to ever say I told you so. Webby is fine and all but JB is a good man." Toni followed me into the closet and stretched his arm across the doorway, blocking any escape.

"Look. I'm a grown-ass woman. I don't need you telling me what to do. I got this!"

I plucked a purple miniskirt from the hanger and threw it at Toni. He barely dodged it as it sailed to the middle of my bedroom and rested in a pile on the carpet. Toni rolled his eyes in defeat and exited the closet with a huff.

I felt guilty for going off on Toni because I knew he was just trying to help. Unfortunately, I didn't need any help when it came to Justice or Webby. I had both of them eating out the palm of my hand. One of these men was going to pay off. Within minutes of our fight, Toni and I were laughing at a reality show on television as if we'd never argued.

I slipped my forty-inch hips into the purple miniskirt I'd thrown at Toni. I finished the look with a black bra underneath a white see-through blouse and pulled my hair into a slick ponytail while Toni polished my look with smoky eyes and deep purple lips. This look was sure to get me noticed at Club 126 and I couldn't wait to have all eyes on me.

Club 126 had a line wrapped around the building when Toni and I pulled up. The lights from inside the club leaked out onto the pavement in shades of red as the music beckoned us from the sidewalk. I threw the valet driver my keys and sashayed to the front of the line. The door to the club resembled a dark cave until drunken patrons escaped and colorful light and thumping music burst out onto the street.

"You on the list?"

A huge, muscular man with a tight black spandex shirt stood in front of Club 126. The bouncer looked me up and down then assessed Toni behind me with a grimace.

"Nicole Bunn plus one," I stated with authority.

He looked down the list, his pen sliding over the pages. I could have stood in line if I wanted to wait all day for his illiterate ass. I rolled my eyes impatiently as he slowly slid open the velvet ropes. The beat was pumping loud in the club and women danced seductively in shiny leather boots in human-size birdcages hanging from the coffered ceiling. There was no question why this was the hottest club in Atlanta. A sea of beautiful people swayed in all directions to the rhythmic music. Men and women laced the dance floor and clung to each other like their lives depended on it.

"Look at all that booty meat," Toni said, his glossy lips turned up into a tight frown.

Toni wore his high heels tonight, so we carefully bumped through the crowd looking for the bar.

The bar was nestled under blazing red lights, making it look as if the bartender was enclosed in red prison bars. He served a flaming drink through the lasers to a wide-eyed lady. We made it to the bar just in time to see the lady leave her spot carrying the flaming drink at an arm's distance. We struggled to snag the newly vacant space.

"Sexy Nicole Bunn and Webby in the building!" the DJ roared into the microphone.

"What the…" I turned at the sound of my name to spot DJ Cringe hunched over the DJ booth, pointing at me across the club like he hadn't dissed me a couple weeks ago.

I gave a fake smile and waved to DJ Cringe as random partygoers made their way to the bar to greet me. I hugged as many people as I could and heard all the comments about my booty that I could stand. One girl even had the nerve to walk away reassuring her boyfriend my booty was fake. *Haters.* I shook my head. Toni found a way to get our drinks from the bar, so I downed mine in two gulps.

"You better slow down on the liquor. I don't want to carry you out of here."

The sound of Webby's voice made the hairs on my arm stand up.

"I might want you to carry me out of here."

I spun around to eye him seductively. Damn, he was sexy. From his rustic Bed Stu loafers to his black V-neck shirt wrapped tight around his tattooed biceps. He looked good enough to eat.

Webby flashed that white smile as he gave me a quick kiss on the cheek.

"Come on over to VIP. I was beginning to think you were gonna to stand me up."

"Me? I wouldn't have missed your release party for the world."

I followed Webby to his crowded VIP area two steps up from the main floor, cornered off by velvet ropes.

Webby and I assembled ourselves in a dark corner of the U-shaped couch and waited for Toni to grab another drink. Toni had been stifling his attitude unsuccessfully since Webby approached me at the bar. He rolled his eyes and smacked his glossy lips at everything Webby said. We realized we weren't going to have any fun with him lingering around with a judgmental look painted on his face.

"Toni, can you grab me another amaretto sour? I'm parched," I asked with the sweetest face I could muster.

"Can't moneybags over there get you one?" he said.

I smiled at Webby, who was chuckling to himself. "I'm sorry, Webby. Toni…can you *please* get me a drink?" Toni didn't fall for it as he looked at me from under those dark lashes but he still stalked off into the crowd with an attitude. With him gone, I was relieved to be alone with Webby.

"Thanks for inviting me to your release." I blushed and looked out on the dance floor. DJ Cringe had the women kicking their shoes off, sweating their weaves out and having an absolute ball.

"I didn't think you would come. I know you probably have more exciting things to do on a Saturday night."

"I make it to things that are important to me." Now it was his turn to blush.

"Well I'm glad you did." He paused. "Can I ask you something?"

"Sure." I looked into his dark eyes that seemed so filled with curiosity. He leaned closer to me. My knee rubbed against his.

"What do you want from me?" His eyes locked on to mine and I struggled to find a good answer.

"I want a friend."

"A friend?" He chuckled to himself. " I'm going to be completely honest with you, Nicole. I can't be your friend."

"Why not?" A hint of attitude poked through my demeanor.

"Calm down, Nicole. I'm just saying I can't be your friend because I'll never stop trying to have you for myself...unless you have a man, then I can try to respect that and back off."

"No restraints over here." I wasn't going to lose my chance with a celebrity that had the total package. I'm no fool.

He still had those dark eyes locked on me as he inched closer. Before I could react, his lips were pressed firmly to mine and his hand was gripping the back of my neck tightly. His tongue danced along the edge of my lip and darted in and out of my mouth, searching its new territory. My chest heaved as I tried to catch my breath. I was instantly horny. No, this man could not be my friend. Definitely not.

Mali

∞

Today was the day. I'd continued to push it back for four weeks now. I was thrashing around the dorm room looking for my favorite jeans when I remembered I'd worn them on the bus ride to AU. My mind seized the memory of my mother standing on the sidewalk at the bus terminal with tears in her eyes. I remembered feeling so helpless for her. I dreaded the day I'd have to call her because I knew it was only a matter of time before she made me feel guilty for leaving or I'd receive bad news that I couldn't handle. School was going good since leaving my family in Bremerton. I was excelling in dance class, already outshining the other students in the freshman-level introductory course. I was holding a solid B in psychology class and even managed to make a few friends in the process. So why was I so scared to call home? *Just do it*, I thought with a sigh. I palmed the room telephone and punched the glowing numbers hesitantly.

"Hello?"

My mother sounded like she had just rolled out of bed. I glanced at the clock glowing in the dim dorm room. Oops, it was seven in the morning back home.

"Sorry to wake you, Mom."

"Mali? That you?" Her voice was more alert.

"I forgot about the time change. I was just thinking about you," I said softly into the receiver.

"Oh, Mali. I haven't stopped thinking about you. How's the university? Are you making friends?"

"I'm making some friends. My roommate is pretty cool."

I glanced at Carey's empty bed, covers kicked in a pile showing her apparent struggle to wake up this morning. She had rushed out about an hour ago, still dressing as she slammed the door and sprinted for chemistry class.

"That's good, sweetie. And the school? Is it what you expected?" Her voice cut through my thoughts. I scanned the room for my jeans.

"It's more than I expected, Mom. The dance studio is huge. I've been dancing just about every day since I got here."

The excitement leaked out of my voice and hung in the air.

"That's good. Maybe you will come visit soon? I feel like I haven't seen you in years."

"How're things at home, Mom?" I hedged the question carefully.

A long silence lingered. I looked at the phone to make sure I hadn't accidentally hung up. I could hear my dad cough softly in the background, so I knew she was waiting in silence for him to fall back asleep, her hand over the receiver. Her voice sounded tired again when she answered.

"Have fun at school, sweetie." She sounded finite in tone. I knew it was time to go. She didn't want to wake him or talk about it what we both knew was still happening at home. So I ended the call with a brief "See you soon" with more confusion and sadness than when I called. My mom had survived the first month at home alone or she'd found a way to hide the pain from me. On the inside, I was glad she didn't talk about the abuse. I'd lived too long caring for my mother, protecting her from the rabid animal she claimed to love. I couldn't fathom the thought of hearing that he'd laid his hands on her again and I wasn't there to clean her wounds and tell her it'd be okay in the morning like I always did. Maybe things were getting better. I wanted to believe they were getting better.

I dialed Jacinta Mack next, hoping my good fortune would continue and she'd finally answer my calls. After four rings, her jubilant voice mail echoed through the receiver. I guess I'd leave another message.

"Mack, it's Mali. You know, your best friend?" I said, thick with sarcasm. "I've called you for going on three months now. I think it's time we talk. I've started at AU and have lots to tell you. I miss you. Hope everything is okay. Talk to you soon."

I had to be in psychology class at eleven so I hightailed it from the thick double doors of Cramer Hall and scampered across the grassy front lawn with fifteen minutes to make it across campus. My phone vibrated in my bag. I ignored it but smiled at the thought that it was my mystery man. My heart jolted with guilty pleasure. I couldn't wait to get to class to check out the text.

The yard was quiet as students carried their books, chatting happily to each other in the fall breeze. I was still thinking about the text from my mystery man when I spotted Carey across the yard making her way back to the dorm. She was walking with her head down and didn't see me wave. She looked pale under the sun and her eyes darted across the grass, deep in thought. I hadn't seen Carey upset before but it looked like something was definitely bothering her. Carey being upset was the equivalent of upsetting the Easter Bunny. As she looked up toward Cramer Hall, we caught eyes and I waved her over to walk with me. She jogged lazily to the crosswalk and quickly fell in step.

"Chemistry let out early?" I asked, glancing at my watch.

"No. I was late. So Mr. Bach kicked me out." She was fighting back tears now.

"Oh no. I'm so sorry, Carey. I can't believe he did that." I snuck a glance at my watch. I had eight minutes left. If I didn't make it to psychology class, we would both have a free afternoon. I picked up my speed. Carey kept up without missing a beat.

"I can't miss class, Mali. My mother will kill me!"

"Carey, you do realize you're in college, right?"

"Yes, but…" The lightbulb went off as the realization hit her. She smiled a bit under the embarrassment.

"Just follow the syllabus and complete the book work. You won't fall behind," I assured her with a nudge. Her face brightened back to its normal glow. The Energizer bunny was back.

I secretly regretted helping her. I kind of enjoyed seeing her like the rest of society with all its imperfections. Carey was sheer perfection in everything she did. She was smart, witty and outgoing—oh, and a future neurosurgeon, if that wasn't enough.

The glass doors to the Brigg building were propped open as multicolored advertisements waved in the breeze, attached to almost every inch of glass. The Brigg building was a hundred years old and still creaked and groaned throughout the day. The building seemed old and dilapidated in comparison to the new modern construction that sprung to life around campus. The glass windows were thin and long with metal that looked worn and tattered by the elements. The concrete-and-glass, two-story exterior was reminiscent of a World War Two bunker. The dying plants in the corner of the foyer hung over the large pots in despair while old pictures of administrators and department heads clung to the shabby walls and looked aged by the layer of dust that never seemed to be wiped clean. It was a depressing building but most freshmen had at least one class here until construction was completed on the Frank Meyers building across campus.

I waved to Carey as I took off in a light jog toward the entrance of the Brigg building. Behind me, I heard Carey yell, "Thanks, Mali! You're the best!" as I entered into the air-conditioned foyer of the Brigg building. My class was on the second floor so I climbed the steps two at a time and was able to find my seat by the time the second hand on the clock hit the twelve. On time, I said to myself as I relaxed my breathing. The Brigg building lacked the luxury of an elevator so I had a morning workout, two times a week, by climbing the steep stairs.

"You okay?" There was a wide but muscular man sitting behind me today. That seat was normally empty, so it startled me to hear a deep voice so close to my ear.

"I'm fine. Thanks." I caught a glimpse of his kind, dark eyes and goofy smile.

"I'm Deuce. Everybody calls me Big Deuce, though." He stuck his hand out next to my chair.

"Nice to meet you, Big Deuce."

I eyed his rippling arms under his green T-shirt that read "Rock My World" with a picture of Earth sliced in half by a guitar.

"I saw you at the welcome party," he whispered quietly. "You looked amazing."

I felt my fingers brush the curls that hung in my face, trying to hide my flushed cheeks. Luckily, I was able to get through psychology class without much conversation from Big Deuce.

When class ended, Big Deuce slid from his seat coolly and exited the classroom without saying goodbye. I gathered my textbooks and eagerly checked my cell phone. Indeed, a message from my mystery man awaited me.

U look beautiful 2day

I smiled absently, exiting the classroom.

"Mali!"

The echo of my name in the wide hallway startled me as I approached the top step. I spun on my heels to see Big Deuce standing in the corner hidden partially by the classroom door.

"How'd you know my name? Are you stalking me now?" I rolled my eyes and continued down the stairs. Big Deuce was beside me jogging down the steps before I could look up.

"Stalking you? If I thought you'd like it…I just might." He gave that goofy grin again. I couldn't help but laugh. "I heard your name in class."

"Don't you have another class to get to?" I asked after we walked out onto the yard.

"That depends. Do you have another class to get to?" He looked at me with a sinister look then laughed wholeheartedly. "I'm just playing with you. I'm not a stalker. I just want to get to know you."

"Why do you want to know me? Because you thought I looked 'amazing' at the welcome party?" I mimicked his words. "Give me a break. Who names their child 'Deuce' anyway?"

"First, I'd like to get to know you because you seem interesting…different from the other girls. I saw you at the welcome party and knew I had to meet you." He smiled widely then continued, "And Deuce was the name my father gave me. He named me Deuce because I was the second attempt at my mom and him having a child. She passed away during my birth." Big

Deuce looked across the yard blankly then snapped back to the conversation just as quick. I was mortified by my bad joke.

"It's better than being named Two, right?" he continued lightheartedly.

His laughter made me feel better. His spirit mimicked Carey's in an odd way. They both glowed with life.

"Sorry about the joke on your name. I didn't mean to…" He waved away my apology without response. It must've been tough growing up knowing his mom died so he could live. I thought of life without my mother and felt a deep sadness.

"Tell you what, Mali. If you go to dinner with me, we can call it even." Big Deuce smirked and looked at me out the corner of his eye.

I couldn't help but notice the flirtatious looks women sent him as we walked toward the center of the yard. I was slowly getting the feeling that he was definitely a ladies' man and no stranger to the chase. We were standing in the middle of the yard as students crisscrossed our path on the way to their next class.

"Nice try. But I'm not interested." I continued walking toward Cramer Hall.

"Then can we hang out as friends?"

I shrugged my shoulders. "I don't know. We'll see." I hoisted my heavy messenger bag over my shoulder.

When I looked back, Big Deuce was still standing in the middle of the yard with a strong, almost calculating determination flooding his dark eyes. I could see he was the type that always got what he wanted. Too bad for him—he wasn't going to conquer what he had his sights set on. He could have all the women at AU he wanted. But he wouldn't have me.

Justice

∞

Practice was excruciating. I'd been brutally pounded by the defensive tackles all practice long. It seemed like the defensive squad was trying to send me a message that I wasn't the only one worthy of ESPN highlights. I rubbed my lower back in remembrance of the tough hit that landed me on the grass hard. The clapping of cleats against the tile floors echoed throughout the dank locker room. Dirt and tufts of moist grass clung to the checkered tile in patchy clumps as each player stripped their cleats from their tired feet. There was a strange feeling in the locker room today. Something was off. I knew my mind hadn't been fully in place during practice. I'd missed three tires in the tire drill and face-planted in the dirt when my cleat caught the edge of the last tire. Beyond the embarrassment of the team and coaching staff watching, I was pissed that I was letting Nicole get under my skin. Nicole had a way of causing fights just to kiss and make up and it was becoming a tired act. I felt like it was time to close the curtains on her dramatics but the only problem in confronting her was that I hadn't heard from her all week.

I dodged Coach Dempsey for most of the week after practice since I knew he wanted to drill me about the draft. I couldn't get Nicole off my brain. With the scouts calling and the coaching staff breathing down my neck for a follow-up performance to last game, the pressure was becoming too much to juggle. Luckily, I was at the height of my game as far as the media could tell. Even Big Deuce couldn't cheer me up with his antics.

He was preoccupied with some new girl in his class and I didn't have time to hear about his next conquest. I was too focused on my own problems. Nicole wasn't making our relationship any easier by staying at the club all night then dismissing my calls and text messages. I was debating on stopping by her place later and asking her what was up with this new communication method. If the shoe was on the other foot, Nicole would be up at the stadium causing a scene, cussing and fussing. Like a typical diva, she hated being ignored. Yet she had no problem subjecting me to it whenever she wanted. I sat in front of my locker and massaged my temples. This girl was going to be the death of me.

"What's up, man? You acting like the world is gonna end over one bad practice." Big Deuce was leaning on the empty locker next to mine.

"Nicole's not answering my calls or texts."

"Don't worry about Nicole. She'll come around. They always come back."

"I don't know, Deuce. It feels different this time," I responded. Why would Nicole be so distant? I know our conversation didn't end well after the last game but I was upset, not her.

"Why don't you go by her spot today? You can talk it out in person."

I thought about what Big Deuce said. Going by Nicole's place was the best thing for me. I couldn't take another practice like today, wincing from the pain in my back as I stood.

"You're right. I think I'll stop by her house when I leave. What do you have going on?"

Deuce answered quickly, like he'd been waiting on me to ask. "Man, I met the finest chick you will ever lay your eyes on in psych class the other day." Big Deuce leaned back on the locker and rubbed his palms together like he was imagining a juicy steak.

"Psych class? Man, I thought you dropped that class for the third time?"

"I was about to go to Mrs. Lane and tell her I wasn't going to make it again this year when I saw the girl from the welcome party! You know, the one that was dancing in the blue dress?" I remembered her clearly.

"She goes to AU?" I retorted.

"Yeah, bro. And I talked to her and she is…" He rubbed his chin, thinking of the right term. "She's definitely a healthy challenge, so to speak." He smiled wide and I could tell the dog had found his squirrel. If Deuce caught a squirrel scurrying by in the corner of his eye, he can't help but chase it. Unfortunately, that dog will usually keep chasing the squirrel right across a busy intersection. One point for the squirrel and a miserable loss for the dog. I could see Deuce was totally invested in his squirrel.

"So I guess you finally have some motivation to pass psych this semester?" I laughed as I pulled my shower bucket out of my locker.

"Most definitely! I'm going to study hard and long to pass this psych test." Big Deuce slapped me hard on the back, laughing at his own sarcasm.

"While I'm studying the psychology of a fine-ass woman…you need to be teaching yourself how to pick them legs up when you run. I think my big ass could've beat you in the forty today," he joked as we headed to the crowded shower room. Big Deuce did have a way of making things seem a little better. I had almost forgotten about Nicole. Almost.

The hot shower made my back feel better but yoga usually loosened it up. I did a few stretches while the scalding-hot water flooded over my body and relaxed my aching muscles. The other players were used to my odd stretching rituals in the shower. When I first started on the team, the players would look out the corner of their eyes, speed wash and scamper out of the shower room with their towels wrapped tight to their waists. Now, they continued talking and laughing among themselves as if my yoga poses were perfectly normal. I finished drying off the last beads of water and SNAP! A towel cracked through the air and pierced the back of my thigh with a stinging fire. I yelped in response to the heat radiating from the wound. I heard Big Deuce snicker behind me as the other players erupted into unruly laughter. Sometimes this team was the best and worst thing that ever happened to me.

"I'm going to get you back. Remember that!" I looked at my wound swelling with angry redness.

Big Deuce was mimicking my yelp to the rest of the team, ignoring me completely. I shook my head, plotting on how I was going to get him back.

After pulling on some vintage Levi's and a red, short-sleeved flannel, Coach Dempsey cornered me at my locker. I was pretty sure he wanted to talk about my dismal performance at practice today. Big Deuce had managed to get some laughter out of me earlier but I was pretty sure Coach Dempsey was set on smothering that laugher with his criticism.

"JB, I need you in my office…now." The emphasis on *now* meant I better be in his office before he got there. So I left my shoes off and padded to his office tucked far down the hall behind the shower room. The door was ajar and I could see that he had the television playing old football tapes. His huge game binder was open on his desk with his reading glasses slipped into the middle of the oversized book. I crept in slowly and sat down in the leather chair across from his desk. Within seconds, Coach Dempsey burst into the room, shut the door quickly and took his seat behind his desk. He was moving like lightning and by the look on his face, I could tell he wanted to jump across the table and pound me.

"What the hell was that in practice today?!" he roared. He was not attempting to keep his cool.

"I…" He turned his head and raised his hand.

"I'm going to tell you what that was in practice. That was you…pissing away your future! JB, you have all the tools you need to succeed in this sport but your mind is the only thing you can't get a handle on." He jagged his temple in emphasis. "I don't care if you broke up with your girlfriend or if your family dog died…you give me one hundred fucking percent on that field! You understand me?!"

Coach Dempsey was teetering on the edge of his seat, jabbing his finger roughly into the playbook on his desk.

"Yes, sir."

He leaned back, smoothed the lines in his shirt and loosened his buttoned collar, probably in an attempt to release some steam.

"There is a scout for the Panthers coming to the school on Saturday. You need to be at your best. The shit you pulled today in practice ain't gonna cut it. You got that?" He slowly shook his head with a sinister rhythm, never tearing his eyes from mine. "Don't screw this up for us."

"No, sir. I won't."

"Damn right you won't. I've been watching some film of you the last few days. You have to get higher on your extensions. I need your head above the ball. We lost some catches last year due to mere fingertip grips. If Rainier throws it too high, I need to have confidence that you can catch it."

"I can do it, Coach. I can work on some jumping drills this week," I assured him.

"Yeah, you do that, but I also have something unorthodox in mind for you." His wrinkly eyes squinted like he was assessing if I could handle the secret he was about to tell. "I want you to take dance class."

I almost choked on my own spit right there in front of the coach's gleaming eyes.

"Dance?" I muddled.

"Do you remember Walter Payton? You remember how he could collapse around the ball almost like a cocoon? No one could get the ball from Peyton, let alone stop him."

"What does this have to do with dance class, Coach?"

"Since the 1970s football players have been taking dance and yoga to keep them flexible and loose while taking a hit. I want you to take a dance class to get your feet moving, your leaps higher and your focus stronger. You have mastered the tire drills already so I need you to refocus, trick your mind and body into reacting differently. This is a critical season for you and for the team. If we bring home the championship this year, there's a lot of good things that can happen for this program." Coach Dempsey was back to the edge of his seat but with more eagerness than anger.

"You know I'll do anything for the team and this program, Coach. If you think it'll make me better and has the potential to bring us to the championship, I'll try anything once." I looked at the coach skeptically.

He nodded and pulled out a tiny white notepad from his shirt pocket. He quickly scrolled across the page and passed me the paper. I looked at the numbers in blue ink.

"It's the number to the dance teacher. She'll get you started. I've already talked to her and she's expecting you. Don't let me down, JB. This is our season."

Coach Dempsey stuck out his long, slim hand and gripped mine with a strong shake. I folded the paper, swiftly exited his office and walked through the empty locker room. I felt like I hadn't inhaled inside Coach's cramped office. I slipped on my shoes, jammed the phone number into my back pocket and grabbed my gym bag on the way out the locker room. I thought I was under pressure from the scouts but now Coach Dempsey was putting even more pressure on me by adding another training day to our already grueling schedule. This season's practice schedule had me drowning and there was no one to throw me a life jacket. My classes were suffering because I was falling asleep during lectures. Granted, Coach had the highest expectations for me but I didn't see how jumping around with a bunch of girls was going to make me a better ball player. I sat in my black Impala, in the middle of the stadium parking lot, trying to get my head together. I needed to release some of this pressure. My first stop was the source of my bad day.

I gunned the engine and pulled out of the parking lot onto Main Street. I was two blocks from Nicole's apartment. It was time to get our relationship back on track. I couldn't go another night with an empty feeling in the pit of my stomach wondering where she was and what had her so upset with me. I accelerated through the narrow city streets. I wasn't sure if I had it in me to have another angry confrontation with Nicole but I knew my focus wasn't going to fully recover until she and I were on the same page. Nicole always blew up in anger when she couldn't get her way, even when she was the one at fault. I mentally accepted the challenge as the Impala maneuvered down Nicole's street. There was one thing I did know: Nicole owed me an explanation about why she wasn't returning my calls. I was going to get an explanation one way or the other.

Nicole

∞

I couldn't believe how amazing my night was. I danced around the kitchen in my tank top and panties, trying to decide if I wanted Cinnamon Toast Crunch or Peanut Butter Crunch for breakfast. I grabbed my favorite bowl from the cabinet and fished for a clean spoon on the drying rack. Peanut Butter Crunch sounded good. I curled up in front of the television and clicked through the channels as I munched on peanut-buttery goodness. I reminisced about last night, staring blankly at the flickering screen of morning talk shows.

Between doing dishes and cleaning my filthy kitchen, I was surprised to see a text from Webby.

DINNER?

Of course ;)

I was contemplating which dress I would wear when there was a soft knock at the door to the apartment. When I cracked opened the door, a man in a cheap black suit left a large box with a sparkling pink bow on my welcome mat. I waited for him to reach the stairs to the parking lot before I grabbed the box and eased back into my house. I slowly unwrapped the pink bow and pulled opened the oversized box. Inside was a long, elegant red dress. I knew exactly who it was from. Webby was the only man with enough style to dress me. I pulled the dress to my chin as a reveled in the reflection of the floor mirror, envisioning how it would look on my body. The price tag waved lazily on the neckline of the dress. I tried to focus on the $1,200 tag but my eyes kept blurring. I laughed aloud, jumping across the top of my bed like a teenager, thrilled by the expensive gift. At the bottom of the box were silver strappy heels, perfectly sized and dazzling even in the dim overhead light. I plunged onto the cheetah bedspread as my heart pounded in my chest like I'd run a marathon. I wasn't sure if it was because I'd leaped three times across a queen-size bed or if I was excited about the date with Webby. I peeked out my bedroom window at the parking lot below and observed the man in the suit standing next to a black Lincoln near the curb. I smiled gleefully as I texted Webby.

Thank u 4 the dress and shoes!!! They are beautiful. ;0)

Within seconds, his response vibrated in my hand.

Anything 4 you Baby. A beautiful woman deserves beautiful things.

A girl could get used to this

That's what I'm hoping

I won't disappoint you

I doubt you could

Is that my car downstairs?

Of course. Your chariot awaits

See you at 9, my Prince

Til then

His text messages made me dream of sharing another kiss with him. He knew the right things to do to make me feel like a lady. I sung along to the radio as I showered, shaved and toweled off. I wished Toni was here to do my makeup as I leaned toward the mirror. Toni would have a bona fide fit if he knew I'd been hanging out with Webby since the release party. So I'd tackle this gorgeous face on my own tonight. After dusting shimmering silver powder over my lids I blew a kiss to myself.

"Beauty doesn't take much work after all," I said to the mirror.

I slipped into the slinky red dress and heels. My waist was pinched tight by the fabric but I sucked in my belly and twirled in the mirror. The dress was perfection, falling on my curves like it was made especially for my body. I sprayed two spritzes of perfume on my wrist and fanned myself. One last turn in the mirror showed that my hair cascaded perfectly and my firm rear was giving me just enough bounce to make Webby drool. Yummy, I thought as I locked up the apartment and pranced to my chariot.

When the car pulled up to the restaurant, I spotted Webby waiting outside near the valet looking delicious in a blue fitted suit that hugged his muscular frame in all the right places. His dark skin was smooth as velvet as he waited curbside for the car to pull around the valet. I stepped out of the black Lincoln under the lights of the awning, and my dress shone. Everyone waiting for their cars stopped to stare. I swished my hips confidently as I grazed Webby's cheek with a kiss. We rode the crowded glass elevator to the top floor and everyone inside spilled out into a futuristic foyer. The smell of delicious food wafted around the room and seemed to settle like a fog. My mouth watered as we were led through lines of tables by a thin hostess dressed in her funeral best. We stopped at a small table that overlooked the shining city of Atlanta. The Sun Dial rotated around the entire tower for breathtaking panoramic views of the city over a first-class dinner. Webby and I talked closely at the table as a jazz pianist played soft music in the background. We told stories about our past against the backdrop of a city that spread for miles. Webby pointed out all the places he'd been in Atlanta and which ones he was going to take me to. I smiled so much during our conversation my cheeks cramped.

"So tell me about your parents," Webby said, chewing on a piece of bread.

"What's to tell? They died when I was young. I have a younger sister but I don't get to see her. Not that she wants to see me anyway."

"Sorry to hear about your parents. That's pretty messed up. Why won't your sister see you?"

"She has a new family. She got adopted before me, stopped writing and calling. When I was old enough to find her, I went to see her and she wasn't my sister anymore. Changed her name and everything." Talking about it made my appetite fade.

"That's crazy. It's like she's trying to erase her memories by becoming someone new," Webby analyzed.

I wiped my mouth with a napkin. "What about you? What's your story?"

"My story? Well, I don't know my dad. Sucker never cared enough to be around til I made it big. So he don't exist to me. My mom…" He put his fork down with sadness in his eyes. "She's in rehab. She got heavy on some drugs after I made it and stole a few mill from me. So I put her in rehab to get cleaned up."

"She stole a couple million dollars from you?" I asked incredulously.

"Yeah. It was crazy. But that's my mom, you know. I only got one." He smiled and motioned for the waitress.

Webby ordered every meal I found interesting on the menu until our table was filled with plates of roast duck, braised chicken, surf and turf along with asparagus and corn medley. My dress was aching to bust open as I tasted everything on the steaming plates as the waitress slid them on the table. Webby continued talking about his childhood and how fame can distort things in relationships, change people for the worse. All I wanted was fame and he was complaining about having it? I listened intently to his stories, which revealed a lot of hurt behind the betrayal of his ex-girlfriend and his manager.

"I couldn't believe that everyone in my life had betrayed me." Webby scraped his food across the plate, still not eating. "It made me go a little crazy. It was right after my mom, you know?"

"Trust me, I know betrayal more than you know." I thought of Justice and swallowed. "But there is something to always remember…the things that hurt can either destroy you or make you stronger."

Webby smiled up from his plate. "Aren't you a wise young soul? How did you get so much wisdom at twenty-one?"

"I've been through things. I've lost people that I cared about. I know what it's like to feel like you have to go into the world alone."

"You don't have to do it alone, Nicole. Let's do it together." Webby reached for my hand across the table. "I just can't understand how none of those knuckleheads at your school didn't wife you up by now."

"Those are boys…I need a man that can take care of me the way I deserve," I said confidently.

"I can promise you one thing. If you are honest with me and you ride with me, I'll ride with you."

I tried to hedge the relationship conversation by nodding emphatically. I wasn't equipped to tell all my secrets. Not now. Not when things were starting so well with Webby. The last thing I wanted to do was complicate things by talking about my six-year relationship with Justice. So I excused myself to the bathroom and looked in the mirror at my reflection. What was I doing? How far was I going to go with Webby? I polished up my makeup, spread on some lipstick and told myself, *Stop being a broke bitch and get this money.*

Webby didn't seem to mind my expeditious exit or my brief hiatus. When I returned to the table, he had a baby-blue box wrapped with a similar pink bow sitting on the tablecloth. I smiled as I sat down slowly.

"What's this?" I grinned as I fingered the box.

"It's a little gift for a very special woman in my life. Before you open it, I have a confession to make." He dropped his head slightly before raising his dark eyes to meet mine. "Nicole, you've been such a blessing in my life. I thought that after my ex, things weren't ever going to be right for me again. I felt like I couldn't trust even the closest people to me."

"I'm sorry…" I offered. He raised his hand to quiet my apology.

"Nicole, I'm telling you this because I feel different with you. I think about you all the time. Even when we're apart, I find myself wishing you were near me. So this gift is a reflection of how much you've inspired me in such a short time." He pointed to the blue box across the table.

I released the bow and carefully opened the lid on the box to find a diamond bracelet shining under the lights of the restaurant. My eyes watered at the sight of the sparkling diamonds and I couldn't help but lean across the table to taste Webby's juicy mouth. He welcomed the kiss fervently. I didn't want to stop kissing him after seeing the beautiful gift but for fear of creating a scene, I fell back in my seat, breathless. He was really working hard for my heart. Webby smiled across the table from me as if reading my mind.

∞

The television clicked to *The View* as I finished my bowl of cereal. I knew I had to stop reminiscing about Webby or I was going to get caught up. I didn't want Webby to have the upper hand in the relationship because every woman knows she has the power of the P-U-S-S-Y until she gives it up to a man. With Webby's endless gifts and sultry kisses, he was going to get it and get it good. I was still worried about Justice, though. I couldn't dodge him forever. I settled into the fact that I was going to have to choose between Webby and Justice eventually. I decided to ride this wave of excitement as long as I could and get as many perks as possible before the choice had to be made.

I examined the red dress that I'd thrown over the edge of the couch last night and fingered the severed price tag that was balled up on the cushion. *It was $1,200.* I smiled to myself and shook my head. I'd have to work four promotion gigs to pay for this dress myself. The shoes lay haphazard in the corner of the living room like a second thought. I remembered kicking them off as I stumbled through the darkness, trying to undress last night. We'd talked until the Sun Dial kicked us out, made out at Webby's mansion until I had to call it quits. Leaving him yearning for more was an integral part of the plan. I was still a little giddy as I pranced into the kitchen to clean my cereal bowl. A knock on the door interrupted my wash, so I toweled off my wet hands. A second knock rang out, harder this time. Was it another gift from Webby? That would be icing on the cake if it was. I crossed the living room and stood in the foyer, unclasping the safety lock. I cracked the door slightly.

"Nicole. Let me in."

Justice was standing in the hall and he didn't look happy. I tried to shut the door quickly but he nudged his shoe in the cracked doorway and I felt silly trying to push against him.

"What do you want, Justice?"

I walked into the living room and leaned my hip against the back of the couch. The door slowly swung open as Justice walked over the threshold and shut it softly behind him.

"You weren't going to let me in?" He looked shocked.

"I wasn't dressed." I motioned to my lack of clothing and as result, crossed my hands over my chest tightly.

"Nicole, don't give me that. I've seen every inch of your body for the last six years. What's going on with you?"

"Justice, I'm tired." I was feeling backed into a corner and I didn't like it.

"Then go to sleep," he said smartly.

"You know what I mean."

"Tired of what? We're doing good one minute then the next you don't answer my calls or text messages." He put his hands in his pockets and leaned against the front door. The space between us felt like it wasn't enough, even though he was far enough away that I couldn't touch him. I watched him visually analyze the room as he stood as still as a statue.

"I don't know what's going on with us, Justice. I'm feeling like I need a break." The words came out like water from a faucet. Smooth and easy. I felt relieved when I said it, as if I'd yearned to say those words for a while. I could see his jaw clench and unclench as I waited for his response.

"So who bought you that dress? And those shoes over there?" He pointed at the silver heels in the corner. I scrambled for an answer.

"A friend."

"A friend, Nicole? Are you cheating on me?!" Justice's face hardened. His Asian eyes were no longer as deep as pools but instead held a cold, sinister gaze.

"No. I'm not sleeping with him. It's someone who's interested." I looked at the shoes in the corner and smiled. Without warning, Justice was standing in front of me, breathing heavily. I had never seen him this mad at me before.

"You're a liar! You don't answer my calls and you're getting gifts from another man? You ain't nothing but a slut!" I could feel the spit from his words sprinkle my face.

The anger boiled within me at the sound of his words. Before I could stop it, my hand darted out and slapped his smooth, brown face with a loud clap that could be heard next door if they listened close enough. His eyes returned to mine even darker than before as he held his face where I hit him. I had never hit Justice before. The shock was tattooed on both our faces. Before I could utter an apology, Justice had his thick hands wrapped around my throat, squeezing. My legs kicked at the back of the couch, trying to gain some type of ground or leverage. Justice's eyes were empty as he flipped me over the edge of the couch and pressed me hard into the seat cushion. I grabbed his wrists and tried to pull my neck free from his grasp, without luck. I tried to scream but only gurgling sounds projected through the room. Tears streamed out my bulging eyes and I could feel the light fading into darkness. As my fight grew weaker, Justice's glassy eyes blinked twice as if he realized that he was seconds from stifling every ounce of life out of me. He released me from his grip and looked at himself with his arms outstretched, as if he was in someone else's body. I gripped my bruised, tender neck and puffed heavily until my wind was back. Justice came toward me in apology. He grabbed my wrist and eyed the diamond bracelet that still hung there from last night. I snatched my wrist from his grasp.

It took all my energy to squeak through my anger, "Get out of my house with yo broke ass! You can't do half the shit he can do for me! Weak-ass, broke-ass, wannabe baller!"

Each word came out broken and less forceful than I imagined. I tried to push his chest away from me. Get him out of my house. But he took every push like it didn't affect him. I crawled across the couch to keep a barrier between us. Still, he remained six inches from my face, his fists clenched into tight balls. I was starting to panic. What if Justice went over the deep end? He could easily crush me with his thick hands.

"Nicole, you're never going to find a man that loves you more than I do. You're going to give up six years of our lives for some gifts and a few dollars?!" he snapped.

"It's not the gifts! It's how he makes me feel when he touches me." Justice curled over and grabbed his knees. I could tell this was crushing him from the inside out, but I had more to tell him. "He knows how to make me feel like a woman, not a little girl. I'm tired of you! Tired of these damn football dreams and being broke all the time! I have to work and go to school to maintain a damn life for the both of us. I can't do that shit anymore! It's time for me to be spoiled."

I thrust a hand through my hair that had gotten tangled during the scuffle and watched Justice's back heave slowly as he tried to breathe through the weight of my words. I didn't care anymore. I wasn't going to let him get away with choking me without him feeling my pain. It was a small price to pay, I thought as I rubbed my neck. I was happy to get the proverbial monkey off my back. Now, I could focus on my new relationship.

"You're a spoiled brat. You think everyone should cater to you and what you want. What about everyone else, Nicole? What about what I want!" Justice straightened to look in my eyes. His anger simmered below the surface.

"I don't care what you want! You're like a little puppy that keeps coming back. Just forget about me! Forget about us!"

"Nicole, you're making a big mistake." Justice stepped back. "Does he even love you?" His eyes burned with the pain of the question.

"He's going to fall in love with me. I know it." I tried to sound convincing.

"He doesn't love you, Nicole! Men that buy your love are going to bill you one day and I hope it's a price you're willing to pay." He clutched his chest, which was now rising and falling quickly. "Real men lead with their heart."

"I don't need a love lesson from you, Justice! If he wants to buy my love, it's for sale. Free love ain't got me anything but broke. Look at you! You're *chasing* the dream. He's *living* the dream." I paced around the room. "Leave before I call the cops and put an end to your sorry-ass career." I pointed at the door.

Justice's body seemed to float like a ghost to the door. Without a look back, he was out of the apartment and the door swung shut with a hollow *thud*. The living room seemed to swell and vibrate around me with the anger of the breakup hanging on the wind thick as cigarette smoke. I wrapped my arms around my body and swayed as I replayed the fight in my head like a bad dream. I felt the tinges of loss deep in my belly as I scanned the room for something…anything. I settled for collapsing on the couch. I grabbed the red dress that had become balled up on the corner of the couch in the scuffle and raised it to my face. I could smell my sweet perfume and Webby's faint cologne lingering on the threads. The dulling thoughts of Justice and our breakup made my heart throb as I padded to the bathroom to examine my neck under the bright bulbs. I noticed two long, purple bruises on the front of my neck rising to the surface of my skin, pounding with dull heat. I replayed the fight with Justice in my mind as I searched for my foundation in the drawer and blotted the artificial color over the bruises. I stared in the mirror at the slight dark mark that peeked through the matte foundation. *I have to look good tonight when Webby picks me up*, I thought to myself. I knew if he saw these bruises he would question my loyalty. I had successfully hidden the fact that I was in a long-term relationship with Justice and I would do anything to make sure I didn't turn Webby into the arms of another woman. I just knew he could give me the life I desired. The life of a princess. All I had to do was play my cards right.

Mali

∞

It turned out to be a very dreary, rainy day at Atlanta University as I plodded through soggy grass en route to dance class. The large drops of rain fell on my hooded sweatshirt as I dodged puddles that looked too deep to step in. I actually liked rainy days. It was the world's way of washing everything clean. I knew how beautiful it was going to be when the rain subsided and the clouds opened up to reveal beautiful rays of sunlight. The smell of soaked wood and fresh grass would blanket the air. I envisioned the flowers and trees would shake free of their wetness in the gentle fall breeze while the tiny birds would visit them after the storm. But currently, I was getting soaked to the bone as I half walked, half jogged to the Denman building. The Denman building housed the school's first and only dance studio. The studios were crammed in the rear corner of the building while the theater and drama stages lined the entryway, reminiscent of Broadway theaters in New York. The building was actually quite amazing in structure since it carried a historic regality that so many other buildings on campus lacked. The cold, wet wind ripped through my thoughts as I gripped my sweater tighter. *My chance to perform on the Denman stage isn't too far away*, I reassured myself. It was a stretch to dream that my mother and father would travel to see me perform so I discarded it for an idea more likely to happen, like pigs flying.

Mrs. Della-Rose, my dance instructor, was working on her second full-length dance theater play. Her first play, *The Kindness of Foes*, was recognized in *Atlanta Magazine* as "creating groundbreaking artistry in dance and theater" and awarded last year's Best Performance Award for the Teen Division, Best Urban Play and was nominated for an Emmy award. I remembered my first day in dance class as students chatted with one another and stretched their limber bodies against walls, poles and barre. The class quieted to a hush as Mrs. Della-Rose wheeled in a squeaky TV cart and the video sprung to life. I watched in amazement, my mouth gaped open, as the story on-screen told of the skill of such great dancers. Their limbs stretched and rolled against each other, the pain evident in the hard lines of the dance. The stage lights cast shadows of their bodies in larger-than-life movements against the white background as they tumbled into embraces and effortlessly leaped in unison. Mrs. Della-Rose's original numbers were well known nationally so she maintained a network of ambitious working dancers. Her eye for creating dance stars and spotting talent earned her program top honors and recognition. She clung to me after the first few classes and immediately thrust me into her intermediate course. She pushed me until my knees buckled and screamed "Again!" as my feet cried into the wooden floor on most nights. There were senior-level students but others were actual working dancers that she invited to participate in the course. She'd said they were there to mentor but from the looks of things in class, the mentors were too busy trying to be seen by Mrs. Della-Rose to care about the new dancers. In dance, the competition was fierce. I had to fight for my spot in the intermediate class—which was limited to invitation only—and an invite could be retracted at any time.

I entered the studio to find the intermediate dancers already in full swing, literally. Swing class was scheduled for today but I was pretty sure I wasn't late as I rechecked my wristwatch. Yes, I was on time. I eyed the room suspiciously and caught sight of Brianna dancing near the front of the room. Brianna was Mrs. Della-Rose's protégé, or her brown-nosing, backstabbing slave as I liked to secretly describe her to Carey. She returned my devilish stare as I pushed angrily through the locker room doors and started

stripping my wet sweatshirt over my frizzy bushel of curls. I knew
Brianna was the cause of my lateness. She was in charge of Mrs.
Della-Rose's calendar and, conveniently, she'd forgotten to send
me any updates on scheduling. She'd been in competition with me
since Mrs. Della-Rose complimented me during contemporary
class. Contemporary dance was my bread and butter, so to speak. I
kicked off my waterlogged boots and slipped on my cotton toe
socks. I was going to make sure I did my very best today, just to
spite Brianna. I walked back into the studio with fire in my eyes
and a new motivation toward greatness.

After dance class left all of us heaving and aching in
clusters around the studio, Mrs. Della-Rose finally called it quits.
She clapped her hands twice, just loud enough to make us
straighten our backs into ready position.

"Good class. Please work on your technique for this style.
Timing is everything!" She strutted around the class, eyeing each
dancer. The class grew even more silent. "We are here to make
history, people. Remember that when you come out on this floor."

She eyed a dancer next to me and rolled her eyes
distastefully. The dancer cowered under Mrs. Della-Rose's
appraisal, her head dropped so low in shame that I thought she
might become a turtle in her oversized T-shirt and leggings. I
straightened my back and stood majestically, pressing my bust
forward at the thought of Mrs. Della-Rose assessing me next.

"Brianna and Mali?"

Instantly, my eyes darted to Brianna in anger.

"Stay after for a minute. I need to talk with you both."

Brianna gave a smug grin and nodded at Mrs. Della-Rose's
request. The class was dismissed with a wave of her hand as she
strolled lightly as a seasoned ballet dancer down the hall to her
office. The dancers looked back over their shoulders as they exited,

worried for the fate of the two of us. Mrs. Della-Rose was a perfectionist in her own right but all the dancers knew she was very blunt and callous with her assessments. Maybe years of being in the dance industry had made her insensitive to the woes of budding young dancers, or maybe she just stopped caring about being liked and instead held on tight to her numerous achievements.

I approached Brianna as she guzzled her water bottle in an attempt to avoid what she knew was coming. "Why did class start early today?" I tried to suppress my anger through clenched teeth.

"Class didn't start early. Are you stupid or something?" She stared directly into my eyes. "You were late."

"You and I both know I wouldn't be late if you had emailed me the update like everyone else." My voice was beginning to rise. "I just happened to be the only one that didn't get the message, huh?"

"Look, I know that you were put in this class by Mrs. Della-Rose but honestly, no one else here can see why." Brianna stepped in close enough that I could feel her breath on my lips as she spoke. "You'd be better off finding a new course. Better yet, a new major."

"You don't have to want me here. Mrs. Della-Rose has made it clear that she wants me in this class. And fortunately, she's the one with the awards on the wall, not you. So you can keep trying to get me kicked out but at the end of the day…I'll still be a better dancer than you. Unlike your personality, you can't fake talent."

I bumped Brianna's bony shoulder to remind her that I wouldn't ever be backed down by a skinny, snobby, second-rate dancer. She gawked in disbelief as I stormed off toward Mrs. Della-Rose's office.

She sat in her office quietly, seemingly oblivious to the tension as Brianna and I sat across from her desk. She was still so graceful even though she had stopped dancing professionally more than ten years ago. Her ebony hair fell around a petite, pale face. She reminded me of the cuteness of a small mouse with her large, dark eyes and long, pointy nose that always looked pink at the tip.

"Brianna and Mali, how do you think the course is going this semester?" Her abruptness startled both of us. I glanced over at Brianna to see if she was going to bring up our altercation in the studio today. She showed no signs.

"I feel like you are doing an excellent job, Mrs. Della-Rose. The routines are challenging. The students seem genuinely interested in the program…for the most part, anyway." She glanced toward me quickly.

"Mrs. Della-Rose…" I started but was cut off.

"You two have been distracting each other in my class and I will not have it." She leaned back in her chair and rested her hands on her lap. Her voice was controlled and soothing.

"Mrs. Della-Rose, I would never intentionally distract your class," Brianna urged. Hopefully she could see through Brianna's lies like I could.

I leaned back in my chair and waited for Brianna and Mrs. Della-Rose to finish. Brianna wanted to steal the show again and in this circumstance, I would gladly give it to her. I learned from dealing with my father not to speak unless directly addressed. Otherwise, you could be picking up your teeth off the living room carpet. I was pretty sure Mrs. Della-Rose was not going to reach out and slap us both for our disruptive rivalry but she could provide a nice slap to my scholarship. So I figured being quiet might suit me better. After minutes of listening to Brianna rant, I sensed Mrs. Della-Rose growing agitated by Brianna's unabashed apologies and constant reminding of how much she loved the program.

"Quiet, girl." Mrs. Della-Rose rolled her eyes at Brianna's incessant voice and smoothed her hair behind her ears. Brianna struggled with one last "Sorry" before fading into the silence.

"Mali, do you have anything to add?" Mrs. Della-Rose asked.

"Ma'am, I think you know how I feel about this course and about dance in general. I came to your class with the hope of fine-tuning my skills with great mentors and peers." I glanced at Brianna out the corner of my eye. " I apologize for any interruption I caused."

I wanted to say so much more. I wanted to beg that she not suspend me from class or lose respect for me as a dancer. I needed her courses to keep my scholarship and my skills developed each time I stepped into the studio under her guidance. I wasn't ready to give up yet.

Mrs. Della-Rose looked thankful for my short and sensible response. She answered, "Well, I do know that both of you love this course but I do feel that one of you has been digressing, while the other is progressing. Progression is a sign of a great dancer. They continue to learn new techniques and push the limits of their abilities. You see, dance is a lifelong journey." She eyed both of us, back and forth, for what seemed like hours.

I could feel my heart thumping in my chest, trying to escape through my throat. The lump in my throat burned. I was kicking myself for not pleading my case like Brianna had. Apparently, another useless teaching from my dad, I thought. Even miles away he still had the ability to make me scared to speak my mind. My tunic seemed too tight on my body and my hands started sweating profusely. I could not lose this scholarship. I was not going back home to my mom and dad. I'd get a job bussing tables or scooping up dog poop before I caught a bus back to Bremerton. How could I let Brianna get under my skin and destroy my focus? Yes, she was annoying and conniving, but that wasn't enough to change the way I felt when I danced. I waited patiently for the worst, for Mrs. Della-Rose to kick me out of her course.

"Mali, I never thought you would behave this way after seeing that initial fire burning in your eyes. You were late to my class, which is another slap in the face to my program. But we'll get to that soon enough." I shrunk down in my chair and hugged myself as Mrs. Della-Rose continued, "I have great expectations for you but unfortunately, this isn't the class for you."

A tear cascaded down my cheek. I could see Brianna's smug face from the corner of my eye. She relaxed her rigid back slightly. A very subtle sigh of relief, I was sure. My mind was reeling on how I was going to pick up another class this late into enrollment and prove myself to Mrs. Della-Rose. Losing this course could set my goals back tremendously. I wanted to be in her stage play next year and being kicked out by the choreographer and director was more than a major setback.

I dropped my chin in defeat as Mrs. Della-Rose cleared her throat. "That's why I want you to practice with my senior dance troupe on the weekends as well as moving to my contemporary dance course on Mondays and Wednesdays. We need to really hone your natural talent in contemporary dance. I think you will grow tremendously given the right challenge."

I felt my body surge to life before I realized I was standing in front of Mrs. Della-Rose's mahogany desk with my tears wet on my cheeks in utter disbelief. I replayed her words again and again in my head as I looked at the edge of her lips flicker into a slight smile.

"Thank you so much." I smiled.

As quickly as I had seen it, her smile was gone. She was staring at Brianna, poised in her seat with her long neck extended. Her face displayed the same disbelief as mine, and then a hint of fear flushed her pale cheeks.

Mrs. Della-Rose continued as I found my seat and smiled to no one in particular. "Brianna, I'm very surprised at how this year has developed your skills. You've come from the best school and I have the highest aspirations for you in my ballet course." Mrs. Della-Rose smiled curtly. "With that said, you have been slacking on your timing with my new corps of dancers in the advanced dance course and I've been made aware that you have not been playing well with others in the intermediate class." I could feel the tension radiating from Brianna with each word that Mrs. Della-Rose spoke.

"As my aid, it is important for you to motivate the students and foster their love of dance. Instead, you fail to send emails, argue openly in the studio and fail to control your own distaste for any form of healthy competition."

I was breathless. How did Mrs. Della-Rose find out about the missed emails? I surely hadn't told her about the wicked things that Brianna said and did while she left us in her care. Had she been doing this to others? Brianna sat rigid in her chair and succeeded in wiping her face clean of any emotion. She stared straight ahead as if being badgered by an intimidating drill sergeant instead of a mousy-faced, petite lady. Mrs. Della-Rose picked up a paper on her desk and slid it in Brianna's direction. It settled on the end of the desk for a long moment. Brianna sat still as a stone and did not acknowledge the paper that was clearly intended for her.

"Brianna, on the paper you will find a release from your duties as my aid. You are still welcome to attend the class in a student capacity. Of course, I would like to keep you in my advanced ballet course."

She turned her beady brown eyes in my direction. "Mali, please stay for a moment to discuss." With that, Brianna snatched the paper from the desk and exited without a glance in either of our directions. The door slammed loudly behind her as the faint sound of her bare feet slapped against the linoleum floors, echoing down the hall.

"Mrs. Della-Rose, I am so grateful for the opportunity. Again, I'm so sorry for any interruption I caused." I tried to contain my excitement so that my apology sounded sincere but it didn't work too well. I was too elated to be in her contemporary course, since it was a known fact that those students usually ended up in the play.

"Mali, you have to learn a thing or two in this business or this business will swallow you up. One, don't back down from a challenge. There are many people like Brianna in this business that don't want to see you succeed, so you need to make sure you are always early, ready to dance and on top of any changes within the studio. Second, you have to dance with that fire in your eyes. It's undeniable to anyone who watches you. You understand?" Mrs. Della-Rose smiled kindly.

"Yes, ma'am. I understand."

"Since you will be working with my senior group over the coming weeks, I have a special challenge for you. If you complete this challenge, it can be a great addition to your skills and I think it will exercise your skills in patience tremendously." I was wiggling in my seat from the suspense. She continued, "I have a friend that needs a favor. Will you help?" Mrs. Della-Rose was very vague but the mystery had me intrigued. I knew that I could use the opportunity to prove to Mrs. Della-Rose that I was dedicated to the program if I accepted, so I did.

"Sure. I'll help. What do I need to do?" I quizzed.

"Be at the studio on Saturday morning at 7:30. I'll fill you in on the rest before then." Mrs. Della-Rose revealed a coffee-stained smile.

"I'll be there," I said over my shoulder as I closed her office door behind me.

I couldn't believe my good fortune. When I was out of sight, I gave a few arm pumps to celebrate my great luck. I wondered what the favor was and what I had to do but I imagined it revolved around dancing since I was meeting her at the studio. I imagined she would whisk me away to the Fox Theatre to work on a solo dance as the star in her next play. I twirled in happiness in the doorway to the locker room. How great would that be?

The locker room held the faint scent of musty socks, sweat and deodorant. I wondered how often they cleaned this place because the smell always seemed to linger. I opened my locker door and jumped back from the sight of my usually neat locker that now looked like a bomb had exploded inside. Shards of ripped paper were scattered about. The contents of my backpack were spilled and in a large heap at the base of the locker. My school papers and notebooks were ripped clean of all sheets—only the bindings still clung to the front covers. My school assignments were ruined. I grew angry thinking of the amount of time it would take to re-create the work. Who would do this?

There was a sign scrolled in red marker on a sheet from my psychology homework, taped to the rear wall of the locker. "KARMA IS A BITCH" echoed in the locker room as I read the note aloud twice, trying to calm my beating heart. I spied the locker room for anyone lingering in the aisles and listened closely for any signs of the intruder. The room was empty. I could hear the constant *plink* of an annoying water leak dripping in the showers but no sound of anyone lurking nearby. I inspected pieces of the torn paper sprinkled in a wet substance resembling saliva. I pinched the edges of the paper as to not touch the spit and vaguely made out the wording. Brianna had done this. The ripped shards were her release from duty that Mrs. Della-Rose had slid across the desk only moments ago. In her anger she must've destroyed weeks of my notes and research, wrote the eerie message and spit on my things as a final show of her disrespect. I couldn't imagine Brianna being so angry and embarrassed that she'd have a full-blown temper tantrum. Was this what I could expect as I moved forward in my dance career?

I hadn't told Mrs. Della-Rose anything about her vindictive ways. She probably couldn't remember all the people she'd screwed over to get her aid position and because of that, she didn't know who the real person was behind her firing. But I was pretty sure that fact didn't matter to Brianna. I could tell by her angry overtaking of my locker that I'd see her again and it wouldn't be pleasant. She may have been slightly embarrassed today but deep down she's majorly psycho.

Justice

∞

I love Saturday mornings when the world is buzzing outside my apartment window. The sounds of cars passing on the street and the chatter of passersby in the alleyway below my bedroom window. Unfortunately, it was Saturday morning and the sun was not up yet because no one in Atlanta was up this early that has an ounce of sense. I kicked back my comforter, leaving the warmth of my soft bed to drain the night's liquor binge from my system. The bathroom was filthy as I lifted the urine-stained lid with a fingertip and drained my main vein. I'd really let this place go since the breakup. I'd promised myself I'd clean up my act last week, yet this week I wasn't feeling any better. So I stayed up last night drowning my sorrows in vodka until I fell asleep on the couch with *Martin* reruns blinking into the darkness of my living room. I woke with a massive ache in my neck and a queasy stomach. I barely recall stumbling to the bed in a heap before I fainted into the deepest sleep I'd had in a while.

I looked at my reflection in the mirror and was worried with what I saw. My facial hair had become shaggy and overgrown on my cheeks and chin since I had given up on using a razor for two weeks. I rubbed my bloodshot, tired eyes and shuddered at how I was letting myself go. My hairline had grown rough around the edges of my forehead and the hair was starting to look curly instead of wavy. I hadn't had the energy to do much of anything since the breakup, not even practice. Coach was threatening to suspend me from the next few games but I knew he was bluffing to make me answer the phone. I didn't have a solid backup on the field and Coach loved winning more than he loved his own kids.

I just kept playing it over and over in my mind, her telling me that she was with someone else. How could she do that to me when I'd been nothing but faithful to her? The memory of her eyes watering in fear as I gripped her neck scared me. I'd never felt so much rage off the field. On the ride home, I made a solemn vow never to trust my heart with a woman. I was too good for any of these women at AU. All they really wanted was to be seen on my arm and use me until they found something better. Women like Nicole were bloodsucking and heinous with low morals and no principles. They would open their legs for the highest bidder, just like she had. I had to protect myself. Things were eventually going to blow up big with my football career and then it'd be even worse. More hoes, more thirsty bitches and I wouldn't get taken on a ride again. Big Deuce assured me that there was nothing better than being single. He had been single his entire life and, ironically, I used to preach to him that his lifestyle would get old or he'd get old, one or the other. Now I was starting to see I was nothing but love struck and he was right all along. I was embarrassed to tell him what happened but like a true brother, he was there to pick me up.

"Can you believe she was cheating on me?" I breathed into the phone, waiting for Deuce to respond on the other end.

"Look, I can't answer that. You know I've never been a fan of hers. I can say this, though…I'm glad you're free now."

"Deuce, I ain't worried about these females out here." That was the last thing on my mind.

"I'm not talking about that. I'm just saying, you need to clear your head and she wasn't helping you with that. She wasn't nothing but a distraction."

"You're right. Good thing is, I don't think any of the boys on the team are going to be able to take me out on the field. I got too much damn anger in me right now."

"That's what I'm talking 'bout. Use that shit to make you better." I could sense Deuce smiling into the phone.

"I can't believe I put my hands on her, though." I felt sick thinking about the look on her face as I squeezed her neck.

"Look, I can't condone violence but…chicks like Nicole need to be snatched up." Deuce tried to console me but it wasn't working.

"I'm 'bout to lie down for a while. I'll talk to you later."

"Imma come by there tomorrow."

"Yep," I said as I disconnected the line and lay on the couch.

I still couldn't shake this feeling in my heart, though. I wouldn't let Deuce know that I was still yearning for Nicole every night when I lay down. I kept thinking about never feeling her soft, silky body again or hearing her laugh so loud it hurt my ears. I still burn up on the inside when I think about another man hitting it from the back like I used to. *Forget it, I'm not shaving today.* I pushed the razor to the edge of the sink and pulled out my toothbrush instead.

I was out of the house in record time and pounded heavily down the stairs to the parking lot. My car was lazily backed into a nearby spot and looked like how I felt. Every inch of the car was covered with a thick layer of dust from the rain that beat down all last week. I hadn't even attempted to wash it…or drive it, for that matter. I stayed in the house, skipped classes and ate fried chicken that Deuce dropped off on one of his frequent checkups. He said some chick had made it for him and wanted to make sure I wasn't about to commit suicide or starve to death. I laughed when he said that to me but honestly, losing Nicole felt like I was dying slowly anyway.

The ride to campus was short and quiet. I didn't bother turning the music on in the car because my head was already aching from a hangover and lack of nutrition. I didn't have much food left at home so I'd have to grab something on campus. I stopped by the only place open this early on a Saturday, GiGi's Coffee House. GiGi's was attached to the library and served pastries and coffee in a French setting. I ordered two pastry puffs and a large caramel macchiato. The clerk shot a surprised glance over her shoulder, stunned by my unusual, disheveled appearance. I casually pulled the hood of my sweater over my head to hide from her assessment. Some days I wished I could blend in with the crowd. The clerk was quick and efficient in getting my macchiato, so I headed back into the gloom of the early morning toward the Denman building.

I never had classes in the Denman building but the entryway made me stop and take a look around. The majestic entry opened to a long hallway cloaked in heavy red velvet drapes along numbered stage doors. The small windows of the building didn't allow much light in, so the hallway seemed to carry an ambiance of mystery and seduction with its dark brown walls and glowing sconces. I slowly continued down the corridor, eyeing each doorway and its signage. Stage 1 had a play scheduled for next week called Les Misérables. I'd heard of that play before but couldn't put my finger on where I'd heard it or seen it. I continued reading each doorway until I stopped at Stage 4, the last stage. I didn't know there were so many stages in this building but clearly, I was missing out on a lot of stage plays. Nicole would never have gone to a stage play for fun. In our many years together, we never once went to a play and had stopped going to the movies once we entered college. I usually caught up on movies at home alone while she worked at a promotion or modeling gig. It always baffled me how she dreamed of being an actress yet never sat down to watch a movie or see a stage play. I gritted my teeth as the memory of

Nicole made me feel queasy. Maybe I'd start a new hobby of going to plays—a fresh start, a new me. I tried to push Nicole out of my thoughts as I descending the stairs to Studio 1. Studio 1 was supposed to be the place to meet my new dance instructor. I was told by Mrs. Della-Rose her name was Miss Mali Struthers and she was a dance student volunteering her time to help me out. Mrs. Della-Rose was a thin lady with scrawny arms that hung with loose skin as she patted me on my shoulder and gave me the same look a grandmother gives her grandkids when they show up on her doorstep.

"I'm glad I could help Coach Dempsey…and you, of course." She was sitting behind her desk when I visited her. "I've paired you with one of the brightest new dance students at AU. She'll teach you the basic skills that will meet Coach Dempsey's wishes. So please apply yourself to the program and don't waste her time."

"I won't waste anyone's time. I'm dedicated to football, Mrs. Della-Rose, and I appreciate any help I can get. I'm not sure how much dance will help but…" I shrugged.

"It will only be as good as your application of the training. If you apply yourself, you'll see results," she said in her straightforward manner.

She continued on about the instructor but I tuned out her voice halfway through the conversation every time she uttered the word *dance*. Thoughts of Nicole dancing on TV interrupted my focus. I had to get better with shutting Nicole out of my life and my mind. Even now, I felt like I wanted to call her or text her to let her know I hated her for what she'd done to us, our future plans. But I knew cutting contact completely would be the only way I fully got over her. Big Deuce had even gone so far as to delete every trace of her from my cell phone. Little did Deuce know I still had racy videos of Nicole doing unspeakable acts stored on my computer hard drive. I admit that I watched a few since the breakup but I was very close to purging myself of those too. I was slowly beginning to realize that Nicole was never in my corner—she just wanted to be along for the ride to see what she could get from me, and now, someone else.

I was nearly fifteen minutes late for the meeting with the instructor when I finally pulled open the door marked Studio 1. The small studio looked like a room from an insane asylum or fun house with white walls and mirrors. A bar attached to a mirrored wall ran the length of the studio and sitting with her back to me, a lady stretched her arms toward her pointed toes.

"Sorry I'm late."

At the sound of my voice, she turned toward the door. Instantly, I noticed it was the girl from the welcome party. Her face was breathtaking even in its raw form. She had no makeup on her bare, brown face and her eyes looked bright, lively and ready to work. Her wisps of curls fell in soft ringlets around her hairline with a puffy bun atop her head. I realized I was standing in the doorway like a star-struck homeless person in sweatpants. *Damn, I should've shaved.* I still clutched the empty coffee cup and paper bag that held the last pastry. I'd devoured the other one on the way over.

"If you're going to be late, a call would be nice." She slowly rose from her sitting position and walked to me with her hand extended. "Mali Struthers."

Her hand felt so tiny in my bearlike palms but her grip was tight and confident.

"I'm Justice Bradford. Your student, I guess."

"Nice to meet you."

"Sorry for being late." I kicked myself for repeating the apology again. She must think I'm a dumb jock already.

"You said that already." She smiled. Mali walked away as I eyed the gentle sway of her hips in her black spandex tights.

As I did, she turned and looked at me in disbelief. "You do realize there is a mirror right there…" She pointed at the mirror that caught both our reflections. I was draped in an old sweat suit with overgrown hair while she looked dazzling in black tights and a loose-fitting, lime-green tunic. I pulled my hood down in embarrassment at being caught ogling her stealthy curves and rhythmic gait.

"Come on. Don't get shy now. We have lots of work to do today." She placed her leg effortlessly on the stretching bar and reached for her toes. Her hand actually went past her toes. Amazing.

"I brought you a pastry," I lied. I held up the brown paper bag to show her that I indeed had something inside.

"It's a little early to be teacher's pet, isn't it?" she muttered as she switched legs and stretched deeply. I smiled in my hoodie at my unsuccessful attempt at flirting. It had been a while since I was allowed to openly flirt with any girls.

"Just think of it as a peace offering," I said.

"So are you going to stretch with me? Or just sit there like a bum? You know, I could make you a 'won't work for food' sign if you need it…" she joked and placed a hand on her hip.

"Well, what do you want me to do first? You're the instructor, remember?" I teased.

"First, you can take off those ole-school, ran-over sneakers and lose the gangster hoodie while you're at it. Next, come sit down so we can work on some stretching drills." I smiled at her and began kicking off my Jordans while stripping the hoodie over my head. Even with a T-shirt and sweatpants, I could tell my muscular body made her uneasy. Now it was her time to squirm. She averted her eyes to the floor as I walked over to her and sat on the floor to begin stretching.

The stretching drills were not brutal but it was difficult to stay focused as she mimicked each movement slowly so I could do it properly. Mali was a timeless beauty. Her light brown skin and thick lips showed traces of her African-American heritage while her long curls and saucy personality breathed life into what must be Spanish heritage. Her body was lean and strong but she still had a softness that made me feel the need to protect her.

"So where are you from?" I was aching to know more about Mali.

"A small town in the middle of nowhere. And you?" she said without raising her head. She was focused on pointing her toe and raising her leg in a big, circular motion while hopping on one foot. It looked like she was doing a martial-arts kick from a Bruce Lee movie.

"I'm from Florida. I went to a big high school there. I was blessed to make it out with a scholarship, actually." I reminisced on the nights I'd lay in bed, unable to sleep, because I was stressed about getting a scholarship. Glad those days were long gone.

"Yeah. I was pretty excited when I got a dance scholarship here. You can't even imagine the small number of dance programs in this country. I think I applied to them all." She smirked. There was something hidden in her words I wasn't able to grasp. A sadness, maybe.

"What about your parents? Do they come here to see you?" I could see the pain flicker in her eyes as she contemplated the answer.

"No. They don't." She pushed herself from the bar and kicked her legs high in the air. They sailed like butterfly wings as she landed softly on her feet and posed with her hands held high, wrists turned outward like a gymnast.

"Why not?" I asked, confused.

"Because they just don't! Do you always interrogate everyone you meet? Or am I getting special treatment?" she snapped.

"Sorry for asking. I didn't mean to offend you."

"You ask a lot of questions. I think we're done for the day," Mali stated matter-of-factly.

I glanced at the clock on the wall almost as if to challenge her. I still had ten minutes left. Before I could look back she was picking up her sweater from the corner and gathering her things. I quickly slid on my shoes and grabbed the paper bag with the pastry from atop my sweatshirt.

"Don't forget this." I extended the paper bag at the doorway.

"Oh. Right." Her voice was flat. She grabbed the bag while she tried to avert her eyes from my apologetic gaze.

"Sorry if I said something wrong. I didn't mean to upset you."

"I'll see you next week," she replied coarsely. She exited the studio before I could reach down for my sweater and meet her in the hall.

I felt like I was chasing Cinderella as I tore through the Denman building entry hall looking for her. I jogged out to the parking lot and there was no trace of Mali. She must've been on foot. I raced to the Impala and gunned the engine. I pulled out in the direction of the shuttle bus stop on the opposite side of the Denman building. I had gotten there too late. The bus peeled away from the curb as I rounded the corner to see Mali with her headphones plugged in her ears through the tinted-glass windows of the shuttle. Her face was tight as she leaned her head back against the seat as the bus accelerated and turned from view.

I hadn't noticed that the sun was finally shining and the campus was now bustling with activity. Students laughed animatedly as they strolled down the sidewalk; others that had exited the shuttle stop were waiting for me to drive past before crossing the street. I hadn't realized I was sitting in the middle of the lane, watching the shuttle drive away. Something struck me as intriguing about my new instructor, Mali. She was so mysterious. I played back our conversation in my mind and smiled. I hadn't learned anything about her at all from the entire training, other than the fact that she was an amazing dancer. Her wittiness kept me laughing but her sadness when I brought up her parents only made me wonder what had happened in her past. I needed to know more about Miss Mali Struthers.

Nicole

∞

Costa Rica was refreshingly beautiful as I stepped off the private jet and onto the runway. The island air drifted through my hair, whipping it around my face while the sun kissed my skin with its radiant warmth. Flying to San José on the jet made the island seem quaint yet full of tree-lined hills, warm tropical water and lush jungle space. I was eager to set foot on the ground and explore all the streets of San José. My bliss was abruptly interrupted by the sound of Webby's assistant, Veronica, and her friend Joy stumbling off the plane and talking loudly as if we were in a packed nightclub instead of a quiet runway. I rolled my eyes at the thought of Webby employing Veronica, who had started this melee from downing one too many drinks before the plane had even taxied the runway strip in Atlanta. Webby descended the stairs of the aircraft, close behind, looking like a superstar in linen pants with a straw hat sitting on the back of his head. He chewed on a toothpick and looked good enough to eat with his dark skin glistening in the sunlight. I smiled seductively at him and dodged the drunken ladies heading toward the welcoming sounds of Spanish music. I rushed through the corridor marked "Arrivals," trying my best to put distance between me, Joy and Veronica. Sensing my rush, Webby caught up to me and nonchalantly put his arm around my shoulder.

"What's the rush, babe?" Just the feel of his skin so close to mine made wetness seep from around my thin lace panties. Damn, he was sexy and being filthy rich ain't hurt either.

"Just ready to get you home," I said without hiding an ounce of seduction.

The trip to Europe last week hadn't ended well. He'd made me wait in the hotel for a week by myself before he rushed in and whisked me on a flight to New York. I pitched a fit the entire eight-hour flight until he promised to make it up to me.

"We have to first make a stop at Las Corpras Bar for a signing. Then I'm all yours for the night. I promise." He kissed me softly on the cheek and patted my behind.

"Do I have to go to Las Corpras with you guys? I have a couple things I want to do to get ready for tonight."

"What are you planning, you little naughty girl?" Webby's eyes danced in delight at what he imagined to come.

"Don't worry about that, baby. Just know you'll love it." I slipped my hand into his back pocket and snuggled close as we strolled to the customs agents down a private sector of the airport.

"Alright then, you don't have to go this time." He kissed my nose and hoisted our bags onto the customs counter. "You know that I love you being with me. I gotta keep my eye on you, pretty girl."

The custom agents worked quickly, only stopping to glance once or twice at Webby, who was already on his cell phone talking with his management team. They had flown out two days earlier to prepare the room and venue for Webby. The airport was empty and quiet on the private entrance side as we rolled our bags to the awaiting vehicle. Tim, Webby's main bodyguard, rolled his massive body from the driver's side of the SUV and held the door open for us as we piled in. Tim grabbed our carry-on luggage like he was cleaning up a room full of children's toys and tossed each one in the trunk effortlessly, before pulling the SUV from the curb.

"Webby, I can't wait to get to Las Corpras! It's going to be fantastic. They got everyone on the guest list to attend." Veronica seemed to snap into work mode almost as quickly as she got drunk on the plane.

I could see why he'd hired her. She was about her business. You wouldn't think she'd graduated at the top of her class at NYU by looking at her dressed in a tight, black maxi dress with hair weave almost touching her waistline. I thought the whole purpose of fake hair was to fool people, not look a hot mess.

"I got the seats all set up for the VIP area tonight. The list is already in to Joe over at Trinkets. So we shouldn't have a problem getting everyone in." Veronica continued scrolling down the list on her BlackBerry.

"Trinkets? I thought it was Las Corpras tonight?" I chimed in.

"It is. We have Las Corpras then Trinkets." Veronica looked over her sunglasses at me in the rear of the vehicle.

"That sounds like a strip club," I wondered aloud.

"Right again," Veronica said and turned back toward her BlackBerry.

I eyed Webby in the front seat. He didn't turn around even though he'd heard the whole conversation. I'd have to work this out when we got to the villa.

Veronica's friend Joy was sitting next to me in the last row of the SUV, looking out the window. She looked like a round-faced baby and couldn't have been more than eighteen or nineteen years old. I wasn't much older but I'd reveled in the fact that I looked mature for the type of business I was in. The moment the music artists or directors thought you were an easy lay was the moment they stopped paying you top dollar. I had one rule: Never sacrifice my money for a man. Even though Joy's facial features were round and soft, her body was voluptuous and busting from every seam of her summer dress. She opted for a pink, paisley-print dress that clung too tight to her bosom and rose too high up her thigh. It was cute on her, though, I had to admit. She reminded me of a page from a Victoria's Secret catalog with her softly tanned skin and youthful appearance. The dress was too sexy in my opinion but Webby hadn't glanced sideways at her the entire flight, so I wasn't tripping. She eyed me assessing her outfit and slyly pulled down the hem of her dress with a shy smile. She rested her hands in her lap, most likely a feeble attempt to keep her dress down under my scrutiny.

"That's a cute dress." She attempted to make conversation by complimenting me.

"It's from Prada...this season's summer edition," I answered smartly.

Webby had purchased it specifically for this trip. Joy let her eyes fall to her own dress then back out the window at the passing businesses and storefronts. It wasn't that I didn't like Joy. I just didn't like her kind around my man. I glanced at Webby in the front seat talking quietly with Tim. I was giving my best effort to try to fall in love with him since, on paper, he was everything I needed in a man.

Thirty minutes later, the SUV swerved into the parking lot of a sprawling villa overlooking the beach and all of us spilled into the grand foyer. Tim stuck with me and Webby while Veronica talked with the rental agent. She returned quickly with the key and Joy followed close behind her.

"The rooms are ready. Fridge is stocked and bathrooms too." Veronica handed me the key and tossed Tim the remaining key.

Webby was already climbing the steps to the master bedroom as I kicked off my sandals in the foyer and rushed behind him like a child on Christmas morning. The villa was like a huge toy, waiting to be explored. My toes settled into the plush carpeted hallway that led to the only door on the second floor. The door creaked slightly as I pushed it open. The massive, California king-size bed was built with indigenous wood that swirled like marble into four bedposts. A wooden nightstand flanked both sides of the bed with fresh orchids in a large, white vase sitting in the sunlight pouring through the windows. As I explored further, the door clicked closed behind me. I spun to see Webby standing in front of the door with his belt unbuckled, hard penis protruding from his zipper.

"Come give me what you know I've been waiting all day for." He reached out his hand to me.

I grabbed it softly and gently fell to my knees. I knew what he wanted. He wanted to feel the inside of my mouth again. I learned early that it was important to be skilled at making a man come quick and hard. That's why they always come running back. And that's why I have a credit card with his name on it.

I searched for Webby's stiff member in his jeans with only my lips. When I found it, he moaned deeply under the feel of my slick mouth against his taut skin. I could feel the pulse of his heartbeat in his stiffness as I released his bulging package from its prison and bobbed up and down in rhythmic motion. "Yes, deeper," he whispered as I engulfed him into the back of my throat. I pushed him to the farthest region of my mouth without gagging and vibrated my tongue gently. He loved when I gagged, so I inched him deeper until my throat reflexed. "Baby, damn, you gonna make me come all over your face."

I pounded him faster into my mouth, only breathing on the down stroke. I could feel his hands entwined in my hair, gripping my scalp, trying to hold on to his sanity. He always wanted to last long but I knew the trick. With one quick stroke, I grabbed his balls and pulled gently. Instantly, my mouth filled with warm juice as the overflow seeped from the sides of my lips. Webby collapsed to the carpet, breathing heavily, still convulsing slightly.

"That what you wanted?" I asked in a whisper.

"Hell yeah," he breathed.

"You owe me. So don't forget that when it's time to go shopping." I strolled to the bathroom without waiting for his confirmation.

I rinsed my face with water, avoiding all the areas not affected by come. I didn't want to do my makeup over again. It's hard to re-create perfection. In the mirror, Webby was behind me, naked and glorious in his dark skin. I looked at us both in the mirror as he nestled against my hair. We were the perfect couple. Webby kissed my neck and disappeared into the bedroom.

"Babe, you want a hit?" Webby yelled into the bathroom.

I found Webby crouched over the nightstand near the bed with a white, powdery substance in four neat lines, one halfway gone on the glass top. Webby smiled that gorgeous smile and held a rolled-up hundred-dollar bill in his fingertips.

"I don't do drugs," I said.

"Neither do I. I'm just doing it to have a little fun. I'm not an addict or anything. I just want to share something with my girl. Something special."

"Don't that stuff make you crazy?" I was curious.

"Nah. Not really. You just feel happy and full of energy. It's nothing bad. It's only bad when you don't know when to stop," he answered easily.

"I don't think that's a good idea, Webby."

"Look, just try it once. If you don't like it, then don't do it anymore." He extended the rolled bill again. What was the harm in trying it once? He was right, I could stop whenever I wanted.

"Just once," I assured him as I pinched the bill between my thumb and index finger.

"That's my girl!" he cheered as I sniffed one line of powder.

It burned like fire at the back of my nostrils and then faded into a feeling similar to eating ice cream too fast, like a brain freeze. My head swelled with pressure and my body felt like it was vibrating on its own. I lay back on the bed and let the vibrations drift from my head to my fingertips and then the tingle tickled my toes. I laughed aloud.

"This feels so fucking crazy…like I'm in another universe," I said to no one in particular.

"Welcome to my world, baby. Welcome to my world," he said, unhooking my bra and pulling my shirt over my head. We made love like jackrabbits and the powder made me feel every stroke, kiss and nibble with passionate intensity. We finished breathless and satisfied.

Webby and his crew left the villa an hour later to meet his manager for the signing at Las Corpras. Joy and I hung around the villa in boredom for about thirty minutes until we decided to hit the beach at the bottom of the hill. I was still feeling a little tingly and giggly after doing the line with Webby but I was starting to feel more like myself, just better. I changed into my bathing suit and cut-off shorts then Joy and I started hiking down the steep, winding road to the beach. The beach entrance—or what looked like the entrance—was two trees with their branches tied together to make a walkway. We walked under the entwined branches and out onto the warm, sunlit sand.

The beach was in full swing as we stood there in awe at the amount of action happening right below the house. We couldn't see any of this from the villa's large bay window overlooking the ocean. Tanned men in small swim shorts were kicking a soccer ball back and forth while women played volleyball, kicking up sand as they ran. The water was lapping quietly on the shore and surprisingly, no kids were around. It looked like the ultimate adults' party. A few men glanced our way and said things in Spanish under their breath. They were ogling our curves while trying to remain focused on their soccer game, so I smiled at the men, trying to make friends with the locals. I felt free as a bird in the sunshine and I was looking beach-body-ready in a bikini top and ripped jean shorts hiding Brazilian-cut thongs. Thank God I kept the food at bay because my stomach was flat even though I was majorly hungry. Joy twisted her waist as she walked around in ripped Daisy Dukes. She got a lot of attention from the beach dwellers as she hid behind her oversized sunglasses. She was a formidable sidekick after all. We settled on a plot of sand that looked like it had gone untouched by the locals and spread our blankets out neatly.

I squeezed my titillating booty from my shorts before settling on my towel. I settled into my spot to get a dark island tan while I was here, proof to all the haters that I was lying on the beach while they were slaving away at their jobs. I didn't realize that my undressing had caused a major uproar on the volleyball court. Women were slapping their men upside the head as they eyed me suspiciously. I looked over the edge of my sunglasses and shook my head at them. I didn't think that helped the situation because they spat at the ground and stomped away with their men in tow. First time I'd ever cleared out a beach, I thought to myself. Joy giggled at their response while she undressed and lay on her stomach. Her booty was perfectly shaped and her waistline was so tiny. It looked unreal.

"Are those implants?" I had to ask.

Joy giggled again and without pause answered, "The breast are but not the butt."

"Damn." We chuckled together at the inside joke. In Atlanta, butt implants replaced breast implants as the new hot surgery. It wasn't extraordinary to see women in Atlanta with grossly oversized, gargantuan booties.

As I sat talking to Joy, the afternoon sun faded to the dusk of the evening and tanned people peeled their sandy towels from the shoreline and made the short walk down the covered path to the street. Joy and I had enjoyed the day as we watched men and women romping and water fighting in the warm ocean water. We chatted as old friends might but I remembered to keep my guard up. I had been in the music industry business for a while and I knew all the tricks women used to get close to an artist. Joy seemed genuinely interested in being my friend but I knew that could change in an instant, as soon as she found something she wanted— my money or my man.

Earlier in the day, we'd managed to buy a few mixed drinks from a bar nestled beneath a green, leafy roof held up by bamboo rods. I was starting to feel the effects of the fruity alcohol and the unrelenting Costa Rican sun. As I stood to gather our blanket, my ears rang painfully loud. I squinted my eyes to see Joy also gathering her items next to me in the sand, oblivious to the sound. She slipped back on her tiny shorts without pause as the loud ringing quieted in my head to a low, bearable pitch. I definitely had too much to drink and probably needed to lie down before Webby returned from Las Corpras ready to party. I didn't want to ruin our special evening together by being a sourpuss.

The massive villa's emptiness seemed eerie as we opened the door and tossed our sandals aside in the foyer. The darkness of the sunken great room made me feel small and vulnerable as I looked out at the waves lap against shore. Three windows let in just enough moonlight to cast shadows against the enormous stone fireplace. Joy and I bounded down the two steps that led us into the carpeted living space which housed a large, burgundy-colored, U-shaped sofa. I settled on the curve of the sofa and tried to breathe deeply to ease the headache that now pounded my head. I hadn't realized that alcohol, cocaine and sunbathing on an empty stomach was such a horrible mixture.

"I can't believe we sat in the sun for, like, five hours." Joy curled like a kitten by my feet and yawned. "You feeling okay, Nicole?" She seemed genuinely worried about my state as I massaged my temples and opened my half-slit eyes.

"I'm doing alright. My head is ringing from those damn drinks. How many did we have anyway?" I tried to count in my mind but gave up quickly since thinking seemed to hurt too much.

"I dunno. Maybe six or so. I wasn't counting." She giggled.

"I need to relax. Webby should be here soon and I don't want to have this headache when he gets here. I think the sun zapped everything out of me."

"You want some tea? I think I saw some in the kitchen earlier. Chamomile and green tea, I think."

"Green tea, please." I laid my head back on the couch cushion as Joy bounced from the couch and tinkered in the kitchen for what seemed like ages.

"Here you go." The steam billowed from the tea cup and I could smell the honey before I took the first sip.

"Thank you. This is good tea."

"Oh, no problem." Joy settled back at my feet.

"I hope you don't mind me asking, but how old are you?" She looked too young to buy drinks but she had bought her own on the beach.

She giggled. "I get asked that all the time. I'm twenty-two. I graduated from NYU with Veronica."

"NYU? I was going to go to school there. What did you study?" I asked, intrigued that she'd graduated from such a prestigious school.

"I graduated with a bachelor's degree in film and television. I want to make movies, write scripts."

"That's pretty cool. I was heading down the same path but I came to AU to…" I paused, "…to follow my ex-boyfriend. I started working in the music video business shortly after I was seen at a modeling fair."

"I wish my story was that simple." Joy smiled and leaned her head against the couch.

"What's so complicated about it?"

"I was taken from my parents when I was young and put into foster care. I ran away at sixteen and caught a bus to New York. I was doing whatever I could to survive. Stripping. Sleeping with clients. Whatever it took to make a life for myself." She wiped her brow and continued, "I decided I wanted to go to college after a year of sleeping in different beds and worrying about getting raped, so I got my GED, applied for scholarships and got into NYU by the skin of my teeth. I kept stripping until I met my ex-boyfriend and he paid the rest of my way."

"So your boyfriend doesn't mind you being in Costa Rica for a week?" I was floored by her story.

"I don't have a boyfriend anymore. I graduated so I wasn't going to keep stripping or sucking his dick for tuition. When

Veronica told me there might be work in Atlanta, I hopped on a flight. So here we are."

"Damn, you had a tough start." I shook my head in awe.

"I really loved your video with Webby." She ignored my comment completely.

"That's where we first met. I was lucky to meet him."

"You know, I really came on this trip to meet Webby." My eyebrow rose at the sound of my boyfriend's name on her lips. "No, not like that! I came to pitch a story for him. I wrote a script and I want him to help me get it started." She held her hands up in defense.

"You mean, you need money," I cut to the point. Suddenly, I wasn't so relaxed anymore.

"Of course money is a part of a project like this but I also need producers, actors…"

"What kind of story is it?" I interrupted, becoming more interested.

"It's a story about a basketball star that cheats on his fiancée with multiple women. All the women end up with children and he leads double and triple lives to hide his infidelity." Joy's face lit up with excitement as she explained the plot. I grew more and more interested as she continued. It sounded like a great story for the big screen.

"So what do you want Webby and me to do?" I questioned.

Joy leaned her head on her hand and simply said, "Help me any way you can."

I was beginning to think there was more than met the eye with Joy. She was clearly beautiful, smart and motivated. I started thinking of a plan to see her script and somehow get on board with it before Webby could take it over. I knew if he got his hands on it, he wouldn't want me to get any money off of it. He didn't like me working since we started dating so I was pretty sure he was going to snatch this project from my reach as soon as he caught wind of it. Webby bought everything for me so that I'd never ask to work—and I wasn't complaining about that part—but he was trying to keep me out of the limelight and not in it where I should be. I wasn't sure if his new attitude was simple jealousy or some form of control. Regardless, I wasn't going to let him sidetrack me. I had to get this money.

"I think I can help you with the movie," I finally said in the silence.

"Really! That would be awesome." Joy was almost bouncing with excitement on the couch.

With Webby flying me around the world on his promotional tour, I hadn't had time to work or even go to school. I was pretty sure I'd been dropped from every class. Missing weeks on end would do that to a student. I made a mental note to have Webby pay the school bill since he contributed to my absence. Doubt he'd have a problem with that.

"I need a little time before you tell Webby about the movie. I want to see if my connections can work first."

"Sure. Anything you need. I'll do it," Joy assured me.

It might be time to get in touch with Will and possibly get Joy an introduction. I had to make sure Will Dunkin hadn't forgotten about his finest protégé since he was my best connection to the industry. School and modeling was not going to make me the money I was seeing right now being Webby's girlfriend. If I played this right, I could make some serious cash and have my name in the credits of a movie.

"So we have a deal? No Webby until we get an answer from my connects?" I waited patiently as Joy put her finger to her chin as if wondering what to say.

"Deal." She jutted her hand across the couch and shook mine emphatically. The deal was sealed.

I hated to steal business from Webby but he'd be proud I took initiative in growing my business while he toured around the world with his music. Who wouldn't want a boss chick like me on their side, right?

Joy was brimming with anticipation as I explained that I'd try to get her a meeting with an exec. I felt awkward doing an underhanded deal with a woman I met only hours ago…but when I saw an opportunity that could change my life, I capitalized on it. Hopefully, Joy and I would have a mutually beneficial relationship and make loads of money on this project. Now all I had to worry about was getting her in front of Will Dunkin after I'd been avoiding his calls for weeks.

We both stole away to our rooms to shower and get refreshed for the evening. As if by miracle, my headache was fading but my mind was still racing with ways to make money from Joy's movie project. I couldn't stop fantasizing about my name in the credits of an actual movie. I'd left behind my scholarship in New York to follow Justice's dream to AU but now, I wasn't going to let another man divert me from my destiny.

I twisted the chrome knob for the shower and undressed in the oversized bathroom. A soak in the tub might have been nice but I really wanted to get back downstairs to chat with Joy. I was interested in hearing more about the movie. The shower created billows of steam and left the room feeling more like a sauna than a large master bathroom. As I grabbed the towel from the bed, I saw that Webby had left the nightstand slightly open. As I peered inside, I saw the small vial of cocaine. *No, I shouldn't. Wait, why not? Hell, this is a time to celebrate!* I unscrewed the vial and poured only a tiny ball onto the nightstand. I used my nail to chop it up into a skinny line like Webby had earlier.

"To new beginnings…" I whispered and snorted the skinny line quickly. I felt the tingle in my body and knew that tiny little line wasn't going to hurt anything. It was much smaller than the one Webby had made.

The shower was large enough for three people and had four showerheads strategically placed to make it a spa-like experience. I stepped under the powerful blasts of water and exhaled as my body relaxed under the intense warmth and pressure. I leaned on the shower wall as the warmth overtook my body and closed my eyes in thought. A movie deal could be big money. How was I going to seal this deal?

I must've imagined the soft hands sliding down my spine and stopping above the curve of my buttocks. I moaned under the feel of the angelic touch. The warm hands streamed up my back and to my neck and kneaded my tense shoulders. A soft kiss landed on my nape and stirred me from my trance. I turned to see Joy, naked and glistening under the wetness of the shower. Her large, perky breasts heaved in anxious anticipation as she rubbed her palms down my smooth bosom, stopping at the nipples only to tweak them with her fingertips.

"What are you doing!?" I asked, surprised at her aggression. I reached for the shower knob and her hand shot to mine rapidly. She held my hand softly but firmly enough to stop my advances.

"I want to make you feel good, Nicole." Joy's eyes were intense and needy. I could tell she wanted me with all her being.

"Joy, we can't…"

"Nicole, I want you. Just let me have you…just once."

I could feel my face growing red in the shower from the heat between our bodies and the sheer emotional discomfort of Joy rubbing me so softly. My mind was screaming to stop this seduction but my eyes took in her beauty and my body sighed against her touch. I was even more embarrassed over the swelling of juices between my thighs at the vision of Joy's nakedness. Her straight hair was beginning to turn wavy in the steam of the shower as she suckled her thick, pink lips to my erect nipples. A moan escaped my lips and echoed against the hollow shower walls. My moan gave her more conviction as she slid her fingers into my core. Within minutes, my hips were circling to her beat, grinding to her rhythm. She slithered her tongue to my pink button and sucked gently while pulsing her fingers inside me. I couldn't hold on to sanity. The shower was spinning and my body was reacting in ways I'd never known it could. I held the shower walls to stabilize myself but the ecstasy was overwhelming. Her tongue gyrated and swirled until my screams filled the bathroom and I collapsed in a ball at her manicured feet. The shower spread water over my head and body, shielding my shame from Joy. Joy snuck from the shower and padded out of the bathroom before I could lift my head to speak. But what could I say? *Thanks? That was fun?*

After gaining enough confidence to exit the shower, I dried myself and looked at my ruddy face in the mirror. What was I doing? Did I just cheat on my man…with a woman? My cheeks were flushed with embarrassment and elation. Joy was my first female encounter and I was in shock at how great it felt to come so hard that I'd collapsed. I'd never had a man be able to make my body *sing*. *It's not cheating when there isn't any intercourse,* I rationalized. Webby would probably have loved to see what just went down in the shower. Unfortunately, he would never know. Every woman needs her skeletons in the closet. I just hoped my closet didn't get too full.

Mali

∞

No snow was falling in December on the Atlanta University campus. I pulled back the dark purple curtains and looked out from the dorm room window at the empty grassy area below. Condensation dripped from the window and made Cramer Hall look like it was crying tears of loneliness. The holiday season wiped the campus clean of students and teachers. The dormitory halls were quiet and empty as students ventured home for the holidays. It was five days until Christmas and I felt like I was aching for school to start again instead of waiting for Christmas morning to get here. Growing up, I never really had a true Christmas like the ones I saw on television or heard about from Mack. My family never had a tree and I didn't hear many Christmas songs unless my mother was playing "Noche de paz," the Spanish version of "Silent Night," lower than a whisper while she cooked in the kitchen. Surprisingly, I'd usually get a gift from my mom which she conveniently stashed under my bed while I slept on Christmas Eve. While most kids ran to look under the tree on Christmas morning, I leaned over the edge of my bed to hold a single gift given by my mother. It was always something small, of course, since she never really had her own money. I remember when I was thirteen I received a small porcelain jewelry box with a blue dove painted on the lid. I felt like a big kid, no longer a baby, for receiving something so delicate and breakable. It was small enough to fit in the palm of my hand, so I used it to store delicate rings or bracelets. I glanced at the blue jewelry box on the nightstand and sighed heavily. Memories of the holidays always had a bittersweet edge. I loved how my mother could make Christmas special but I hated that I never had a regular Christmas like every other child. Never did I find a bike with a big red bow or a doll that I dreamed of from the television commercial under a colorful, brightly lit Christmas tree. I gave up hope on ever having a Christmas like that after turning thirteen because my father had settled on squashing any remaining hope I had left to be an ordinary kid. I never knew my mother was secretly saving money until I received that blue jewelry box, which must've been the most expensive gift—maybe $30—that I'd ever received. In his drunkenness, my father had stumbled into my bedroom to find me reveling at the new jewelry box. Without a word, he snatched the box in his grimy palm and slapped me across the cheek.

"Where'd you get this?"

I held my cheek, trying to hold back the tears and the urge to run. "Momma," I stammered.

He stormed to the kitchen to find my mother cleaning the tabletop of scattered crumbs and used napkins, remnants of her holiday chicken dinner. Even on Christmas night, he questioned her, vigorously and callously, on how she managed to buy the jewelry box without asking him first.

"I always knew you were a goddamn thief! Stealing from my pants like a fuckin' lowlife scumbag. You want my money, huh?" He brutally pushed her into the wooden kitchen chair and it croaked under her weight. I watched from the hallway in silence as he pointed his dirty finger to her cringing face and spat with liquor-stained breath, "I'll kill you if you steal from me again." By the look in her eye, she believed him.

That was the last gift I received under my creaky, wooden bed. I wondered if my mom was forbidden from saving any money or if she was too scared to be confronted by my father for even trying. Either way, I was grateful to my mother for attempting to show me the power of giving whilst despising my father for being so malicious and controlling.

I shook away the lasting memories and settled on my twin-size bed. I was exhausted. I'd spent most of the Christmas break in the dance studio working on a new audition piece. The senior-level classes with Mrs. Della-Rose had turned out to be much more challenging than I'd originally anticipated. I usually found myself in the rear of the studio, practicing moves during the break or being tutored by the senior students on certain jumps and leaps that didn't seem to fall as nicely as theirs. I was especially happy that I didn't have to see Brianna during class anymore. After her locker room meltdown I was worried she'd snap and try to do something outrageous. Her message haunted me for weeks until I realized that she was probably just acting out of anger. I heard from one of the dancers that she still attended Mrs. Della-Rose's intermediate dance class but had a better attitude than before. I didn't know if the better attitude was a product of me not being there to compete with her or if she had finally gotten over her anger of being dismissed as an aid. Hopefully, she'd started putting all her energy toward dancing and ignored any idea of senseless revenge.

Everyone in Mrs. Della-Rose's senior class was very helpful when it came to learning new ideas or pushing the creative limits. I was able to change some of the movements slightly to fit my own unique style and, surprisingly, some of my moves were adopted by the whole troupe and integrated into the set. Mrs. Della-Rose required all her dancers to audition at least ten times in a year.

She said during the end of a grueling session, "To be a real dancer is to know the feeling of failure and triumph."

I thought those were good words to live by, so I started working on my audition piece that night in the dorm. Carey was swamped with her final exams and didn't spare any time from the library so the dorm room actually felt more spacious than normal. I reminded myself to ask her to lunch since I declined her offer to ride with her to Mississippi for the holidays. I didn't think a Cole family Christmas would make me feel any better about my own family; in fact, it would do the opposite. I'd be depressed for weeks.

I started tidying up the dorm, pushing mounds of clothes into a mesh bag to tote to the coin laundry. I had one exam left for my dance practicum tomorrow so I'd reserved time to clean over the holiday break. Next semester's class schedule and syllabi were finalized and it was going to be a demanding schedule. History was my worst subject, so maybe a trip to the library would get me a good head start. I gathered my history textbook, wrapped myself in a warm, wool coat and prepared to head to the library for a few hours before meeting with Justice tonight for training.

The nagging feeling of not talking to Mack kept chipping away at me. I'd been calling my best friend for months and hadn't gotten a response. She hadn't even tried calling me back to check on my first semester. My mother talked to her a few nights a week so I knew she was alive but I still missed talking to her. In the spirit of the season, I'd try to call Mack again and squash whatever ill feelings we had between us. The phone rang twice before a scruffy voice picked up.

"Hello?"

"Mack?"

"Yeah." Her voice perked in confusion.

"It's Mali." I hesitated, waiting for the sound of the dial tone.

"Hey, Mali. What's up?"

Her casual toned confused me. We hadn't spoken for months.

"I've been trying to call you for the past few months. Are you okay?" I quizzed.

"I'm good...just going through a lot. How about you? How's AU?" Mack sounded exhausted.

"AU is going good. I have so much to fill you in on. But what's been going on with you? My mom said she's kept in touch with you but she won't tell me much."

She sighed heavily. "Shannon and I broke up about two months ago. He was cheating. I found out. End of story."

"I'm so sorry, Mack. I can't believe he'd do that to you. What an asshole." I tried to console her.

"Neither could I. I mean, I heard the rumors but I didn't believe them. I trusted him, Mali. *I loved him.*" Mack continued harshly, "You never know who a person really is. One day, you're inseparable. The next day, something better comes along and you're nothing. *Nothing* to them." I couldn't believe that Shannon would cheat on Mack. He was so in love with her in high school, even writing silly poems and giving her his virginity.

"How did you find out?" I questioned in awe.

"His stupid cell phone messages! He was so dumb that he saved every single message for the past three months from some campus slut. Mali, this girl was rumored to be with almost every guy on the basketball team." Her emotional wound flared openly now.

"Mack, maybe it was a mistake. I mean, you guys were so good together," I pushed.

"Mali, it's no mistake. His messages weren't only about hooking up with that slut..." Mack trailed off.

"Well then, what were they about?" I pressed, confused.

"He was telling her he loved her and wanted to be in a relationship with her. He said he was going to leave me, Mali. Leave *me* for her!" Mack cried softly into the receiver. It broke my heart to hear her quiet sobs.

"I'm so sorry."

"No, I'm sorry. I'm sorry for being so mean to you. For being so selfish. I got so involved with Shannon's bullshit and lies that I forgot who was really there in my corner." She sniffed. "I called your mom to help me find a way to call you and apologize but I've never really been good at apologies."

We laughed lightly at her honesty.

"That doesn't matter now. I have my best friend back and I'm here for you whenever you need me."

"I know, Mali. Thank you."

"Thanks for what?"

"For being who you are." Mack and I rarely talked about emotions. It was awkward hearing her express her feelings but it was probably something I needed to hear, being so far away from her. We ended the call with the best intention to talk again in a few days. I sat back down on the edge of the bed after hanging up and took in the entire situation. I couldn't believe Shannon would cheat on Mack after she traveled with him to Idaho to help him pursue his dreams. I pushed the thought to the back of my mind and gathered my books from the bed. Maybe studying would help take my mind off Mack's pain.

The library was nearly empty with only a few students straggling between bookshelves. At least I wasn't the only person on campus that didn't want to go home. I settled on a wooden table in the fiction area and spread out my notebook and text, so I could highlight and write at the same time. I couldn't help but think about Mack's phone call as I stared at the black-and-white typed pages. The words on the page and the thoughts in my head were jumbling together. I laid my head on the book, completely distracted.

I forced Mack's relationship to the back of my mind and focused on practice with Justice later tonight. I replayed the day Justice walked into the studio, late for his appointment. I was in shock when I turned to see that he was the student I was teaching. When Mrs. Della-Rose said she had a challenge for me, I didn't think she meant a challenge the likes of Justice Bradford. I was thinking maybe a high school student with less than desirable skills. Instead, she sent me a gorgeous athlete to feast my eyes on for two hours, twice a week. It's hard to maintain a professional bearing with someone who made me moist when he'd grab my hands to help me up or touch my back to usher me through the door. His skin was perfectly tanned from being outside on the football field and his body looked like it was chiseled from stone as a Greek god. I think Mrs. Della-Rose knew the only challenge Justice was going to give me was the challenge of trying to remain focused. He smiled so wide at my sarcasm and silly jokes that his Asian eyes would slant to small slits in his smooth, flawless face. He'd touched on a sensitive subject in our first session and I hated that I'd ended the session so abruptly. I kicked myself for weeks for overreacting. He probably thought I was a nut job for running out the session. If he knew how often I ran back home, he'd understand it was mere reflexes.

I enjoyed my sessions with Justice but only when he wasn't asking about my family or how I was raised. He had such a perfect family and home life. I didn't want to tell him about the alcohol and abuse. Luckily, over the past six weeks, we'd managed to get him in the best condition of his life. He'd run for the most yards in his career in a single game and had two touchdowns to help the team solidify their spot in the Hawai'i Bowl. He'd called me after the last game with sheer excitement.

"Mali! Did you see the game?" Justice's voice was loud and excited.

"Of course! You had a great game. What was it? Like, 120 yards in one game, or something?" I settled back on my pillow and cradled the receiver on my shoulder.

"Well, you're pretty close but I won't gloat." He laughed hardily.

"You did amazing, Justice. Good job."

"I want to thank you, Mali, for all the training and conditioning. I think it's paying off big."

"You did the hard work. I was just there to get on your nerves most of the time."

"You could never get on my nerves, Mali." His voice was quieter, almost a whisper, then he cleared his throat loudly.

"Doubt it."

"I'm just saying that you're a great teacher. Hey, I'm going to have to get on the bus in a sec. Are we still on for Thursday?"

"Yep. I'll be at the studio at seven. I have to practice for an audition."

"What are you auditioning for?"

"There's an audition for a music video and a television show downtown. Both of them will have lots of talented dancers showing up. It's a huge opportunity to get my name out there. I'm not sure if I'm even ready. Hell, it's only my first year here." I sighed.

"Don't think like that, Mali. You're an amazing dancer. I've seen it myself. It doesn't matter whether you get the job or not. You love to dance, right?"

"Yes."

"Then dance! Stop worrying about the end result. Just have fun with the audition and if they can't see how amazing you are, then they'll be kicking themselves when you're dancing on Broadway in a few years." I was smiling at Justice's reasoning. He knew how to massage the nerves away.

"Justice, can I ask you something?"

"Sure."

"How do you do it? How do you go out in front of all those people and still perform like you do?"

"I just think of something that calms me. Try to remember something calming from home or your family. Just try to relive a good memory from your past."

"What if you don't have any, you know, good memories?" I said cautiously.

"What about your mom and dad? Haven't they done something with you where you can remember being happy?" Justice sounded shocked.

"Not really. I just remember being happy when I dance."

"Okay…then just think about love. Someone you love…" he pressed.

"I've never been in love," I whispered into the phone. "I guess I really don't have much to help me, huh?"

"Uh, I guess not. Good thing you're a strong, talented dancer…you don't even need to be calm." He lightened the heaviness of the conversation.

"My nerves are so bad. I don't think I should audition yet. I'm still so new here. I will just embarrass myself."

"Mali, stop discouraging yourself. You're auditioning and that's it," he said sternly.

"Okay, Justice. I'll do it. But only because you told me to." I laughed. "See you Thursday at seven."

I could feel the giddiness rumble in my belly at the end of the call. Justice always managed to give me butterflies anytime he'd talk to me. I'd never met a man—or anyone, for that matter—like him. He was all the things I lacked. Confident, assured and fearless.

I sat in the library unable to read because Justice had been on my mind since the phone call. My emotions were overriding all rational thought because I had a nagging feeling that Justice might be interested in me like I was in him. I was just a regular girl with a sordid past and he'd had this perfect life and perfect football career; it was so different from everything I knew. Why would he want to be with someone like me? I had nothing to offer him. *He's probably being nice to me because he has to work with me*, I told myself as I leafed through the textbook. Mack came to mind again. I shouldn't get caught up in Justice's web and end up like Mack, torn to pieces by love. But why do I get light-headed at the mere sight of him?

I slammed closed the textbook. Getting Justice out of my head was futile. I couldn't eat without wondering what he was doing. I couldn't sleep without touching myself, imagining my fingers were his lips. And now, I can't even study without thinking about him. My head throbbed with thoughts of Justice as I doodled messy hearts on my notebook. I prompted myself, *don't fall for an athlete*. I repeated it, over and over because my mind and my body were on two different operating systems. Looking at Justice's rippled arms as he stretched during our sessions made me physically melt but when we talked about his relationship with Nicole, I could feel the lightness leave his smile until there was nothing but darkness. Justice was emotionally unavailable and I used that fact to remind me that most athletes were womanizers and players anyway. He probably cheated on his girlfriend just like Shannon had and that was why he didn't want to talk about her. No one wants to admit their wrongdoings, right?

Men keep the emotions out of relationships so that it's easier to use and abuse their prey. My mom was the best example of that. My dad never apologized or said, "I love you" after he pulverized her. It was difficult to look at Justice as a predator like my dad but there was something there I couldn't put my finger on. I remembered asking about Justice's ex during one of our studio sessions but he grew cold and tight-lipped. I grabbed my textbook from the tabletop and slid it in my bag. Where could I go to clear my mind? I walked out the library and headed toward the Denman building.

Big Deuce had become a faithful gossipmonger among the campus elites. We'd gotten closer when he'd shared his notes with me after the locker room incident. I was pretty sure they weren't his notes, since all the *I*s on the notes were dotted with hearts but I was still grateful to be back on track with class and through that Big Deuce and I had grown a little closer. So I took the opportunity to ask him about Justice and his ex, Nicole. Big Deuce shared his very candid feelings toward Nicole. I could tell there was love lost between Deuce and Nicole but he wouldn't tell me exactly what she did to get on his bad side. He rambled on and on that she was "a gold-digging slut that should be horse whipped". I thought his attitude was a bit extreme for someone who'd never had a relationship with her but who knew why he felt the way he did?

Justice

∞

The loneliness was killing me. My apartment was a mess and smelled like a mixture of rotten food and sweaty socks. It probably smelled that way because my gym bag lay haphazardly on the carpet with sneakers and sweaty workout clothes spilling out as if escaping from the stench trapped in the bag. I hadn't attempted to clean the place in the past four weeks. Why should I? I never had any company anyway. No one other than Big Deuce. He didn't really count as company because he always made the place messy when he was over and good company wouldn't normally do that. I wasn't about to clean up after a 250-pound football player, even if it was my house. I flicked through the television channels and stopped on a reality show that showcased two big-breasted women fighting in a restaurant. My cell phone buzzed on the coffee table and I grabbed for it, not able to tear my eyes away from the half-naked, wrestling bimbos.

"Hello?" I sighed, still trying to catch the fight on television.

"Justice?" The voice was very familiar. I sat up and clicked off the television as she continued, "I know you don't want to talk to me but I'm just calling to check on you."

"Nicole, what the hell do you want?" I wasn't going to hide my distaste for the woman who ripped my heart out.

"Justice, please. I was hoping we could at least be cordial."

"Cordial? Really, Nicole? You've got to be on drugs or something to be calling me asking me to be cordial."

"I'm not on drugs," she said defensively. "Look, I'm not trying to fight. I'm just calling to see how you're doing. I still care about you."

"Hmm, let's see. How am I doing? Well, my girlfriend was sleeping with another man, left me to be with him, then to top it all off, she really shows her true colors and makes me feel really small in the process. You know, Nicole, I think I'm doing *great*," I added sarcastically. "Thanks for caring."

"Justice, I'm sorry for the way things went down. I didn't mean to make you feel like that. I just didn't know how to tell you I wanted something else."

"Nicole, how can you say you 'wanted something else'? You were fucking someone else for who knows how long!" The words stung me all over again as I said them.

"Dammit, I'm sorry, Justice! Are you going to hold this over my head for the rest of our lives?" Nicole sounded wounded.

"Nicole…there is no rest of *our* lives."

"You have always acted like the victim and I'm such a horrible girlfriend. You were not a perfect man to me, Justice. Don't forget how you treated me at my house. You put your hands on me!" she screamed into the phone. She was turning into the Nicole I remembered. Angry. Bitter. Misguided.

"Nicole, there is one last thing you can do for me. How about you go outside to that cute little BMW, start the engine and then put your mouth on the tailpipe? That would make me real happy." I let the words drip in sweet sarcasm.

"Justice, you haven't changed a bit."

"Sorry I can't say the same thing about you, Nicole." With that, I had grown exhausted and clicked the End button on my cell phone.

I didn't know whether to feel relieved that she still cared or sad that she'd think I'd go back. A piece of me wanted to love her again but my head kept saying *Don't trust that bitch.* I knew Nicole was missing me and that's why she'd called. It was her way of getting back in my good graces after our fights. She would call, tell me she missed me and make me feel bad about whatever role I played in the argument. She would never actually fess up to anything she did wrong. I wasn't going to let her manipulate me anymore. Especially not after she cheated and left me for another man. I didn't realize that I'd been sitting on the edge of the couch the entire conversation. My neck was tense as hell after her phone call.

I looked at my cell phone again as the home screen lit up. Two missed text messages. One message from Monica, a chick that'd been flirting in the gym since she found out I was NFL bound. She was pretty heavy into working out and her ripped body had the fellas drooling in the gym. She loved to wear little spandex shorts that showed a peek of her butt when she'd squat in front of the mirror. I stiffened thinking about her squatting on top of me. *Ooohhh-weeee.* Monica spelled trouble for a single man.

The second message was from Mali. I opened it quickly.

Audition tomorrow! Wish me luck, buddy!

A smile crept across my lips as I leaned back on the couch cushion, thinking of Mali's text. I reread the message and stopped on the word *buddy.* My jaw clenched in irritation. I didn't want to be Mali's *buddy* but it also wasn't the right time or place to even go down that path with her. My anger at Nicole's call reminded me to never let my guard down…with anyone. Mali was the kind of girl that was genuinely beautiful inside and out. I never had to put up pretenses with her because it felt good just talking about nothing with her. She didn't talk much about her life before AU but that really didn't matter to me anyway. The past was the past. Just like Nicole was in my past and I couldn't care less about reliving my embarrassing past with a blow-by-blow account to Mali. I didn't have to be cool or suave or live up to some crazy expectations with her.

Mali was the polar opposite of Nicole and that made her even more necessary in my life right now. I needed to know there were females out there who still had a bit of decency. With the turmoil between me and Nicole still brewing, Mali could brighten up the dark places my mind got lost in. After Nicole's call, I wanted nothing more than to put my hands around her throat again until I heard a *snap!* But after I read Mali's message, I felt calm again.

I'd be damned if I was going to let Nicole win. Mali found a way to rescue me when I was on the brink of quitting it all. The first day I saw her in the studio, I was contemplating doing something real stupid with my football career because of Nicole. Seeing Mali smile brightly and giggle at our jokes made me want to come to the studio time and time again. She got me back into practicing again, going to class, eating. I still had a drink every now and then to calm the nerves but slowly, my mind was purged of Nicole's poison and I was getting back to being me.

Mali was a good girl but I wasn't ready to jump back into another relationship. So as much as I wanted to pull her close to me while we danced in the studio to taste her plump lips, I kept my distance. I didn't want to get hurt again and Lord knows women can't be trusted. But I couldn't help but wonder "what if" when I was around her. We'd been training for four months and I still wondered whether she realizes how amazing she really is or if she's just being modest. Most of the time, she can't accept a compliment without being negative. If I say she looks pretty, her response is "Oh, this is just an old shirt." It used to bother me until I realized that compliments aren't what impresses her, unlike most women. Unfortunately, I hadn't found out exactly what does impress her but she's mysterious enough to keep me coming back for more, eager to find a way to make her smile. In my heart, I felt like I could trust her but I also trusted Nicole and in the end, I was the one who ended up skull dragged through the deepest depths of depression while she lived it up with some big-time rapper. Thanks to Mali, I was starting to dig out of this hole.

I typed Mali a quick response to her message.

YULL DO GR8. NO LUCK NEEDED. CALL ME AFTER.

I scrolled down to Monica's message and pushed it open.

I'M TIRED OF WAITING. CALL ME. ;)

Monica was cute but damn, this text message made her cute points skyrocket into sexy territory. I hadn't had sex since the last time with Nicole almost four and a half months ago. Monica had damn near begged me to call her after a night at the gym. She'd found out from Deuce that I was single. So I guess that meant I was ready to mingle. She tried every tactic from bending over, to pushing her too-perfect-to-be-real tits in my face as we chatted in the parking lot outside the gym. As the lights had slowly darkened, she seized my phone, punched in her number and called herself. I thought she was a little crazy that night but looking at the text message now, I figured her as a woman with persistence. I was long overdue for some sexual healing anyway. I glanced at my ripped forearm and shook my head, mentally scolding myself for waiting so long. I didn't know how much more manual healing it could take. I hit the button to call Monica and listened to the rhythmic ring in my ear.

"Took you long enough," Monica whispered into the receiver seductively, as if she had been waiting a lifetime for my call.

"What's up? You wanted me to call. So here I am."

"So if I wanted you to come, will you do that too?" I could tell Monica was making a play on words. I liked her style. Straight to the head, no chaser.

"I don't know. I don't come for just anything. It's gotta be something worth coming for." I played the game with her.

"Well, I assure you, sweetie. If you come…over here…then you'll never want to leave." Damn this girl was good. I can't believe I was sleeping on this chick for two years.

"I tell you what…if you wear those little spandex shorts that you've been wearing at the gym, then I'll come over there and show you what I want to do to you when I see you wearing them." A vision of Monica's perky ass straddling the bench press made blood pulse in places I hadn't used in weeks.

"I accept your challenge, JB," she purred. "You know where Seacrest Estates are?"

"I think so. But give me directions just in case. I don't want to keep you waiting." I vaguely knew the name but had never been inside the gated community.

"I'll text you the directions. Oh, and JB…"

"Yeah."

"Make sure you bring your A game."

"You must not know who you're talking to. I know you like to work out and all, but ain't no machine out there that can work you out like I do."

I heard her breathless goodbye and the silence of our ended phone call. Within minutes, a long text message of directions popped up in my inbox. As I shook off the feeling that I was somehow cheating on Mali, I scraped my lazy ass off the couch and turned on the shower to get good and clean for the long-overdue X-rated excursion with Monica.

Nicole

∞

Will Dunkin wasn't especially pleased to see me after three months of not returning his calls. Even still, I put on a happy face and tried to charm my way back into his good graces. He sat behind his overly massive wooden desk with a face that didn't smile like it used to when he saw me. Lord knows I couldn't lose his friendship or his link to the industry. I wiggled my behind into a stiff yet stylish chair opposite his desk and waited. Everyone in the industry knew Will Dunkin and, more importantly, everyone respected Will Dunkin's opinion. If I had a problem with Will then I could literally commit social suicide. All it took was one word of distrust or negative connotation and my phone would stop ringing, dollars would stop printing and cards would get snipped. There would be no more calls to ignore, let alone answer. Will sat still behind his desk and my mind raced with old Western movies featuring two shooters, back to back, ready to turn and fire. Unfortunately, my opponent had way more skill but I was assured that just like with most men, I'd have my way in the end. How I was going to slither my way back into Will's world while also trying to sell him on doing a movie with me was beyond even me. Yet it was worth a stab. And if nothing else transpired, I would at least let him know I was willing to work again since Webby's tour had ended last week.

"Where you been, Nicole?" Will nestled deeper into his large oxblood leather chair.

"Been busy trying to get some new ideas off the ground. How you been, Will?" I tried to change the subject before going into too much detail about Webby. I wasn't sure if he'd gotten wind of our relationship yet.

"So these new ideas wouldn't happen to have something to do with Webby's tour, right?" *Damn*. He knew.

"Sure. Me and Webby have been dating for a while now."

"So you blow off my calls for your new guy?" He rested his hand on his cheek and leaned forward as if I were a child straining to get out of punishment.

"I...didn't..." He waved his hand away and turned his chair to look out at the Atlanta skyline. The dusk had crept in as I waited for our meeting. The city lights twinkled dimly along the darkening skyline and, normally, I would have admired a view like that but I couldn't get past the lump in my throat to truly appreciate it.

"Nicole, we have been in this business together for almost four years. That's a long time in this industry."

"I'm sorry, Will. I didn't mean to..."

"Didn't mean to ignore my calls, miss my gigs and ultimately throw ash in my face?" That stung. I looked at the floor and noted my new, bright red heels Webby had purchased while we wandered around France a few weeks ago. I traded my career for a pair of red heels. My stomach turned at the thought.

"Look, I'm giving you a hard time, I know this," Will continued, "but you are like a daughter to me. I only want the best for you. And sometimes that takes tough love." A flicker of acceptance flashed in his brown eyes.

"You know how hard it is to find love in this industry, Will. I just wanted a chance at something special." That was the key. A sadness glazed over Will's round eyes and he stared out the window with a distant gaze, almost as if he was thinking of someone he may have loved at one point or another. Will had never been married and essentially never talked about a love life or any woman, for that matter. He was an extreme workaholic and knew that in this industry, you sacrificed more than your time to be famous and wealthy. So he had always preached to me about never letting the job make a fool of me.

"So you think you found something special in Webby?"

"I think so. It feels different."

"What about Justice? What happened to him? You used to be so in love with him when you first started working here." He glided his chair closer to the desk and rested his clasped hands on top of his paperwork.

"Justice and I have been over. I outgrew him," I said matter-of-factly.

"What do you mean 'outgrew' him? You came to Atlanta to be with him."

"He couldn't really take care of me. I had different things in life I wanted to do and he was holding me back with his football dreams."

"So you think Webby can take care of you. Better yet, do you think he *will* take care of you the way you want to be taken care of?"

"Absolutely. He loves me." The edge of Will's mouth curled into a slight smile.

"I know Webby and he loves hard and plays harder. I hope you know what you're doing." He looked concerned.

"Don't worry. I have it under control," I assured him.

"I see there's no convincing you otherwise."

"Nope. Not a chance." I smiled.

"Well then, that's all that matters. I wish you the best. If you ever need anything, you know you can come to me." He smiled openly now. Clearly happy that I'd found some ounce of happiness in this industry.

"Well actually…I kind of need something." I smirked bashfully.

"That was quicker than expected." His smile faded slightly but still managed to stay plastered to his leathery face as he leaned back in his chair.

"It's something really big. I have a movie script that I want you to look at. I read it. Fell in love with it. I think you will too."

I reached into my bag and pulled out the script before he could respond. He flipped through the pages, stopping momentarily every couple pages to read deeper. After what seemed like an eternity, he placed the script on his desk and clasped his hands on top of the cover.

"Why do you want me to read this over? Is it a friend of yours?"

"No. Not really. It's someone I met. She was looking for an actress so I read it over. When I fell in love with it, I thought about you. I knew you'd love the story and would like most of all that it could make a great profit." I smiled wide, trying to show confidence even though my stomach was doing backflips.

"It's pretty good. But that's just a first look. You know I have people that handle this stuff for me. But I can get the team to take a look at it a little harder. You say this isn't a friend of yours and you haven't asked to be the lead in the movie, so what do you want out of the deal?" He was a smart man indeed. Nothing ever got past him.

"I want an up-front finder's fee, co-producer title and permanent position on your team."

"Well damn, girl. I was going to ask if you thought this through but I can see you have." He chuckled under his breath and shook his head. "If I didn't know you, Nicole, I'd be scared of you."

"I was trained by the best in the industry." I raised my chin slightly and smirked in confidence.

"I tell you what. I'll run this script by the team and get back to you this week. If…" he raised a crooked finger in the air, "…*if* the script is a go, then I'll get your name in the credits and shoot you a finder's fee. We will have to talk about the permanent position on the team. That's not totally my decision. It takes a vote from all the members." I smiled at the way I'd swung the meeting in my direction. I was unstoppable.

"Okay. That sounds like a deal."

After hugging Will like a child that hadn't seen their parent in years, I kissed him on his smooth cheek and sauntered out of the office with my spirits swirling higher than the penthouse suite of his office building. Once in the parking garage, I immediately rang Joy to tell her that things were moving along nicely. She was so excited she wailed loudly into the phone for minutes before asking for more details.

"He said that he will take the script and have his team review it. I have a good feeling, though."

"I can't believe this could actually be happening," she squealed.

"Remember, keep the news to yourself. We don't want to let anyone know about this until everything's final," I explained. Actually, I didn't want Webby messing the deal up by negotiating his own cut. There were already too many mouths to feed on this project and I wasn't too ready to give up my dream of seeing my name in the credits of a movie. As I peeled the BMW into the downtown traffic, I felt light as a feather. Things were finally coming together the way I had always dreamed. I was a few weeks from being a world-class producer and having the money to take care of myself. I detoured to Lenox Mall and figured I should treat myself to a new purse. I deserved it. Hell, I deserved the whole damn store.

I wanted to call Webby to share the good news but I knew that wasn't a good idea. So I called Justice instead. He was the only person that I always thought to call when I wanted to talk. Unfortunately, he was still scorned over the breakup and hung up on me. Oh well, his loss! Pretty soon, he'd be crawling back, wishing he could have another taste of this. I called Joy back and invited her to meet me at Lenox for dinner. I needed to celebrate with someone who could make me feel like a million bucks.

"Sure! I'll be on my way there in twenty. I have to freshen up."

"Okay, meet me at Tapas Lounge. I'll reserve the table."

"Nicole, thanks again for everything. I owe you so much. I can't wait to start paying it off again." Joy sounded seductive enough to make me swerve into the wrong lane. The car next to me honked in annoyance.

"You don't owe me anything. We both are going to make a nice profit on this," I assured her.

"No. But you didn't have to take this chance. So believe me…I will pay you back. Again and again…" My pussy jittered in the leather seats of the BMW. I reminisced over the feel of her hands on my breasts in the shower, the touch of her tongue against the wetness of my body. I pulled the car over before I wrecked it.

"Joy, what're you doing? You know this can't ever be a *thing* between us, right?" I was fighting my body's reaction to her raunchy conversation.

"I know we could never be a real thing but in the meanwhile, can't we just have a little fun together?"

"Just fun?" I really wanted to feel my body come hard again. It was addictive. I dreamed about it at night then woke up in the morning and daydreamed about it. I yearned to feel it again.

"You know what? I don't feel like tapas. Why don't you come by here instead?" Joy was baiting me. I knew what would happen if I went to her house. It took everything in me to resist seeing her for the past few weeks since our steamy shower episode.

"I don't think I should," I lied as I pulled the BMW back into traffic and made a U-turn at the next light heading toward Joy's apartment. I felt giddy just thinking about being alone with Joy.

"Just come over here. We'll have a little wine and talk. We deserve to celebrate, right?"

"Okay. I'll be there in twenty. Just wine, though. No fun tonight," I warned.

"Of course, no fun. Just wine. See you in a bit." Joy ended the call but I still held the cell phone to my ear, amazed. I couldn't believe what I was about to do. My brain screamed to turn around and go buy the damn purse at Lenox and forget about Joy but my body was on autopilot with Joy's house as the destination.

After wheeling my BMW into the underground parking garage and pacing outside her apartment door before finding the courage to knock, I finally got the nerve. The smell hit me first.

The scent of vanilla candles wafted from the opened door and floated around Joy in a white see-through, button-up top that exposed the perk of her bare nipples. Her shorts revealed smooth, shapely legs and bright pink toenail polish. As I walked into the apartment, she took my purse strap off my shoulder and led me into a living room filled with what seemed like hundreds of candles. Their flames danced against the darkness to an Alice Smith record playing softly in the background. My stomach twisted and turned in anticipation, as if I was on a roller coaster ride. Joy was a unique roller coaster ride indeed. She had the same strengths I did, especially her skill in being fucking irresistible. We were a lot alike and that was scary. I knew the depths I would go to get the things I wanted so I needed to be cautious. I sensed that being around Joy was like living in the red zone. Dangerous.

Discarding my better judgment, Joy found a way to get me undressed and writhing in pleasure between her bedsheets as I had in the shower weeks ago in Costa Rica. I smiled as I felt the unmistakable feeling of climax sneaking up my inner thigh as she touched me in the best and worst ways. I squeezed and pounded a fistful of cotton bedsheets as my body retched in pleasurable pain. Breathless and ashamed, I pulled the sheets over my head. I felt her arm stretch across my side and her head weigh down the corner of the pillow, waiting for sleep to invade me. Thankfully, it took only seconds. Before fully crashing into the sweetest sleep, I heard Joy faintly whisper, "I love you, Nicole." I snuggled deeper into the sheet and replayed her words as I let dreams of Justice envelop me. It felt good to be loved again.

Mali

∞

"Honey, I love those curls all over your head. Too cute!" I eyed the man standing next to me dressed in patterned leggings and oversized feminine sweater. His close-cropped hair was slicked down with shiny gel but his makeup made him look like he could be on *America's Next Top Diva*.

"Thanks. It's natural. Couldn't change it if I wanted to," I returned.

"You should let me beat your pretty little face before the audition." I eased back with a defensive look in my eyes. He continued, "Oh, honey. That's not what I mean when I say 'beat.' That means I can have your face looking flawless...I call it 'beat face'—just think of it like a brand name." He fingered his delicate gold chain, tousling my hair with his other hand.

"Oh..." I shied from his pampering. "You must work here."

"You ain't know? Girl, I'm the lead hair and makeup artist for Will Dunkin. I do everybody who is anybody." He extended his thin hand toward me and I eyed the large opal ring on his index finger before shaking it. "You can call me Toni." The ring was almost as gorgeous as Toni with his false eyelashes fanning deep brown eyes.

The audition was being held in a building that looked like an old warehouse or packing facility. There were backdrops brightly lit in the main studio but the audition would be held in a large, mirror-enclosed studio space in the rear of the building. I was traveling through the main studio looking for the door marked AUDITIONS before Toni stopped me. I wasn't sure if I should take him up on his offer and risk being late. The last thing I needed was to get sidetracked on my first audition.

As if reading my mind, Toni said, "I can have you done in thirty minutes."

I glanced at my watch. I had approximately forty minutes before the audition began. That would leave me only ten minutes to warm up. Toni propped his hands on his hip as I struggled to decide, feigning impatience. Tired of my indecisiveness, he grabbed my hand firmly and jogged with me to his makeup studio down a bright hallway to a door marked MAKEUP. He morphed into work mode as he pushed me into a black swivel chair surrounded by trays of makeup brushes, eye pencils, colored eye shadows and rows of foundation in every shade.

"How long have you been working here?" I asked him as he hurriedly pulled trays from places I couldn't see, tilted my head in multiple directions and made me sit still as he traced my eyelids with a dark pencil and slicked my lashes with mascara.

"Since you been in Pampers," he said, dusting my cheeks with a fat brush.

It all happened so fast that I was determined to believe that only ten minutes had passed since I sat in his chair. He swiveled the chair toward the mirror and my jaw dropped at the transformation. Toni was an expert in his craft because I'd never been this beautiful in my life. Granted, I never wore much makeup before but looking down at my watch, it had taken him exactly twenty-two minutes to completely change my look.

"Just imagine what I could do with a whole two hours…" Toni smirked as he stood behind me, admiring his work.

"Thank you so much for doing this. I wish I could pay you but…"

Toni held up his hand. "Honey, when you do something you love, it doesn't take money to make you happy. All I need is a muse."

I smiled at him and turned back to the mirror, flabbergasted at the sexy, confident woman who stared back. Toni broke through my ogling to remind me, "You better start warming up. I did my part…and now it's time to do yours."

I eased out of the chair and thanked Toni profusely as I backed out of his area and made a beeline for the audition. When I arrived in the studio, there was hardly room to stand due to the number of dancers that had arrived while I was sitting in Toni's chair. Each had their first name and last initial taped to the front of their outfits. A few girls were not dressed to dance as they wore high heels and tight jeans while others were clad in tights and sports bras, ready to dance into stardom. A few men were scattered in the group and commenced stretching in the far corner of the studio. I swallowed hard to ease the tension in my tummy. My first audition and the competition looked steep.

I must admit, Toni's makeup artistry had heads turning when I retrieved my name tag. I guess he was right about having a "beat face." I could feel the eyes of the contestants rolling over my body, assessing my outfit, my makeup. I tried not to cower beneath their curious stares. If I wasn't a threat no one would be looking, I reminded myself. I kept my poise, with my head high and back straight as I noticed many of the directors and producers were watching me intently as I walked to an open space to stretch. In the corner of my eye, I saw Toni slip into the room and sit behind the judges' table next to the other members. My eyes exploded with thanks as he nodded slightly before looking down at the roster.

There were three rounds of cuts in the audition process. The first cut left only fifty dancers in the studio. Luckily, my name was called to continue on. The air seemed to lighten as the second round of terminated contestants gathered their belongings and filed out of the studio, leaving only nine girls and one male contestant remaining in the lineup. We'd practiced choreography all morning but it was time to showcase our individual talents. We were asked to choreograph our own dance to the hit song "Beat Up the Beat" by Webby. I was relieved they'd chosen Webby's song since I'd practiced for weeks on my choreography and knew that it would hit hard in all the right places in the song. Hopefully I'd done enough. I eyed Toni behind the table, marking his page while discarding others into a trash bin behind the table. I gulped, fearful that my bio was the one getting axed. Will Dunkin stood from behind the judging table to make the announcement of the final dancers chosen for the music video.

"Ladies and gent, we appreciate your coming out to the audition this morning. I know you've worked very hard in your craft because you've beat out over one hundred dancers to be in the top ten. Luckily, I have good news for each and every one of you…" I stared at him intensely. "All of you have made it through to work on the video. Being in the top ten allows you to be a permanent dancer with the studio." A sigh of relief flooded the studio as the dancers clapped. Staying composed, I clapped alongside the other dancers, while jumping on the inside at the news.

"But there is one more thing," Will Dunkin continued. "We are currently looking for a lead choreographer. Someone that is professional, beautiful…or handsome." He nodded to the last gentleman left in the lineup. "Someone who can bring a new, fresh style of dance to our videos. Therefore, we will be judging your final solo performances on your choreography skills. Best of luck."

The room fell silent as the dancers' momentary excitement changed to an aggressive determination. We had all forgotten that we had the job we originally came for, and now our sights were set on something bigger. Something I couldn't have imagined was in my reach. I replayed my choreography over and over in my head, hoping it was good enough. I stood in the hallway, shadowing the movements I would do inside the studio. The first contestant had already gone inside to perform as the rest of us waited patiently in the hall for her music to finish, looking around at each other in silence. All of us were hoping and thinking the same thing…*I hope she doesn't get it.*

As each dancer went in, each came out with a look of sorrow or disappointment. There were only three left in line, waiting for our names to be called. Mine was next. My heart thumped loudly in my ears. I strained to remember the moves but I was blanking.

I didn't know what to expect when I skipped into the studio, covering my fear with enthusiasm. I told myself, *keep your poise, Mali.* Will Dunkin sat behind the judges' table next to Toni while three other judges sat to the left. Each judge eyed my body, smiled and whispered to each other. I could see them looking at my head shot on the table and assessing their handwritten notes. I'd make sure they wouldn't need another note because they were going to remember me after today. Time to leave it all on the floor.

"Hello. My name is Mali Struthers. Before we begin, I'd like to thank you, Mr. Dunkin, and your team for the opportunity to work with you. I won't let you down."

Will Dunkin answered, "Thank you, Miss Struthers. I can't wait to see your choreography. Cue the music!"

Toni winked his eye as a sign of good luck, I supposed. I remembered our deal.

Okay, Toni, time to do my part…

Before the song was at the halfway point, I forgot that I was auditioning for the judges' panel. My chest heaved with breathless excitement as I leaped across the hardwood floors and landed without sound. The music infused my arms and tangled them in the air in beautiful shapes as I lifted my leg high to the ceiling. The music took over and before long, I smiled to the judges as the last beat of the song pounded the studio walls. I was finished. I had danced with all my heart and I could only hope that it was enough for them. I bowed slightly as they all clapped openly.

"Please wait in the hall," Will Dunkin announced as I walked to the door.

I beamed and thanked them as I jogged out of the studio and into the hall. The look on both dancers' faces were a mix of confusion, anxiety and determination. I couldn't offer them any solace. I was too excited to be invited to stay. The judges called the male dancer, Bobby, in next. I wished him luck as he entered the studio and shut the door softly behind him.

"So what happened in there?" The blonde woman sat against the wall, fiddling with the strap on her duffel bag.

"Not much. I just left it all on the dance floor." I sighed and slumped next to her.

"Where do you study?" The music bumped the walls of the hallway. Bobby had started his set.

"I go to AU. I'm a dance major."

"A dance major? You're still in school? Is this your first gig?" She looked at me skeptically with her blue eyes.

"Yep. My first gig." I felt uneasy with her eyes boring holes into the side of my head like I was a freak show or something.

"Oh, I'm sorry. I didn't mean to offend. I didn't think you were still in school." She stuck out her hand so I shook it. "My name is Sam, short for Samantha. I guess we'll be working together regardless, huh?"

"I guess so. Oh, I'm Mali, by the way."

The silence between us was awkward and I felt like I was sitting too close to not talk with her but I had a vibe that she was preoccupied in thought.

"One of us might be the boss. That'll be kinda weird," she said, more to herself than to me. I was sure she wouldn't think it was weird if she was the lead choreographer.

"Why would it be weird?" I pushed my sweater deeper into my bag, finding an excuse to move farther away.

"Well, I've been dancing for ten years. It's how I make a living—it isn't a part-time gig for me. So, excuse me, but I don't think college students that still have mommy and daddy paying their way through college can run the show in this business without experience," she challenged.

"Well, I'm sorry you feel that way."

"You'll get eaten alive in this business, little girl. Look at you," she pointed, "you're all meek and mild, timid in the audition. It may be cute for a while but when you get to the heavy hitters, you'll be fresh meat in a pond full of piranhas. I'm thirty-two years old and I can tell you, you haven't seen nothing yet."

"Best of luck to you." I figured ending the conversation would make her shut up. I was right.

She sneered pompously as I walked to the other end of the hall and dropped to the tile floor to wait. Minutes later, Bobby emerged from the door with a large smile spread across his face.

"They asked me to stay!" He smiled. "Your turn." He pointed to Sam as she pulled herself up, stretched her arms over her head and then glanced arrogantly at both of us before disappearing into the studio with a fake smile spread across her face.

"Can you believe her?" I asked Bobby after he jumped up and down in excitement by himself. Sam had killed my high. Maybe she was right, I was in over my head.

"Uh, yeah! Everyone in this industry has a stick so far up their ass that I wanna give them pliers for Christmas." We snickered in the hallway together until he plopped on the floor beside me, waiting for Sam's music to start. Within minutes, the opening bass rumbled the walls.

"So how do you think you did?" I quizzed.

"I did my best. I have acrobatics in the routine, so it was definitely beyond booty shaking and two-stepping. The judges seemed to like it." He chuckled again.

"You know, you seem pretty cool. I wonder why girls in this business can't be more like you." I thought of Brianna and now, Sam. "I guess it's because you're a man and you don't have to deal with these petty competitive catfights."

"I see it all the time in this industry. One girl makes it and another one works twice as hard to pull her down from the top. And don't think that because I'm a man I'm immune to the drama." He shook his head.

"Well, I can promise you, if you get the choreography job, I won't try to step on your toes. If anything, I want you to teach me some acrobatics." I smiled.

"No worries. I don't have many friends in the industry but I can see you're a fresh face to the scene. Literally untouched," he continued as he shook his head slowly. "You might need a bodyguard with the way you dance. You are going to piss off a lot of girls and have a lot of guys trailing behind you or maybe the other way around." He laughed.

"I just want to dance." I blushed. "I couldn't care less about guys right now." *Unless it was Justice Bradford*, I thought to myself.

The music inside the studio stopped and Bobby and I sat silently, waiting to see Sam when she opened the door. The door swung open loudly, Sam grabbed her bag, hoisted it over her shoulder and glared at us sitting in the walkway.

"Move!" she said, stepping over our outstretched legs, clearly on her way out of the studio.

Bobby and I stared in awe as she stomped from the hallway and into the main studio. We heard the slam of the steel front door and the faint sound of a car speeding out of the parking lot. Bobby held his hand up for a high five and said, "Bitch be gone!" and held a silly smirk on his face.

"I guess it's just you and me."

"May the best man win." He smirked at his joke.

We entered the studio hand in hand to face the judges for the last time.

"We'd like to thank you both for auditioning today for the lead choreographer position. Unfortunately, we couldn't come to a decision on which one of you should receive the position," Toni stated.

I looked at Bobby and could see his shoulders slump forward slightly. We'd both worked so hard to make it this far. Why couldn't they choose?

Toni continued, "Both of you did an exceptional job. Mali, you dance with so much passion. Your heart and soul was poured on the dance floor. We could feel every single emotion, every single lyric in the song. You pulled us into the story you were telling. That's a true gift. And Bobby," Toni pointed his pen in his direction, "you have so much power and creativity. You did moves that we couldn't even dream of seeing on-screen. You're so strong when you leap and flip but you look like you're landing on pillows. So soft and graceful. I would love to see an artist or group attempt your choreography."

I could feel Bobby's hand trembling slightly as we stared at the judging panel. We were dreading the news that we would have to audition again, maybe another time after they thought about it more. It was clear-cut enough to know that we were great in our own styles but not enough to choose? I could feel Bobby's hand grip mine tightly as he glanced at me with pure optimism. I could tell by his watery eyes that he was going to take this hard if he didn't get the spot. I didn't even expect to make it on the permanent team let alone lead choreographer so I waited patiently to hear Bobby's name.

Toni whispered to Will Dunkin and pointed at the papers in front of him adamantly. Will Dunkin nodded as the other judges crowded around to listen closely. Bobby and I stood still awaiting our fate as the minutes ticked away. Finally, Will Dunkin held up a hand to the group that was now whispering heatedly around him.

"Mali and Bobby, you're both hired."

I thought I had misheard him. I stood still for a moment, making sure that I wasn't hallucinating when he said we were both lead choreographers for Dunkin Studios. Bobby squeezed my hand roughly and snapped me out of my trance with a bear hug tight enough to make my neck ache. He leaped around the room, extending his long legs into pirouettes and flips with a childlike, gapped-tooth smile spread across his pale face.

"We want both of you to create choreography together using both your styles of dance. I think it will be a breakthrough opportunity for many of the artists that use our services. Please stop into our offices on Friday to sign your contracts and discuss schedules and duties. Congratulations." Will Dunkin looked down at Toni, beaming with pride at the decision.

I blew a kiss to Toni as I raced out of the studio and into the parking lot with Bobby. Sweeping his hand over his spiky brown hair, he offered me a ride in his beat-up Toyota but I declined, hoping to get Justice to take me on a congratulatory date. I was feeling confident, so why not ask him out? I dialed Justice twice, but no answer. I shot him a text that I'd landed the audition and had even more news to share. I pouted, waiting for his reply, but it never came. Dejected, I dialed Mack on the walk to the bus stop. She picked up on the second ring, breathless, as if she was in the middle of working out.

"What's up?"

"I made it." I danced around the empty bus stop.

"Shut up! You made it? I knew you'd kill the first audition!"

"Thanks, but there's more…" I paused for emphasis.

"Well tell me, dammit!" Mack screamed into the phone.

"They hired me as lead choreographer. Can you believe that?" I asked incredulously.

"Yes! Yes! Yes!" I laughed at the sound of Mack doing her happy dance.

The bus was coming so I kept it short. "I was feeling so good…I was even about to ask Justice out."

"You're kidding? I never thought of you as the bold, aggressive type. That's more my speed." She laughed.

"I know, right? But maybe it's a sign because he didn't pick up…and he always picks up."

"Why don't you just ask him out next time you see him? You know, in person, like the rest of us normal people do."

The thought of rejection made me cringe. "No. We're just friends. Nothing more. I don't know what I was thinking."

"Stop it, Mali. You always second-guess yourself. Stop overthinking it and just do it!" That was easier said than done, didn't she know that?

"I've gotta go. The bus is here," I said as it huffed to a stop, door folding open.

"Okay. Congratulations!" she said as I ended the call and plopped on an empty seat.

I wasn't going to call Justice again. He knew I was auditioning today and specifically asked for me to call afterward. Clearly he was preoccupied—but with what?

Justice

∞

I was back. Yes, indeed, the old me had reemerged and nothing could stop me now. After cleaning up my act and making some big strides on the football field, the birds around campus were chirping my name again. I was back in the news. ESPN and SportsCenter had their opinions of the team but I was the highlight on *90 Seconds with Bill Dampier*. I'd been playing better than I ever had at AU. The local news anchors kept saying I was going to lead the team all the way to the championship and maybe even a title. I was watching *90 Seconds* on ESPN, laughing wholeheartedly as Bill Dampier argued the entire ninety-second spotlight against football great Jerry Rice that I would be slotted to rank in the first round of the draft.

The news wasn't the only thing changing around me. Coach Dempsey was like a private investigator since we'd won our division and were headed to the championship. He constantly called to check up on the manager he assigned to me—"out the goodness of his heart," of course. I saw Coach Dempsey pushing some new Cadillac Escalade around campus recently, so I guessed business was doing well on his end too. The Panthers' scout invited me to practice with them over the summer. Coach Dempsey spoke vehemently against it, saying they needed to pay to play. He caught me in the locker room after practice to reinforce his position.

"Don't give them what they want, JB. This isn't first come, first served. The early bird certainly does not get the worm when it comes to football," he advised.

"So when should I start talking to the reps from the teams?" I wondered aloud.

"You don't. Let Jimmy D handle all that." Jimmy D was Jimmy Dagliano, my very Italian and very new manager. He was supposed to find me a proper agent, talk to the teams on my behalf and make sure no one—absolutely no one—got me to sign anything. Beyond the fact that he had an air of a mobster with his wide-leg pants and short-sleeved button-down shirts, I didn't think anyone was going to push him too hard to get close to me. I'd only heard from the Panthers so far.

"Alright. That's cool."

"Just sit back and relax, let them come to you. After the championship, the Panthers won't be anything more than a spot on your dirty drawers." He laughed heartily, showing his gray teeth.

I laughed with him in the locker room but I had a feeling I was going to be rushing his ass to the hospital with a heart attack after the bowl game in a few weeks.

I drove through sprawling skyscrapers and tinted-glass buildings in downtown Atlanta toward campus. I had my music blaring from the speakers as the heat warmed the leather seats. I wanted to have a break and go home to see my family for Christmas but that wasn't going to happen since we were playing in the Hawai'i Bowl Championship in January. The Hawai'i Bowl Championship would be a nice Christmas gift to bring home for the holidays, I thought as I passed the stone-engraved sign at the entrance to Atlanta University.

The campus was hustling and bustling as I pulled slowly around Main Street. People waved from the sidewalk and girls smiled shyly as I passed by, with their curvy hips switching from left to right. I was single, handsome and about to be very wealthy… The world was in my palm. As I drove through campus, I spotted Big Deuce walking with Mali near the front of the Brigg building and honked my horn. They didn't hear it so I honked the horn again. They kept laughing and walking across the yard, oblivious to the sound. Passersby stopped to see who I was honking at and looked around confused. Why was Big Deuce with Mali? I pulled the Impala into a parking spot behind the art building across the street and took off in a trot toward them.

"Hey! What's up?" I half yelled to Big Deuce and Mali. Both looked away from each other, spotted me near the curb and smiled. They actually looked happy together. So why was I trying so hard not to get upset?

"Hey, Justice!" Mali waved happily. Big Deuce smiled as I jogged up to them.

"Where you headed?" I asked them both.

"Probably to the Union to grab some food before my next class," Mali answered.

"You're going to lunch with Deuce? Is this a date or something?" I raised my hands defensively. "I'm not trying to step on anyone's toes." Big Deuce looked confused as I smiled in Mali's direction to keep from looking at him.

"No. We're just going to grab something. It's not a date." She laughed out loud and started walking toward the Union. Big Deuce eyed me suspiciously before falling in step with her. I scrambled to keep up.

"Mali, I'm sorry I missed your calls after your audition. I was caught up…" I stammered. I couldn't reveal that I was banging Monica the morning, afternoon and evening of her audition.

"It's no big deal. I got the job but instead of just being a dancer they wanted to me to be lead choreographer. It's a pretty sweet deal. Deuce actually answered his phone when I called," she glanced back at me quickly, "so he offered to take me to lunch to celebrate."

Deuce stared at me like I had stolen his spotlight. I knew what Big Deuce was trying to do with Mali and I wasn't going to let him do it to her. She was not the type of girl that should be treated like a two-bit whore to be discarded in a few weeks. The thought of him using her like he had so many other women made bile rise in my throat.

"Mali, I apologize for not calling back. I'll make it up to you. Maybe dinner tonight?" I tried to flash my most seductive smile.

"No need," she stated matter-of-factly, unfazed by my charm.

"Hey, man, can I talk with you for a second? I'll catch up with you in the Union, Mali." Big Deuce put his hand on my shoulder as Mali nodded and walked up the steps and inside the Union. When she was out of sight, he continued.

"What the hell is wrong with you?"

"Nothing's wrong. What're you talking about?"

"You're acting jealous of your best friend." He pounded his huge chest for emphasis. "I'm trying to make a move and you're blocking me, bro."

"Look, I'm not jealous. She's just not one of these hoes around campus." I knew I couldn't tell Deuce too much or he'd try even harder to get her, so I said, "I just don't want her to get hurt because she's a friend. I know how you are, Deuce. She's not that type of girl."

"You act like that's your girlfriend or something. It's cool. She's my friend too but I don't keep sexy-ass friends around without trying to hit it every now and again. That's part of the man law. Damn." Deuce put his finger to his temple as if in thought. "You told me that you weren't interested in her like that. That you were just friends. You need to tell me right now whether you have feelings for her or not."

I stood there thinking of all the smiles and laughs Mali and I shared in the studio and over the phone. I knew I wasn't the best man for her because I had no money, no way to take care of her. I couldn't focus 100% on her with my football career about to go into full swing. Not to mention, I was two steps away from leaving the school for good while she was just beginning. Money was the same reason Nicole left and I knew before long, if I let her, Mali would do the same. She'd find someone else who could take care of her and leave me broken, just like Nicole. I knew I had to let her go. She could make her own choices when it came to Deuce.

"No. No feelings for her, bro. My bad. Go ahead and do your thing." I gestured toward the Union.

My stomach dropped when I spotted Mali watching from the Union window as Deuce and I shook hands to seal the deal. As I darted back toward the car, I turned to look one last time at Mali's face watching from the Union window. The look of abandonment darkened her eyes as she turned her face to Deuce as he sat down. It was a look that burned into my soul and I would probably never forget it.

∞

Women always drove me to drink. After leaving the Union, I kept seeing Mali's sad, hurt face in my head. After two hours of wondering if I was right to release Big Deuce's charm on her and lie about my feelings for her, I sat on a stool in Atlantic Station in a bar off 17th Street and downed another glass of rum and Coke. It burned less than the previous two glasses. Occasionally, people passing through the bar would pat me on the back and say "Good game" or "Good job" but I wasn't worried about football right now. I was wondering what Big Deuce was doing with Mali. He could be slick with the ladies and for some reason, they could never resist his comedic charm. I'd seen him love 'em and leave 'em without even an inkling of emotion. I was hoping that Mali was strong enough to see through all Deuce's tricks, for her sake and mine.

"Well, well, well, what have we here? Mr. Justice Bradford?" I turned on the leather stool to see Monica and two of her friends lingering behind me.

"Yes. It's the one and only. What are you ladies getting into tonight?" I downed the rest of my drink, immediately feeling the buzz.

"Nothing too much. Coming to get a drink then off to a party later," Monica answered.

"I see you never have a free Friday night. I'm going to head home after one last drink." I grabbed the freshly poured rum and Coke and nodded to the bartender in thanks.

"I'm always free on Friday for you, Justice. Looks like you might need a designated driver tonight. We wouldn't mind taking the party to your house, you know." Monica ran her fingers down my chest and stopped at my belt as her friends giggled behind her. This girl was a straight freak. She would have pulled my junk out in public if I hadn't stopped her hand.

"Is it going to take all three of you to take li'l ole me home?" I teased. "Have y'all been drinking tonight?" They were a little too giggly to be sober.

"Oh noooo...of course not. We have fun in our own little way." Monica leaned to whisper in my ear, "Bet you didn't know ecstasy could make you last...all...night...long." She sucked my earlobe with each word, sending a chill down my spine.

Monica glanced at the two slightly taller girls standing behind her. One girl smirked seductively in response to my rhetorical question. She was tall and slender with long arms and legs like a supermodel but she stood rigid and poised behind Monica. Her pinch of a nose on white porcelain skin made her look doll-like while the other girl was much less delicate with a sharp jawline and chiseled features. She was clearly a workout buddy of Monica's as her dress pulled tight against thin, straight hips and muscular thighs. I wouldn't have normally looked twice at her but under extreme intoxication, she had a sexy way about her. She smirked under my obvious visual assessment of her body as Monica continued to lay on the charm.

"We wouldn't be real friends if we let you drive drunk. Now would we?" Monica sat on the empty stool next to me and swiveled toward the bar. Her friends collapsed around me on either side and eyed my body like hungry vultures. If I let these girls loose in my house, this was going to be a very long night.

"I could drive you home. Brianna can help you up the stairs and Dena can put you right to sleep. See, you need all of us."

The girls smiled shyly at Monica's insinuation. I wasn't going to turn down my first foursome. What kind of fool did they take me for? I'd been a fool for far too long with Nicole. It was time to start living in the moment again. Time to start enjoying the fruits of my labor.

"I *am* feeling a little buzzed. Maybe that wouldn't be such a bad idea, ladies. Can't have an all-star getting picked up for a DUI right before the championship, can we?"

"Yeah, we're Good Samaritans," the muscular girl said with a smirk.

I left cash on the wooden bar and walked out with Monica, Brianna and Dena in tow. They giggled together the entire way to my apartment, each one taking their turn landing wet kisses on my face and neck. I was nudged in the middle seat between Monica and Dena as Brianna drove cautiously through downtown Atlanta until she inched into the parking space at my apartment building. I'd had just about enough groping of my package and sloppy kisses when the doors to the car finally swung open and I was allowed to escape. I could tell these girls were living on the wild side so I tried to call Deuce to come by the house but he didn't answer. I guess I was going to handle this one all alone.

As promised, Brianna, seemingly the only sober one, helped me up the stairs to the apartment since the liquor made me feel like I was wearing cement shoes. I was feeling a little unstable but not as much as Dena and Monica seemed to be as they struggled up the stairs behind me. Brianna fluctuated between helping me up two steps and reaching back to grab Monica and Dena as they walked up two steps bursting into raucous laughter while stumbling over each other.

Finally, we toppled into the apartment's darkness and I reached for the light switch only to find Monica's warm hand covering it. She laughed into the dark, grabbed my outstretched hand and slapped it to her perky breasts. The softness of her breasts in my palm made me forget about the damn lights and focus on nothing but her...for the moment. My eyes focused in the darkness and I could make out the shape of each woman. The streetlights' glow seeped through the closed blinds and cast shadows across the colorless walls of my apartment.

I felt Dena's muscular arms as she eased herself to the floor in front of me and released my belt buckle. Monica was fervently devouring my lips and neck as I scanned the room for the other girl, Brianna. She sat on the couch, in my favorite spot, silently watching us. She watched the girls attack every inch of my body vigorously before slowly undressing herself. Even in the darkness I could tell that her body was beautiful and elegant. She stretched her long legs across the couch and spread open her flower for me to see. I squinted in the dark and caught a glimpse of her pink flesh beaconing me to *come hither*. I released myself from Dena's monstrous mouth and peeled Monica's lips from my nipple as I walked in a trance to Brianna's awaiting cocoon. She swirled her tiny fingers in the juices that awaited me and offered her finger to a hungry Monica. I watched with my pants bunched around my ankles as Dena and Monica consumed Brianna hungrily. Her delicate body looked like a sacrifice to the gods as she sprawled across my lumpy couch and moaned softly with each slurping of her nipple or bite of her thigh. I slowly paced to the awaiting jezebels, dropped to my knees and feasted on Brianna like she was purifying waters and could save me from all hurt and pain I'd felt for so long. I found her flower petal deep in the meadows of her flesh and plucked it from her soft spot as she sang a song of joy into the darkness.

Monica, Brianna and Dena took turns satisfying their insatiable appetites until I had nothing left to give. We poured onto the carpeted floor of the living room, exhausted. I felt empty. Emotionless. This was how I wanted to feel. How I needed to feel right now. But I never thought I'd feel so alone in a room full of naked women. I couldn't get the morning out of my head as I lay on the floor staring up at the ceiling fan that whispered around the room, fanning the funk of sex.

How did Big Deuce get so close to Mali? He'd switched his class to get closer to her but Deuce did that kind of stuff every year. It wasn't enough to alarm me. I didn't think Mali would actually fall for his charm. The air seemed thick in my throat as I swallowed to keep the emotionless feeling in my body. I strained to stuff all thoughts of Mali into a deep place within my soul. I scanned the three women that lay naked and unashamed at their wild ways. Why would I want to worry about love again when I could have nights like this?

Nicole

∞

The smell of sizzling bacon made me pull the thick down comforter from over my head. I squinted into the sunlight that shone through three huge windows in Webby's bedroom. The birds were chirping loudly in Sandy Springs, Georgia, this morning. I loved mornings like this but a small part of me hated to remember where that love began. I remembered waking up to perfect mornings like this while I grew up in my father's old farmhouse in Douglasville. He'd have something cooking on the stove for me and my younger sister, Lola, most mornings. It could be fresh eggs from the henhouse, homemade sour cream pancakes or fresh bacon slices. At the time, I didn't grasp that he was a wonderful dad for cooking us breakfast every morning before school. Not until he was gone did I miss those breakfasts together. I swallowed back the tears. *It's only you now*, I reminded myself. I had to beg, borrow and steal to get a man to cook something these days; Daddy surely wasn't around to do it. The modern man thought hot dogs and toast with jelly counted as cooking a gourmet breakfast. I rolled off the edge of Webby's large bed and covered my nakedness with a pink silk robe he'd purchased in Europe. It felt cool against my skin as I stretched before heading into the bathroom. I heard pots and pans rattling in the kitchen downstairs and realized that Webby wasn't the type to cook anything. So I was sure he'd asked the chef to cook us breakfast even though he was usually off on the weekends.

I padded down the sprawling u-shaped staircase that surrounding a dazzling crystal chandelier and stepped onto the cold, marble floors of the foyer. The cold jolt forced me to tiptoe into the open living and dining room which switched to warmer hardwood floors. I internally scolded myself for not putting on slippers before coming down. What could I say? It was the country girl in me. The living room was a mix of colorful abstract paintings that hung high on the walls and neutral-toned modern furniture that looked as if it was purchased by the Jetsons. I heard the faint sounds of Leela James's rendition of Sam Cooke's classic song "A Change Is Gonna Come." It was my favorite song. The only song that made me feel I could make it in this world, no matter the obstacle. It was the song I played over and over from the first night I slept in the orphanage until I was taken to a foster home. That song had gotten me through nights when boys would slide their hands in my pants feeling for my treasure as the foster parents slept. I cried so much until I was adopted that I vowed never to cry again…and I hadn't since.

Still, I was surprised Webby remembered after all these months that I loved that song. I couldn't wait to wrap myself in his strong arms and plant kisses all over his handsome face for remembering something so special.

I rounded the corner to the expansive gourmet kitchen to find Joy chopping onions and dicing green peppers. An omelet bubbled in the iron pan behind her. I stood inside the threshold unsure of whether to speak to her or turn and run from the house in terror. What was she doing here? She gave a dazzling smile as she tossed the vegetables into the pan.

"Rise and shine, sweetheart!" She bounced like a child and embraced me in a hug that felt more like a straitjacket than anything else. She looked as if she had just rolled out of her bed as well. Her hair was pulled into a knotted bun atop her head and she wore short cloth shorts and a midriff Atlanta Hawks top.

"What're you doing here, Joy?"

"Cooking you breakfast, silly girl!" She pinched my nose like a child and bolted to the pan to flip the omelet before it burned.

"You know what I mean. How did you get in here? Where's Webby?" My confusion was slowly turning to agitation as I looked around the house for an escape route.

"Oh. Webby called Veronica and wanted to talk business over breakfast. So I thought," she put her finger to her cheek as if still in thought, "maybe I should make you breakfast. I knew he wouldn't bother to bring you anything back. He *is* a man, you know." She giggled at her own joke. If she wasn't normally attached to Veronica's hip, I might have been a little skeptical.

"How did you get in here?" I asked again, pointing in the direction of the front door.

"Pretty easy, actually. Tim remembers me. He let me in. I told him my girlfriend wanted to see me." She smiled absently as she continued cutting vegetables for the next omelet.

"You're not my girlfriend, Joy. You're just my friend. You know that, right?" I pressed.

"I'm a girl and your friend…a girlfriend. God, I'm just playing with you! Why are you so uptight?" She stopped chopping and pointed the knife at me. "Do you need a massage or something?"

"You should have called me before coming over and doing all this." I gestured to the spread of food on the oversized island. Fresh fruits spilled from porcelain bowls, crispy bacon strips and fluffy pancakes stacked high sat in the middle of the island. It looked like a meal for a family of ten, not two women.

"It's no problem. You know I don't mind doing it. You've been such a great friend and I wanted to tell you the good news in person since I doubt you heard it yet, sleepyhead."

I eased to the leather stool in front of the island and held my gurgling stomach, waiting for the news she had to share. I must've looked like a starving child on television because she laughed loudly and urged me to start eating.

"So what news do you have?" I said between bites of bacon and syrup-laden pancakes.

"Well, I got a call from Will Dunkin last night and he said they want to move forward with shooting the movie! They are cutting the check for the advance today!" She jumped up and down in her midriff shirt that barely contained her bosom.

"What? Are you serious? That's better than good news…that's amazing news!" Her enthusiasm was infectious as we danced around the kitchen until we bumped into each other in laughter. As we clung to each other breathless from our celebration, Joy pressed her lips against mine.

"Not here, Joy. Not like this. You know that." I jolted back without warning.

"Don't be scared. He won't find out. Our secret is safe," she breathed. She leaned in for another kiss and I let her mouth press aggressively into mine, letting me know she needed me. Of all the people in the world, she was the only person who ever needed me for anything so I gave in to her seduction. She moaned as our tongues darted into each other's mouths, playing a game of chase. Before long, she'd led me back to the bed I'd left, buried me in the covers so deep that no one could hear my screams of ecstasy.

∞

I woke up sweating my ass off beneath the down comforter. I snatched the cover back to reveal Webby unbuttoning his trousers in the bathroom. I pulled the covers back up slowly. *Shit, where was Joy?* When I fell asleep she was wrapped around me like a cashmere sweater. *Ok, slow down, Nicole. He doesn't know anything.* I quieted my breathing and listened as Webby stepped into the glass-enclosed shower and I heard the light bang of the door closing behind him. I quickly snatched my phone to see if Joy had called me after her sneaky exit. There was only one text in the inbox and it was an alert from the bank. I pushed it to review the message. A deposit was received in the past twenty-four hours. It was the typical alert set up to remind me when I receive checks from various jobs. I thumbed the app for the bank, punched in my password and almost dropped the phone at the sight of my account. I brought the phone closer to my face to ensure I saw each and every digit of the $183,478.12 balance. I did the math in my head and realized that the $180,000 payment was from Dunkin Entertainment. I kicked off the covers happily, just in time for them to fall to the floor in front of Webby's naked body.

"What you so excited for?"

He startled me. I hadn't heard him come into the room. He was standing at the foot of the bed with small drips of water still cascading down his barrel chest and rippled abdomen. I wiggled deeper into the bed under his questioning, searching for a story he'd believe. I definitely couldn't tell him why I was really excited.

"I'm happy to see you, of course!" I lied as I snuggled up to him, sniffing his shower-fresh scent.

"Oh yeah, I had a meeting this morning with Veronica. We've got the video shoot for the new single coming up soon. So I needed her to get with the stylist. What you been doing all day besides sleeping?" he said with a hint of attitude.

"Maybe I need my beauty rest." I hugged him gently. "I had a wonderful dream." I hid my devious smile by resting my head on his shoulder. Little did he know, my dream involved Joy in this bed and it was oh so hard to wake up from.

"I can't tell you the last dream I remembered." He looked to the ceiling like he was trying to recall it from memory, and after a minute or so he gave up. "I have dinner being prepared downstairs. So throw something on and let's eat." He smacked the meat of my rear before disappearing into the closet.

I waited to hear him rummaging through the drawers before I dug for my cell phone I'd tucked under the pillow. I found it, erased the text alert and nudged it onto the nightstand. That was close, I scolded myself. I needed to get better at bending the truth or I'd lose everything I worked for. I dug in the nightstand where Webby kept a small stash and snorted a few quick sniffs before dinner. I was feeling like a million bucks in seconds.

The dinner was prepared by the normal chef and the smell clung to the air like precipitation after a morning rain. I could smell the fresh herbs and spices that laced the chicken cutlets even though my nose was still numb and tingly. My stomach grumbled with the thought of tasting the tender meat since I hadn't eaten anything since breakfast. I smiled at the thought of Joy's breakfast. I envisioned her bun bobbing atop her head as she chopped vegetables and danced around with the skillet sizzling. Webby's voice broke through my thoughts and reminded me to stay focused on dinner, not breakfast.

"You okay?" he repeated.

"Hmm? Yeah, I'm fine. The food smells so good."

"You're probably starving. I should've brought you something back from the restaurant. My bad."

My mind flashed to Joy. "Don't worry about it. I found something to eat."

Webby nodded as the chef simultaneously placed our food in front of us in the grand dining room. The walls were covered in a velvety wine color with abstract paintings that showcased multidimensional greens, oranges and golds surrounded in thick black frames. A dark iron chandelier hung from the center of the massive stained-wooden table. Webby sat at the head of the table while I took the seat on his left. The high ceilings and wide emptiness made the table for fourteen seem too small for the room. Steam rose from the piping-hot sautéed vegetables and chicken. The meal looked healthy, which usually meant it was nasty to me, but I knew this chef could throw down in the kitchen after the past few months of staying at Webby's house. My little apartment didn't have the same appeal as it once had before coming to a mega mansion in one of the most elite neighborhoods in Atlanta. Webby was still paying the rent at my place but I only went by to check the mail occasionally.

"Something on your mind, Nicole?"

"Nothing really. Just admiring the meal. You know how much I love to be pampered." I smirked as I gobbled a forkful of chicken that was too hot on my tongue. The flavors burst in my mouth and I moaned at its tenderness. Damn, the chef was good.

"And I love pampering you. I have to be honest with you about something, though…" He placed his fork on the side of his plate and leaned back in the leather chair. Honest? My breath caught in my throat as the food I was chewing lodged in my cheek. I wouldn't dare swallow yet.

"There is a reason I had this dinner made for you. I really want to tell you how much I've been thinking about our relationship the last few months." I swallowed slowly.

The last thing I wanted was to have another conversation with Webby that I had to wiggle out of. He continued. "I can't stop thinking about you. All day long I wonder what you're doing when you're away from me. It drives me insane sometimes because I know you're beautiful and men want you. I can't help but spoil you because I know that's what you like and I don't want to lose you. Is that a bad thing?"

I almost choked at what I realized was not a joke. I stifled my laughter long enough to notice that he had a serious, concerned even, look on his face. How could I explain to this man that there was no way to spoil me too much? Well, I could tell him outright but then who wanted to be that transparent?

"Babe, I love everything you do for me. It's what a real man should do. And just so you know, there is no man that could take me away from you."

Perfect. I added just enough ego stroking to make him think he was the one that actually thought up the idea of giving me gifts. Inside, he knew the truth. No cash. No ass.

"I felt like we were getting a little distant after the Costa Rica trip." He put his palm to my cheek. "I won't lose you, Nicole. And more importantly, I won't ever let you go."

His sincerity was cute but also a little scary.

"I'm not going anywhere. If you continue to treat me good…I will treat you even better." I smiled.

"I'm sure I can do that. Matter of fact, I have my second confession."

"What is it?" I asked, hesitant to hear it.

Webby grabbed my wrist and led me through the kitchen and outside to the expansive balcony overlooking the manicured lawn. The pool glistened under the dimming sunlight and the sounds of the hot tub bubbling could be heard in the distance. Nightfall was beautiful when you actually stopped to see it. Webby's dark skin caught the lights from the pool as the reflection danced across his strong features. He was truly a handsome man. He looked down at his land and used his fingernail to scratch paint from the wooden railing, staring in the distance. I waited patiently until the silence was too maddening. As if hearing my thoughts, he stood tall and slipped his hand around my waist.

"Nicole, I want to let you know that you mean the world to me...and I love you."

The crickets stopped chirping and the sound of an airplane in the distant sky sounded like a whisper on the wind. The world seemed to revolve in slow motion as the words escaped his lips. I had been waiting patiently for months to hear those words. So why did I feel like I'd just been hit by a bus?

"What? Are you sure?" I couldn't stop it before it came out. I scolded myself for my misstep.

"Yes, I'm sure. I don't give my heart to just anyone. You've proven to me that you have my back. I can trust you. And that means more to me than you know after what I've been through."

He kissed me but my lips wouldn't kiss back. My conscience spilled over into my thoughts. Joy raced through my mind, the movie deal, Will Dunkin, the hiding, the lying. I felt sick.

"Nicole, what's wrong?" He pulled away.

"I just need a little time. Everything is just coming at me all at once."

I couldn't think under the weight of the conversation. He turned back to the railing and stared off into the distant overgrown field behind his property.

"I'm not saying that I don't feel the same, I just need time to take it all in."

"It sure sounds like you don't feel the same. What is there to think about? Either you love me or you don't. It's not a thought. It's a feeling." Webby glanced at me before turning back to the house and disappearing inside.

I turned to look out over the pool as the water quivered in the breeze. I wished I was strong enough to tell him that I loved him in my own way but I knew he wouldn't understand that. The only person I thought I'd loved was Justice and after a while, that didn't even feel like true unconditional love. He hated me now and that was all because I betrayed his trust. Joy was the only person I trusted and felt truly understood me but there was no way I could be in love with her because she was a woman, right? I shook the thought away. What the hell was wrong with me? I had a rich, devoted, handsome man and I couldn't find it in my soul to love him.

I looked out over the pool and remembered my mother with her long dark hair swinging in the breeze at the farm. The sun would always catch her in just the right light to make her smile seem dazzling even though she was an avid smoker. She was gone long before I could really understand the cancer that was painfully killing her body and diminishing her playful spirit. She was like a leaf falling from a high oak tree in September. Fragile and floating around the house until she dried and cracked under the pressure of cancer. My dad couldn't show us the love we needed because he was engulfed by sadness of her deterioration and his helplessness. Cancer took away all the happiness left in our home. He tried hard to focus on me and my sister, Lola (or whatever her new name is now), but he failed to really allow us into his heart, probably from fear of eventually losing us too.

My dad provided for us but there was never anything affectionate or emotionally gratifying in the house after my mother's death. We walked around the farm aimlessly, trying to avoid each other. Trying not to talk about Mom's death or show our feelings, thinking life would go on normally without her if we waited long enough. I wasn't sure if it was the house that reminded Dad so much of her scent and her smile or his daughters' faces that made him turn away from us. Little did he know that each night he'd muffle his cries in the garage standing beside Mom's old Buick, we'd still sit at the table waiting on him to occupy the third seat. The dinner table became a lonely place with one too many chairs. Before long I started setting the table, saying the prayers, and Dad never emerged from his bedroom.

I took care of Lola and the farm after school while he worked late hours at the supermarket until he collapsed on that dirty supermarket linoleum with pain shooting from his arm to his neck. The last thing I remembered when he died in that rickety old hospital bed when I was sixteen was feeling like I wanted to hug him but would never get the chance again.

I couldn't tell Webby about my sordid past. I wouldn't give him that power over me. I wondered how Webby could love someone he knew absolutely nothing about. Didn't he know I was damaged goods? I didn't realize I was crying until the tickle of my tears stung my neck. I palmed the tears away and stared into the darkening thicket at the edge of the property willing myself to be strong. *No tears, dammit.* I'd guarded the door to my heart since Dad left us to foster parents. I'd managed to guard my heart for years even though Webby was knocking for me to open the door again. I couldn't allow him in because only the pain of abandonment still lived there. I promised myself when I entered foster care that I wouldn't leave myself vulnerable. If I never let my guard down I wouldn't have to ever worry about anyone abandoning me again. *The most important thing to remember is to always be the first to leave*, I told myself. *If you leave first, you hurt less.*

Now Webby was pressuring me to give in or lose him. But it was only a matter of time before the love bug turned into an angry, resentful hornet. I wasn't going to lose my lifestyle, so I bucked up and realized it was time to play the game. He had been everything I could have asked for—the perfect man to give me the lavish lifestyle, fast cars and gourmet meals. There was no more time for tears. It was time to strategize.

The night had crept in while I stood there lamenting the unpleasant past and the fast-approaching future. I knew it would only be a matter of time before Webby found out about all the lies and betrayals going on behind his back if I didn't start cleaning out the bones in my closet. The first bone to pick was with Joy. It was time to cut her off before she ruined everything by confusing me into thinking I was in love with her and not Webby.

Mali

∞

The high of being a choreographer for one of the largest and most prestigious studios in Atlanta had not worn off in the past three weeks. Between Mrs. Della-Rose pushing me to perform in her class, working after school at Dunkin Studios for hours with Bobby and bumping Justice's training to once a week, I was surviving on pure adrenaline. The beauty of it all was that I was doing exactly what I wanted to do. Dance.

It was Saturday morning and I finally had a day to myself. January had come quickly and rejuvenated the campus. It was back to being the main stomping grounds for the young and fashionable; the cliques and jocks were back in full effect. Last night, Bobby and I met at the studio to finish out our choreography for Webby's new music video. We were scheduled to teach it to the rest of the dancers on Monday. Will Dunkin said to be ready to shoot in two weeks, which meant I was going to be sweating, nervous and anxious for the next fourteen days. I wasn't worried about the dancers picking up the routine as much as I was worried that Will Dunkin and Webby wouldn't approve of the routine we'd put together. Then we'd be back to the drawing board or, worse, fired. Toni sat in on our final run-through last night and clapped vigorously while Bobby and I sucked in air at the end, winded by the physical intensity of the routine. Toni had an eye for talent so we asked him to critique what we had. We tweaked a few things from his appraisal and ended with an ironclad plan for Monday. Toni assured us Will would love it but I was still nervous about revealing our first choreographed piece for a major rap artist and media mogul. I only hoped it was good enough.

I stopped Bobby in the parking lot as I waited for the bus. "What do you think Will Dunkin and Webby will say when they see it?"

"They'll say we're the greatest team they've ever seen." Bobby smirked and unlocked the door to his car.

"Seriously, you're not nervous? Not even a little bit?"

"Mali, you gotta understand something about dance...you do what you feel and it will be interpreted a million different ways. Who knows? They could love it or hate it...but at the end of the day, we gave it our best." He blew me a kiss and folded his tall body into his tiny car.

I waved when he honked as he pulled out of the parking lot. I stood there thinking about his words. He was right. We'd worked day and night for weeks on a routine that would only play in a five-minute video.

Outside the dorm, the cold winds rattled the windowpane and dislodged frost from the glass. I tucked the covers into the mattress and tidied the space surrounding my bed. I stared at Carey's perfectly aligned textbooks on her nightstand and shoes lined up at the end of her bed. She was so organized. I shook my head as I picked up old running shoes, foot powder and a rolled-up pair of used socks and stuffed them in my closet, slamming the door shut before everything spilled out. My cell phone buzzed on the nightstand as a text symbol appeared on the screen. My mystery man made sure to text and call every day since our first conversation. It was weird to expect to hear from a man I'd never seen before but what else was I going to do? When Justice wasn't around to talk to, I could always count on him to be at the other end of a text or call. I palmed the cell and quickly opened the inbox.

Waiting for my response was a message.

What R u doing?

Nothing. Cleaning. U?

Thinking of u…as always.

You r so sweet. Feels good 2 be thought of.

Then u should feel good ALL the time.

I smirked at the message and fell back on the bed to chat a bit longer.

I do.

I have a question for you.

Shoot.

Why don't u ever ask to meet me???

The question caught me off guard. I thought of the best answer for a while until I realized the truth was probably the best move in this situation.

Becuz I don't want 2 b disappointed.

U think I would disappoint u?

Idk. That's why it's hard. I've learned not 2 have expectations 4 men.

Why is that?

Becuz u only get hurt or let down when they change.

I won't change.

U don't know that.

Just as I finished typing, I heard Carey's key in the lock and she slid into the room. Her fluffy parka filled the entire doorway and her nose was red from the cold wind. She shrugged the coat from her shoulders and hung it in her closet. Her roots were based in Mississippi, so I was pretty sure the wind chill in Atlanta made her feel like she lived in Alaska. I looked down at the phone and no response popped into the inbox.

"Oh my gosh…it is cold as ever out there." Carey sat on the edge of her bed and pulled her big boots off. She looked as if she was going sledding with all the armor she had on for the cold.

"That's why I have every intention of staying in today and catching up on some old TV shows," I added.

"Nooooo…you can't stay in all day! We have to hang out tonight. We haven't hung out together for so long!" Carey was trying not to whine but she failed miserably. I had to admit, we hadn't hung out for weeks. Either she had to study for some big test or I was at the studio late.

"Carey, I'm tired. You know my crazy schedule. I just don't have it in me tonight," I said as the phone buzzed to life in my lap. I looked down to find a message from my mystery man.

I want to see you tonight. It seemed to float on the screen. I swallowed in desperation. Was it finally time to see this person that I shared so many things with? What if he was hideous? What if he really was a stalker? Well, he did actually talk with me for weeks. Maybe he was a stalker with a lot of patience? My heart raced at the thought of meeting him. What if we didn't get along as well in person? If it didn't work out, I wouldn't have any text messages in the morning, no uplifting words during a crisis. Could I risk it? Risk it all to satisfy my curiosity?

Carey was still complaining about hanging out tonight but her voice sounded muffled outside my thoughts of meeting my mystery man. I slowly typed back, *NO* and released a sigh of relief.

I wasn't ready to meet him. I wasn't sure if I was ever going to be ready to meet him.

"Hello? Mali? Are you listening to me?" Carey stopped moving around the room and rested her hand on her hip, just like her mother would.

"Oh. No. I mean, yes, I'm listening. Wha—what did you say again?" I was still tense as I waited for his response.

"I said do you want to go to the coffeehouse with me tonight? I really don't want to go by myself."

I knew that if I didn't go with Carey to the coffeehouse, I wouldn't have any excuse to tell my mystery man a reason I couldn't meet him. So I had no choice but to agree by reason of self-preservation.

"Of course I'll go with you tonight. Coffeehouse? Sounds fun." I sighed under my breath and I eyed the phone for a response.

His response was simple. *Why?* I had saved myself from lying to him by agreeing to go with Carey. I was relieved that I'd thought ahead.

I'm going with roommate to coffeehouse. Maybe another time...

With that, the conversation was done. I was officially going to the coffeehouse with Carey and I had bought more time to get comfortable with the idea of meeting my mystery man, once and for all.

Carey was so excited about the coffeehouse that she slipped on her headphones and danced around the room preparing her outfit for the night. I, instead, curled up on my bed and trailed off into thoughts about Justice. He'd been so cold when he told Big Deuce that we were just friends and that he didn't care if Big Deuce dated me. Deuce told me over lunch that he had received

Justice's blessing that day outside the Union to take me out to lunch, or even dinner. I sat across from Deuce smiling on the surface but hurt brewed deep in my bones. I fumed that he could pass me off in such a way after all the time we spent together. I wasn't a car that Big Deuce could borrow. I was right in assuming that Justice had no feelings for me. It took everything in me not to dial Justice's number and scream to him that he was a fool for not noticing that I loved him. I couldn't imagine what would have happened if I told him I was falling in love with him. That would have been a rejection I might not have made it back from. I couldn't continue loving a man that only wanted my friendship. I could feel Justice's rejection eating away at my happiness. I was depressed for days after the stunt he pulled at the Union with Deuce until my mystery man was there to pick me back up.

"So you think Deuce is telling you the truth?" he had asked me one night.

"Sure. Why would he lie?"

"Why would he lie? Hmm, let's think about that for a second," he said sarcastically.

"Okay. Okay, I get it. Maybe I was a little hasty with believing Deuce. You're right, he's probably not the most reliable source…but I saw Justice with my own eyes. I'd have to be blind to not see that he passed me off," I said, trying not to be sad all over again.

"I know you like Justice but he doesn't seem like your type."

"You mean I don't seem like his type," I corrected.

"Stop doing that. Stop putting yourself down," he whispered. "He'd be a fool not to love you."

"Thanks. You always know how to help. Are you ready to tell me your name yet?" I asked again. He'd eluded the question in every conversation.

"I like the name you've been using...Mystery Man." His laugh was almost musical. "It makes me sound debonair and intriguing."

"Wait, you mean to tell me you aren't really debonair and intriguing?" We both laughed.

I had trailed so deeply into my thoughts that I hadn't realized I'd dozed off until I awoke to Carey's persistent nudging of my side.

"Wake up, Mali." Carey rocked me gently.

"I'm up. I'm up," I said, rubbing my eyes.

"It's time to get ready. The coffeehouse opens at eight and I want to be there for the free coffee bar."

"Coffee bar? I'm glad I got a nap if I'm going to be sucking down coffee all night." I groaned and sat up slowly, kicking back the covers bunched up around my feet.

"No worries. You will love this place. It's live poetry and artist night. So there should be some pretty cool live entertainment." Carey rummaged around in her closet for something near the back. She brought out a tattered notebook with pages stuffed, curled and ripped inside the book.

"What's that?"

"It's my old poetry book. I used to write when I was a kid. Our family went to this therapist and she made us all write in a journal about our feelings. I used to write a lot but not so much anymore."

"That's pretty cool. I love poetry but I can't really write it. Are you going to read some tonight in front of everyone?" I peeled a pair of jeans and chunky knit sweater from the closet.

"I think so. I'm going to give it a try. I've never performed in front of anyone before. My family hasn't even heard any of this stuff." She looked nervously at the book in her hand.

My life always played out onstage and in front of people except instead of words, I used my body. So I was shocked that Carey had an artistic side, a side so different from what anyone would think, since she was a witty brainiac ninety percent of the time. Maybe going to the coffeehouse was not a bad idea after all.

After braving the chilly walk to Carey's little VW from Cramer Hall, we chatted until she pulled into the parking lot of the café. From the outside, the building looked closed as no light peeked through the windows. As we got closer, the muted sound of a horn and saxophone floated on the air from inside the café. The building itself was cramped in a slither of space between a large mechanics shop and a hair salon with a huge sign that read HairScape. Carey pulled open the wooden plank door that held no signage. Cigarette smoke wafted out the open door as it swung open to reveal an overweight black lady with fuchsia lipstick slathered across her thick lips and greasy bangs plastered to her dark forehead.

"You watching or performing tonight?" she said impatiently. I eyed Carey to see what she wanted to do. It was her moment of truth.

"She's watching," she pointed at me, "but I'm performing." She held up her weathered notebook as if to prove she was ready.

"Okay. That'll be three dollars for her and one dollar for you. Put your name here." Her long, colorful nails pointed at a book that held about ten other names. Carey responded by sliding a wadded-up five-dollar bill on the counter and inking her name quickly. Once we walked off from the glare of the cashier, I bumped Carey playfully.

"So you're really gonna do it, huh?" I asked.

"Yep, I think I'm ready. Thanks for being here with me." She smiled shyly and found a table in the dim, smoke-filled room.

Although there were only ten names in the performance log, there had to be almost seventy people slammed together in the slim space of the coffeehouse.

Carey said, "I need more than coffee to get through the night," as she disappeared into the crowd standing around the bar. People chatted around the coffeehouse in small groups as the space swelled with creativity. A man with long dreadlocks wrote vigorously in a notebook between pulls of his cigarette while other people sketched on notepads with charcoal sticks. A woman with a large untamed afro and big wooden earrings laughed openly with a thin man in wire glasses, half her size and weight. An odd pairing on a normal day but in here, it seemed normal. The atmosphere was definitely full of positive energy.

I felt a tap on my shoulder and spun to see a tall, lanky man standing behind me with a shy smile. I vaguely remembered him as he sat down in the seat Carey had left.

"Craig?" My mind jumped back to the tall man that had helped me move into my dorm room. Carey's brother.

"Hey. You looked a little confused there for a second." He brushed his long hair from his eyes.

"I didn't recognize you. It's been months."

"Yeah, it's been a while. I've been real busy, though. You know how it is." He scanned the room, maybe looking for Carey.

"Carey went to the bar to get her coffee," I said as he stared off into the crowd. "Do you come here often?"

"I come every month. I actually started this event at AU. The owner is my roommate's dad. So he lets us use the space sometimes." He nodded at a person walking by and kept his eyes on the crowd.

"Wow. That's pretty cool. So you made up this whole idea?" I was intrigued by how young he was to start a business that got this much support from the community.

"Me and a friend mostly." He smiled slightly but it was gone before I could smile back. "Are you going to perform tonight?"

"Ohhhh no. Not me. I've never been one to share my emotions through speech but I can tell you one hell of a story when I dance." He chuckled at my response. It was soft beneath the croon of the horn and saxophone onstage.

We sat there in silence until Carey bounded to the table with two cups in hand.

"Can you believe that I had to wrestle my coffee out of someone's hands at the bar? I'd waited ten minutes for my order and no way was I letting someone get this macchiato from me..." Her vision settled on Craig slumped low in the chair with his legs kicked out. "Craig! Oh my gosh, I forgot to tell you. I am really going to do it tonight."

Craig nodded his head, knowing what his sister meant immediately. She landed a quick kiss on his cheek as his eyes darted across to me. I shifted under his gaze. He had beautiful eyes underneath the long bangs that swept across his forehead. I was sure this wasn't the first time she said she was going to read her poetry onstage nor was it the first, or last, time he'd acted as if he believed her. I sipped the hot coffee and turned my chair toward the stage.

"I've got to go. Make sure you guys don't leave without saying goodbye," Craig said as he made his way through the crowd like a sports car bending around mountainous curves. He was so smooth.

"We won't!" Carey yelled after him cheerfully. She loved her brother. He glanced back briefly and looked directly in my eyes before sweeping his bangs off his face and escaping into the sea of people.

"Your brother is so weird," I said once Craig had vanished from sight.

"I know." Carey grinned and focused her eyes on her notebook.

"Why is he so quiet all the time?"

"He's an observer for the most part. But if he likes you then he's an open book," she said, then almost as an afterthought, "He's been through a lot."

"Like what?" I wondered aloud.

"Hmm? Oh, never mind. Look, there he is!" She smiled toward the stage. Somehow I felt like she was happier to get off the subject than she was of seeing her brother onstage.

The coffeehouse was filled to capacity as Craig hosted the night with his smooth voice on the microphone. He introduced each poet, singer and artist while keeping the crowd snapping their fingers and laughing at his witty humor. I had never seen Craig really come alive before. Onstage, he was carefree, fearless and very different from what I remembered seeing on my first day at AU. He gripped the microphone loosely and swung his arms out to the crowd. "Do you want more?!" he said silkily into the microphone.

The crowd answered with loud claps and yells of "Yeah!" around the dark café.

"I have a very special treat for you tonight. Please give a warm welcome to my sister, Carey. She's a virgin to the mic, y'all, so give it up for her."

Craig's Southern drawl dripped with each word as the crowd clapped noisily for Carey. She stuck her nose deeper into the notebook and averted her eyes from the audience as she stepped softly onto the stage. Silence fell over the crowd as she fumbled with her notebook behind the microphone that now seemed too tall in front of her. She adjusted the microphone quietly and looked out for the first time at the sea of faces awaiting her words. I wanted to run up there and save her. She looked terrified. Craig whispered to her from the edge of the stage but I was too far to hear what he was saying. Carey shook her head and stared at the ground. The seconds were gruelingly ticking away as people in the crowd became restless with the silence.

The momentum was slowing as Craig skipped onto the stage, hugged his sister and said, "She's a little shy, guys. Maybe next time. Give her a round of applause!"

With that the room erupted with the sound of voices from the crowd yelling, "Don't worry, girl!" and, "It's okay, honey!" Carey made it back to our table with a deepening frown on her face.

"I can't believe you were brave enough to go up there," I offered.

"But I didn't have the courage to do it." She looked down at her notebook again. She stuffed pages that had slipped loose back into the book.

"One step at a time." I patted her back as Craig continued to speak onstage.

"Well, everyone, I want to thank you for coming out tonight. Remember, it is very difficult for all the artists to share their heart and soul in front of a crowd. With that being said, I have something I want to share from my heart." The whispers of surprise from the crowd swarmed like bees around the small café. Carey looked up from her notebook in awe. *Was I missing something?*

Craig continued, "For those of you who have been coming to this set for years, you know that I vowed that I would never perform again until I felt inspired. So, I have something to share with you all and for a special someone close to my heart." Carey smiled and nodded at her brother as we watched him step back from the microphone, shake his arms until they were loose like noodles and inhale deeply before beginning his poem.

"I call this poem *Love Awaits*," he began.

"She entered my world
When I was still so cold
And lonely
Her hair was like her body
Curvy, wild and free…
Her eyes like the swirls of coffee
That I'm sure you're drinking…" (he smiled)
"I was ashamed of me
Of what I lacked in bravery
Ashamed that she was beyond me
Until late one night, our souls collided
She called out to me…
On a night when I couldn't sleep
Too drunk on depression to think
Of anyone else…
Not even myself.
But she stormed in, dancing on clouds
Spewing sunshine from her mouth
Saying words about her past

That make me mad
About the way a man treated her
Assuring her I'd never mistreat her or leave her
Only has her pushing me away
So it's time to come clean and wait
Time to stop the mystery from continuing to play
I want you
I need you
Will you meet me tonight?"

The crowd roared with screams, whistles and loud claps. Craig stared from the stage in the midst of the chaos, not at his sister but directly in my eyes. I could not be torn from his stare. I had never imagined that Craig was the mystery man I'd been speaking to for weeks but it was unequivocally him. I swallowed the lump in my throat as I searched for a way to understand what had just happened only seconds ago. His quirkiness had transformed into an intangible beauty as he smiled wantonly and leaned on the microphone stand.

Carey nudged me roughly. "Was he talking about you?!"

I nodded my head slowly, still caught in a trance as Craig stepped off the edge of the stage and disappeared into the crowd that had gathered there to congratulate him. I needed to breathe. I slid my chair back quickly, bumping into a patron before apologizing, and trotted to the parking lot with Carey close on my heels.

"Have you guys been talking behind my back?" Carey seemed to be stung by the idea that Craig liked me.

"No. I mean, yes. I mean…I don't know!" I touched my chest to slow my heartbeat.

"What do you mean, you don't know? What's going on, Mali?" She was confused. She had every right to be. Hell, I was confused.

"We've been texting and talking on the phone for weeks. I didn't know it was him. It was always a mystery."

"That doesn't make any sense. You mean to tell me you were talking to a person that you never saw or met and it gets to the point where he thinks he's in love with you?" She was quelling her disbelief.

"I know it doesn't make sense! God, can't you see that?" I breathed deeply.

Carey patted her forehead repeatedly as if trying to force the unconventional truth into her head. I paced in the parking lot, still reeling from the news that Craig had been my mystery man for months. I hadn't even seen him since I moved in. How could he do this and not tell Carey? They were so close.

"So you never knew he liked me?" My voice cut through Carey's obvious attempt to believe what just happened inside the café.

"Well…" She spun on her heels. "I knew he had a little crush, but…"

"What do you mean, 'a little crush'? Apparently, it was more than a crush." I couldn't believe she had kept that from me.

"I didn't think he would go this far. I thought he was just like every other guy on campus…in love with Mali Struthers." She spread her arms wide and smirked sarcastically.

"What in the hell are you talking about?"

"Mali, you have to be deaf or blind not to notice how the guys are drooling all over you. Ever since the welcome party, your name has been like a wildfire around campus. Hell, people know me and want to be my friend just because I'm your roommate," Carey answered.

I must have been deaf and blind because I never had anyone ask me out on a date or even ask for my number in the months that I'd been at AU. Carey was truly my only friend.

"Carey, I didn't know." I couldn't find the words to make her feel better. Hell, I couldn't find the words to make *me* feel better.

"Mali, you will never get it. You walk around in a daze. People are so interested in knowing you, helping you, but you are so caught up in your own struggles that you don't even recognize that you have something special." Carey crossed the pebbled parking lot swiftly and hugged me deeply. I felt like my mother was in Atlanta, the hug that I always longed to have with her was morphed through Carey's body. Moments later, I realized that I had drenched Carey's T-shirt with my tears.

"If you don't want this thing to happen with Craig, I'll stop it right now. You're one of my best friends and I don't want to hurt you." I sniffled, still huddled close to her in the darkness.

Carey's eyes were magnified as she stared through her black frames into my eyes. "Be happy, Mali. That's all I ever wanted. Stop worrying about your mother. Stop worrying about whether Justice likes you back. Stop worrying if I'll be mad about Craig. All you do is worry about everyone else. But what does Mali want to do?"

"I don't know what I want."

The honesty in her words stunned me. I hadn't really lived for myself. I was just recently learning how to stop worrying about everyone else. My mother and father's deteriorating relationship. Justice and his mysterious past. Will Dunkin's thoughts of my choreography and now there was Craig, my once mystery man turned nepotistic admirer. I never took control of what I really wanted in life, always being driven by the ebb and flow of everyone else's perception of me. I was like a symbiotic parasite attaching to a host, sharing in their problems and triumphs, never having my own identity.

"Well, we have nothing but time to find out, right?" Carey offered softly.

My mind flooded with questions. How did I get so lost? Why was I so damaged? Who am I? In the depths of me, I searched for an answer but I couldn't find one. With that, Carey gripped my hand in hers and led me back to her dusty yellow VW. As we pulled off into the tiny street leading past the front of the coffeehouse, Craig peeked his head out the front door of the building. Just as we accelerated out onto the main street, we caught eyes. I felt a flutter in my stomach and an intense need to call Craig but I didn't. I needed time to think this all through. I needed time to find out what I really wanted.

Justice

∞

Things couldn't be any worse. After my night with Monica and her friends, I couldn't get all three of them to stop calling. Between Monica texting and asking for a replay, Dena leaving messages that she wanted to go out on a date and Brianna calling to say she'd never done anything like that and felt ashamed…I wanted to throw my cell phone across the apartment until it shattered into tiny little pieces. These days my phone never stopped ringing. I heard from Coach, Deuce, the girls. Everyone except Mali. Of course with her absence and the way I had acted in the Union with Deuce, my mind was playing tricks on me. I kept thinking that she and Big Deuce might be a couple and that's why she wasn't calling anymore. Maybe she didn't need me anymore? I knew that wasn't likely because Deuce had never been in anything a person could call a committed relationship. Then I was thinking that maybe she stopped caring about our friendship because I missed a big part of her life when she landed her audition. I felt like shit. I wasn't a good friend to her and I knew she was going to slowly fade away if I didn't change my attitude, and quick. But didn't I want her to just fade away? Wouldn't it be easier to just let us go our separate ways? I toyed with the thought but quickly realized that if I couldn't go five days without talking to her, then I wasn't quite ready to get her out of my system. I didn't have too much time to dwell on Mali—I had to meet the team for the flight to Hawaii. I checked my cell phone one last time and erased the awaiting messages from Monica and Dena without reading them as I rolled my suitcase to the Impala and hightailed it to the arena.

The team gathered onto the chartered Hawaiian Airlines aircraft leaving Hartsfield-Jackson Airport heading toward the Hawai'i Bowl Championship game. It was going to be a tough championship game against Southern Mississippi University since SMU had a breakout season with big early wins. Unlike us, they weren't expected to make it this far but somehow they had and were now matched up against Atlanta University. I couldn't wait to get on the field and play my last bowl game with us spread across my chest. It was my one chance to make a lasting memory at AU before I got to the league. I wanted to be standing there with the trophy held high in my hand in two days. My body surged with the thought of how winning this bowl game could completely change my life.

Within minutes of the plane leveling off, Big Deuce rambled his wide body down the aisle toward the flight attendant station. He chatted quietly for a few minutes then walked back and sunk into the empty seat across the aisle.

"What's up, bro?" He munched on pretzels from a bag that almost disappeared in his huge hands.

"Nothin' much, man. Just getting my mind right for this game." I tapped the thick playbook that was sitting on the seat next to me.

"Well while you getting your nerd game on, me and some of the fellas was talking about hanging out in Honolulu tonight. You gonna roll with us?"

"Nah. I don't think so. I ain't trying to get in any trouble with y'all." I shook my head.

"There ain't gonna be no trouble. You gotta remember, you are rolling with Big Deuce." He pointed a thumb to his chest. "Any trouble I can get you in…I can get you out of." He popped another pretzel in his mouth and smiled.

"Trust me. I know." I laughed, considering telling him about the threesome he missed out on a few weekends ago but thinking better of it.

"Hey, have you heard from Nicole lately?" he said quietly and looked up the aisle. I was surprised to hear her name from his lips. He despised Nicole from their very first meeting almost three years ago.

"Man, she called me talking about she wanted to be friends or to check on me or some shit like that."

Big Deuce contorted his mouth in disgust. "That chick ain't worth the big ass she rode in on." I chuckled at his attempt at dry humor.

"So what's up with you and Mali?" I coughed. I couldn't get her off my mind and I needed to know if they were a couple.

Big Deuce shifted in his seat and leaned on the armrest until I thought it would break.

"Nothing too much, man. She's a cool girl. She's about the only girl I can actually have a conversation with. Except," he raised a finger, "she's fine as all hell. Makes it hard for a brother to focus." He wiped his brow. "She got that dancer's body. You know she has to be flexible." He shook his head back and forth as if remembering her body. He continued looking down the aisle at nothing in particular. Little did he know, I had seen her flexibility up close for more than three months.

"She's a good girl. So don't mess it up with her." I looked out the window at the white, billowing clouds disappearing under the belly of the plane.

I heard the seat rattle across the aisle as Deuce struggled to balance against the turbulence. He slung his arm over the back of the seat next to me.

"You think I don't know you're in love with Mali? Stop playing yourself and try to be honest with her. Like you said…she's a good girl. And what am I gonna do with a good girl?" Big Deuce crept back toward the front of the airplane without a second glance.

Big Deuce was my best friend because he knew me better than I knew myself sometimes. I hadn't told him my feelings for Mali but he knew and if he could figure it out, then maybe Mali knew how I felt too. Maybe she felt the same way? I shook the thought away. I tried to convince myself that I needed to let Mali go and stop toying with the idea of true love. I was so wrong about Nicole, and Mali was going down the same road as Nicole. Dancing in the industry changed Nicole from a sweet teenager to a money-hungry beast that I didn't even recognize by the end of our relationship. I couldn't go through that again, especially not with Mali.

She invaded my thoughts throughout the day, so much so that I constantly waited on a call or text from her. Truth be told, she was the only reason I still left my cell phone on. I would have turned it off weeks ago after the calls started getting more frequent from agents, scouts and groupies. I couldn't face the thought of shutting her out even though she made me insanely jealous of my best friend. I knew I wasn't functioning well with her in or out of my life.

I looked down at the phone in my lap. Thirteen messages were waiting in the text inbox and three missed calls. I reminded myself to call my parents when the plane landed. They called earlier in the week and divulged that they weren't able to make the trip this time due to work complications. But they said they were excited to come to the school for draft week. They mentioned they wanted to meet Mali since I told them about her training me. Unfortunately, Mali tapered our workout sessions to once every two weeks because her schedule changed with the new job. I hid my hurt as best I could when she asked if I cared about the changes to the schedule. I played it cool and told her it was no problem. What I didn't tell her was I felt withdrawal from not seeing her Thursday mornings and talking to her every night. I leaned my forehead against the cool Plexiglas window of the airplane and squeezed my eyes shut. I had to really think about if I needed to cut out all the distractions in my life, most importantly Mali.

As sweet as she was, Mali was the epitome of a bittersweet distraction. I loved when she'd laugh and hide her face behind her hands. Talking to her was the easiest I'd ever felt with a woman but when she was out of my sight, a jealousy raged in me that I'd never known before. I found myself racking my brain on whether she was spending time with other men. I even ventured so far as to drive around her dorm after she said she was leaving the studio to make sure she wasn't lying to me. After I spotted her getting off the bus at the gate, I felt sickened by what I was doing. I couldn't even force myself to pick her up from the gate and give her a ride home. What excuse would I have? The last thing I wanted was Mali to end up like Nicole. I went through hell and back with Nicole before she left me for the first rapper that would buy her some gifts. I couldn't take that hurt again.

It was definitely time for a change. Especially since things were going to be changing with football in the next couple months. ESPN and SportsCenter were now bidding heavily on which round I would show up in the draft. Most game-day hosts were toying with the idea of the second round while others were bold enough to say first round. The final evaluations would come out in January, after all the bowl games. Either way, it looked like the future was leading me out of the darkness and into the light.

The airplane landed in Honolulu after circling twice over the volcanic island smothered in lush greenery and lined in crystal-blue water. The football team spilled out from the side of the plane and onto the blacktop, searching through the sea of baggage that had been laid outside in the sun. I found mine quickly and headed to the charter bus parked on the tarmac. After a short ride, we were sliding our key cards into our hotel room doors at the Sheraton. Big Deuce lurched his wide body into the room and seized the bed near the window by plopping his duffel bag on the mattress. The room was typical, with two beds dressed in white comforters separated by a wooden nightstand. The nightstand held a small lamp and alarm clock. Across from the beds was a large flat-screen television sitting atop an empty dresser. Big Deuce peered out the window at the stunning pool a couple stories below. Tourists lined the pool edge as kids jumped from the springboard into the pool with a splash. The sky was refreshingly blue and tall palm trees waved in the ocean breeze like the picture on a postcard. I spotted our schedule on the writing desk tucked in the far corner of the room with an uncomfortable-looking wood chair.

The team staff had highlighted each event and the requirements of the players. From the notes, it looked like later today, we were scheduled to sign autographs at Hawaiian Airlines Field from 2:00 p.m. to 5:30 p.m. Shortly after, we had a team dinner catered on the beach with a special Hawaiian presentation from seven to nine. An italicized message at the end of the day's schedule stated: *The van will leave the field at 6:30 p.m. promptly.* In bold, capital letters, *CURFEW* was printed next to *11:00 p.m.* Big Deuce leaned over my shoulder and eyed the page for a few seconds. He snorted a response, most likely in regards to the curfew. Then he exited the room without a word. I heard a knock on the neighbor's door and within minutes muffled laughter came from behind the fake landscape painting hanging on the hotel room wall. I placed the event schedule on the nightstand and lay out across the thick comforter. I had about two hours to catch a nap before the van left for the stadium. I drifted off to sleep thinking of Mali and whether she would be watching me play in two days.

∞

After the signing, as promised, the bus promptly dropped us at our beachfront hotel for dinner. The night blazed with flickers of fire dancing wildly atop bamboo sticks lining the central dining area. I sat on a cushion at a low table listening to the water lap against the soft sand of the beach in a soothing rhythm. The evening felt full of energy with the firelit beating drums pounded by brown, shirtless men dancing in colorful garments of bright red, orange and turquoise. The luau was in full swing when we exited the bus and traveled through the sand to our dining area on the beach near the hotel. I sat quietly as Big Deuce leaned to Jack Campbell and started pointing at one of the dancers twirling a baton-like stick in the air and catching it in the crook of her arm. Dancers strutted through the sand with pink-and-yellow flowers wrapped around their waistlines and coconut shells hiding their modest bosom. Their bellies rolled and bounced to the drums and cast shadows from the light of the fire against the white linen attached to the stage that swung in the ocean breeze. The male dancers pounded the homemade drums with their thick, calloused hands and sent thunderous noise into the night sky.

The signing at the stadium earlier had gone well. People were really excited to meet us. The line wrapped around the football field as ushers hoarded people down the line, stuffed memorabilia in their hand and shooed them to the next player. Proud mothers snapped pictures while young girls giggled gleefully at the thought of being next to someone that had been on television. My hand ached after the session was complete and the bus peeled off back toward the hotel. I was excited to finally sit down and relax, take it all in.

"JB, how many autographs you sign today?" Big Deuce and Jack had turned their conversation toward me.

I rubbed my wrist. "More than I care to remember."

"I think I signed like a thousand. Some of those kids were straight-up brats. But some of their mommas were fine as hell." Jack pounded fists with Big Deuce. Jack Campbell was the quintessential playboy. Lisa was his main chick but he never turned away from some pussy. No matter how broke-down the chick looked, if she was offering, he was taking.

"I ain't worried about those women with baggage. Trust me, tonight…I'm going to have all the action I need," Big Deuce interjected.

"What're you going to be getting into?" Jack was immediately interested.

"I'm going to get some of these groupies that was hanging out around the stadium for us and bring them back to the room. It's going to be a good night for us. No doubt," Big Deuce said. Jack nodded his head in approval.

"I ain't trying to be in all that. You know we're playing in a few days and Coach is going to be patrolling the halls like a warden all night," I responded, trying to talk some sense into Deuce.

"Damn. You know he's right. Coach has been real extra these past few weeks." Jack finally sided with me, clearly a voice of reason.

"Gentlemen, I got a Plan B. Don't worry about it," Big Deuce said confidently as he discarded the umbrella in his fruity drink and turned back to the stage to watch the show. When Deuce said not to worry, that meant we were going to be getting in some trouble tonight. Jack shrugged at me across the table as I finished my drink. Both of us were confused as to how Big Deuce would pull off not getting caught smuggling girls into the hotel by the coaching staff during heightened security measures.

I should've stopped wondering how Big Deuce could get things done. After the luau was complete and the coaching staff saddled off toward the bar near the hotel, Big Deuce and Jack guided me back into the hotel lobby.

"What's up, beautiful?" Big Deuce addressed the pretty receptionist behind the desk. She smiled hugely at his compliment.

"Hello, Mr. Deuce McMann. Good to see you again. What can I do for you?" She tried to hide the seduction in her question but surely Deuce wouldn't miss it, no matter how subtle.

"You know, there is something you could do for me, actually." Big Deuce glanced back at Jack and me as we waited patiently for him to work his magic.

"Anything." The girl glanced around the front desk to see if the other receptionists were listening. They were checking in other guests and hadn't paid much attention.

"You got some friends that want to hang out with a couple of ballers tonight?" Big Deuce was laying it on thick. Somehow it worked. The receptionist nodded sheepishly and we departed back to the room. Just as we opened the door the phone rang.

"Hello?"

"Mr. Bradford, this is Talia, the receptionist. Would you like me to bring anything to your room this evening? We have concierge services until midnight." Her words sounded sweet as sugar. Professional.

"Just a few drinks and some food," I said into the receiver. If she was offering, then why not?

"Of course, we will have everything. I just want to let you know that I am a big fan of yours and so is my friend Natasha."

"Natasha, huh? I'm not really trying to meet anybody tonight. I just know Deuce really likes you and wants you to feel comfortable hanging out." I tried to diffuse the meet-up. I wasn't in the mood to entertain the ugly sidekick.

"So are you saying you don't want to meet my friend?" She sounded disappointed.

I felt bad for her. She just wanted to have her fifteen seconds of fame with her girls. "Sure. I'd love to meet her. I'm sure she's a nice girl." I hung up the phone and turned to Deuce.

"Man, you gonna fuck the receptionist?" I laughed.

"Hey, she has all the access and knows all the ways to get around this hotel. She's our best way of sneaking girls in and out of this spot." He slapped Jack on the back as he laughed. "And it don't hurt that she's Hawaiian and I'm trying to get laid." We chuckled at his play on words.

"This girl better not be crazy. She'll have us all kicked out the damn hotel," Jack added.

"She got two days to get wild with some big, strong football players." He flexed his muscles and kissed his bicep. "That girl will be sending us champagne and caviar by tomorrow night." Big Deuce was a riot but he knew how to get anything he wanted with his gift of gab.

Thirty minutes before the girls were to arrive, Coach stopped by the room for his final check. We pushed him out quickly, saying we were settling in early so we could work out in the morning. He bought it as he finished his rounds on our floor and boarded the elevator at the end of the hall. Within minutes of Coach leaving, as if on cue, a soft knock bounced against the door. Talia was the first to enter, all smiles, but her friend Natasha was the one that had all of us standing around with our mouths open. She was like a Hawaiian goddess with tanned brown skin, thick lips and even thicker hips. She didn't spare any mystery with her skintight miniskirt and cropped top that gave us a peek at her chiseled abs. She sashayed into the room smelling like fresh fruit and cotton candy. Her hair was shaved on one side and long waves cascaded down her back almost to her perfectly shaped behind and covered one of her large brown eyes. Another girl entered behind her but no one noticed her much since Natasha was clearly the showstopper.

"So, Justice, I heard you didn't want to meet me," she said with a husky voice.

I swallowed at her aggressiveness. Damn, this girl had something I couldn't put my finger on. "Of course I wanted to meet you. I heard you were a fan."

"Don't try to play me. You didn't want to meet me until just now when you realized I was a sexy bitch." She put her hand on her curvy hip and waited for my response.

"I can't lie...you are very sexy." My eyes scanned her voluptuous body.

She smiled. "Well I think you owe me an apology and...a drink." She pointed at the liquor and juice they had set up on the desk.

"Of course. Anything for the lady," I responded as I poured some V8 juice with a little vodka—okay, a lot of vodka.

She drank it greedily and patted the bed next to her. I sat down on the comforter and she leaned in to whisper in my ear, "I have a secret to share with you. I have an oral fixation which means I always have to have something in my mouth." I leaned back on the bed, resting on my elbows as she rubbed my upper thigh. She wasn't wasting any time as my stiffness rose in my shorts. I glanced at Jack with a girl giggling on top of his lap as he whispered in her ear. His hand slyly massaged her booty and gripped her plump thighs. Big Deuce and the receptionist were already laid out on the bed next to mine, tonguing each other between small bouts of conversation. I guessed the night was going to end fast with these girls. Natasha was already fondling my manhood through my khaki shorts. I leaned farther back on the bed to let her have her way without a fight. Within minutes, she had stripped back my belt buckle and I felt her fat, juicy lips sliding up and down my shaft. I heard the sounds of ass clapping, female moans and wetness in the corners of the room as I kept my eyes shut tight, fighting against her pulsating tongue. I smiled to myself. Big Deuce had delivered again.

Nicole

∞

"It's over," I repeated for the third time. I was crouched over the arm of Webby's brown leather sofa trying to talk some sense into Joy but she was beginning to irritate me.

"Nicole, you are overreacting. Webby just said he loved you because he thinks that's what you want him to say," Joy said into the phone with enough calm to make me want to scream into the receiver.

"I'm not overreacting, Joy. You're not listening to me. It's over. Plain and simple."

"How can something be over before you even give it a chance to start?"

I rolled my eyes. "I can't keep going back and forth with you about this. It's not hard to understand."

"What I understand is that you're scared about this lifestyle. That you want the easy way out and, most importantly, I know what we shared was not just a fling. You love me. I know it." Joy was a master at being defiant. She reminded me a lot of myself except she was delusional.

"Joy. I've got to go." I pulled the phone from my ear and listened as Webby called my name from upstairs.

"Don't make the mistake of losing me like the rest…"

I hung up the line before Joy could continue. I peeled myself from the warm, buttery leather in the dark home theater when my phone buzzed with a text from Joy.

IT'S NOT OVER TIL I SAY IT'S OVER!

I shook my head at the text as I closed the door to the theater behind me. Joy was starting to act like she was starring in a remake of the '80s film *Fatal Attraction*. When I finally made it upstairs, Webby was pacing from the kitchen to the living room with the phone pressed tightly to his ear. I sensed something wasn't right.

"Will, I don't understand how this could happen. We had plans!" Webby growled into the phone. My heart skipped a beat at the sound of Will Dunkin's name. Had Webby found out about the movie deal I had stolen from him? My heart beat a mile a minute as Webby continued to pace and argue on the line with Will. Finally, he ended the call and slammed the phone on the kitchen island hard enough to crack the screen.

"Shit," Webby rumbled beneath his breath. His anger was making the air seem too thick to breathe. I hadn't seen Webby this upset before. Oh God, was this the end? Did he know?

I was scared to ask what the problem was so I stood awkwardly in the living room, waiting for him to rip into me with the worst language he could muster. The seconds ticked away as he gripped the edges of the granite island, breathing deeply and staring at the tile floors.

"Nicole, do you know about any of this? I hate to ask you but…" He clenched his teeth. "I have to know the truth."

I was frozen in place as I tried to make sense of his words. How could he know? Did Will tell him? It wasn't like Will to share business information with people not involved.

"Know about what?" I mumbled under my breath. I would deny and lie if I had to.

"Do you know anything about this business with Will?" His eyes pierced into me like daggers. He had been doing coke lines and it was recent.

"I don't know…what're you…" I tried to grasp for excuses, explanations—anything.

Webby interrupted my thoughts. "What am I thinking?!" He gripped his head like he was trying to quiet the noise. "I knew you couldn't have anything to do with my music being leaked."

A rush of air escaped me. I hadn't realized that I'd been holding my breath until I felt light-headed. He still didn't know about the movie deal or Joy but the stress of it was starting to take a toll on me. I knew right now was not the time to come clean, though. Webby was reeling beyond any anger I'd ever seen.

"Can you believe that my music leaked from the studio? Will said that they tracked the leak back to a computer at Dunkin Studios. I can't believe this shit." Webby shook his head. "Do you know how much money we could be wasting?" His harsh voice echoed throughout the empty house.

"Slow down, baby. Calm down. What happened?" I stepped closer to Webby but was still cautious not to get within punching distance. He looked as if he'd snap at any moment.

"I've been working on this new record for months. We got too much money invested for this shit to leak! It's not ready. The fans are going to hate the unmastered version and won't buy the singles. You know that, though." He paced from the kitchen and into the living room. "The only people at the studio are all people I trust. You know how I keep everything on lock." His eyebrows were pushed together furiously and his mouth twisted into an ugly scowl.

"Well, let's think about this. Who was in the studio?" I offered.

"The usual people. The same folks that are always there. Me, the producers, Veronica, Joy, and you know Tim rides with me everywhere." Webby glanced at the ceiling as if trying to visualize the studio again. "Will stopped in for a few minutes to check on everything. The concierge team was in and out but nothing out the ordinary."

I swallowed the lump in my throat at the thought of Joy being in the same room with Webby. She was a little unpredictable but I didn't think she was capable of doing something as low-down as leaking Webby's music. Or could she?

I couldn't put interest in Joy as a possible suspect by warning Webby because then he'd start asking too many questions that I invariably didn't have the answers to. Plus, if Webby pinched Joy hard enough, there was no telling how much information she would spill. My stomach turned at the thought.

I consoled Webby as he mumbled that he was tired and wanted to lie down for a while. As soon as he disappeared into the bedroom and shut the door loudly, I grasped my phone angrily and headed to the theater room. It was soundproof and I had an inkling that it was the perfect place to talk to Joy. She answered on the first ring.

"Hopefully you called to apologize for hanging up on me," she answered smugly.

"Apologize? Apologize! Are you insane or just trying to tap-dance on my last nerve? Please tell me you did not leak Webby's single," I spat through gritted teeth.

"Geez, Nicole. That's not the apology I was hoping for. And for the record…who gives a damn about Webby's single? You must not have been watching the blogs. The song is tanking miserably." She spoke matter-of-factly.

"You bitch." I could tell by her sarcastic tone that she had indeed leaked the single.

"Name-calling now? First, you want to break up after fucking me, taking my movie and acting like you loved me. Then you want to leave me crushed while you live this perfect life with a washed-up-ass rapper? I don't think so." Joy sounded like she had handed the phone to her evil twin sister. "You're not going to use me, Nicole, like you do everyone else." Her voice was low and sinister, not bubbly and light like it used to be.

"Why are you doing this?"

"Because you love me. I know you don't know how to love yet. I remember what happened with your mom and dad and that's why you can't stand abandonment. I just need to show you how to love. I'll never leave you like that." She sounded like she was having a conversation with herself, rather than convincing me.

"Joy, please don't..." I said, not wanting to think about Momma and Daddy anymore. They were gone.

"I'm not ever going to leave you, Nicole. No matter how much you try to push me away like Justice, Webby and even your sister. I've decided that I'm strong enough to love you." Her voice dripped like sweet molasses on fresh biscuits. Who the hell was I dealing with?

"You have to stop this, Joy. You're going to hurt someone," I warned.

"You're just worried about your little secret getting out, huh? Worried that the world will know that you love me and want to be with me too. I understand that you're scared but I'm going to hold it down for us and anyone that tries to take you away from me, I'm going to make it my personal goal to see them erased." Joy sounded ominous and determined. A chill flooded down my spine at the depth of her obsession.

"Joy, please. Stop this. It's not worth it. You're going to mess up everything you worked for...and for what?" I tried to appeal to her professional side.

"For you, Nicole. It's all for you!" she yelled into the receiver.

I blinked tears from my eyes and mashed the End button on the cell phone. I balled up in the soft leather, gripped my knees like I used to when I was a child and cried openly for the first time since my father's death. My body retched with the fear and anxiety that leaped around inside me. I'd kept it quiet for so long until now. I couldn't hold it any longer. The memories played their mournful song with my heart strings. Hearing Joy say she would never leave me was tinged with a bittersweet taste that I couldn't scrape from my mind, not even with my unyielding tenacity. I regretted walking down that sandy path with her in Costa Rica, sharing my memories, my secrets with her and then, ultimately, my heart. All the small nuances that made me cautious about letting people in were now at her disposal. I'd let her in and she'd abused my emotions so callously. I sniffled into the dark room, glad that it was empty and soundproof.

In the beginning, a small part of me wanted to be wanted by Joy. I liked the feeling of being admired by someone that knew me inside and out. I finally had someone that I could trust with my deepest, darkest secrets, but I was wrong in choosing Joy. Joy was everything I loved and hated in myself wrapped in beautiful packaging. She had the brains, the beauty and the drive that I admired. But her evil nature could not be shielded or controlled, much like mine. I stared at the blank movie screen hanging on the far wall of the modestly decorated theater. I vowed I would not tell Webby about Joy leaking his single. I knew now that she had skipped too far down Crazy Lane to return to any bit of normalcy. She would stop at nothing to make Webby and I sever as a couple.

Luckily, the movie was only a few months from completion and I could be completely through with Joy. I wasn't sure how much longer I could hold her at bay without causing her to be even more reckless. I decided my best counterattack was to contact Will and try to tame the storm before the raging waters came crashing through.

"Will, it's Nicole," I said after his tired voice answered the phone on the third ring. I knew this had to be a long night for him.

"Hey, Nicole. I guess you talked to Webby about the single already?" he said in a huff.

"Yes. We talked. Any idea who'd want to do this to him?"

"I don't know. I've been going over it again and again. I've watched all the surveillance tapes but I don't have cameras in the production studios." I could visualize his droopy eyes looking watery and red with frustration over his first security breach. It could hurt business.

"I hate this happened at your spot. Is everything else moving along okay?"

He chuckled tiredly, realizing why I'd called. "So you want to make sure the movie is still going to happen, huh?"

"Sometimes the best remedy is to finish something." I tried to sound optimistic.

"The movie is still on schedule. We're done shooting. It's going through the full treatment right now. It won't be completely done and ready for viewing until early April," Will said, as if rehearsed a million times.

"Great." I tried to sound nonchalant but inside I was jumping for joy—no pun intended.

"Nicole, I've been meaning to ask you about the writer on this project, Joy. Is everything okay between you and her?" he questioned.

"Why do you ask?"

"She came to see me about working another movie deal. She said she had been writing a television series. You know we haven't stepped into that genre yet." Will hummed on the phone, clearly stalling to find the right words. "When I asked her if you were going to be involved, she seemed pretty adamant that you didn't want to work with her anymore." Curiosity leaked through his words.

"I can't say that she's particularly easy to work with but I definitely think she's…talented." I swallowed my anger at her attempt to backstab me using my own business contact. She was truly out of control.

"So what are your thoughts? You know how I am about my business. If there's money to be made, then I want to be the first hand stirring the pot."

I pondered his words. Will had been a great business mentor and friend to me over the years. I couldn't tell him to run as fast as his old legs could take him away from Joy because he probably stood to gain a substantial amount of money from her work.

"I think you should at least take a look at it. What would it hurt, right?" I offered.

"You're right. If it don't make money, it don't make sense." He chuckled low on the phone. I heard a muffled voice in the background. He covered the receiver and answered back quickly.

"Look, Nicole. I gotta go. I have company."

"Ooohhh. Look at you, Will. Since when did you get a girlfriend and why haven't I met her?" I teased.

"No worries…in due time," he said before hanging up.

When I finally climbed the stairs to the bedroom and sunk into the bed next to Webby, all I could hear was his rhythmic breathing battling with the constant whir of the ceiling fan. I knew that I needed to come clean to Webby before Joy made an attempt at ruining everything for me. I stared across the pillow at Webby's dark, chocolaty face as his naked chest rose and fell calmly beneath the bedsheet. He looked so peaceful in his resting state but beneath the surface, I knew he boiled with confusion, anxiety and distrust over his music leaking. It was still early but I hoped the single would still thrive on the charts, just to spite Joy. I leaned close enough to feel his breath on my lips and kissed him gently.

"I love you," I whispered into his ear. He needed to hear it after what he'd been through. Unfortunately, I was still working hard at making the words ring true.

"I love you too," he whispered with his eyes closed. He wrapped his arms tightly around my waist and I could smell the scent of his chest against my cheek. He kissed the top of my head and within minutes, a soft snore filled the room.

I smiled faintly against his chest but it slowly faded to shame. Would he be able to forgive me for all my wrongdoings? I'd told so many lies in our relationship but hopefully it wasn't too late. Would he cast me away like his cheating ex-girlfriend and best friend, never to speak to me again? I had to think about the perfect time to tell him everything. After the movie was released, I knew it would be time to tell him about how the movie deal came to be. He'd be happy that I made a big move like this on my own, I was sure of it. I still had to find the courage to tell him about Joy and me. I had a few months to figure out the best time to explain it to him. One thing I was absolutely sure about: I was determined not to let Joy force my hand or ruin this relationship.

∞

The Break

∞

Mali

∞

The studio is my refuge. A place where nothing outside its mirrored walls matters. After the coffeehouse exposed my secret admirer as Craig Cole, I had grown adept at finding time to build my choreography at the studio. Staying busy kept my mind from obsessing over whether to speak to Craig again after the stunt he pulled. Carey continued to reassure me that she didn't mind me dating her brother but honestly, it felt a little creepy now that I knew who he was. My roommate and best friend's brother? A guy who literally stalked me for weeks? I muddled through my thoughts as I hit the remote control to start the stereo on the wall. Soft jazz hummed into the nearly empty space.

My life was starting to sound like a Jerry Springer episode waiting to happen. Still, I couldn't stop thinking about the complicated mess that had become my life. After many sleepless nights, I still fumbled through thoughts about both Justice and Craig. Both men had been calling nonstop for two weeks since the coffeehouse became the headliner of the Craig and Mali Show. I spoke with Justice only briefly to congratulate him on his championship win and even that had been a struggle. Every time I saw him or heard his voice, a piece of me yearned to hold him but shortly after came the undying gut feeling of possible rejection. The paralyzing feeling of loving someone that couldn't or wouldn't love you back lingered like a stain on my heart. He begged me to meet up with him so he could tell me something important but I ended up blowing him off and coming to the studio instead. I wasn't ready to deal with my feelings for him and the possibility that they'd never be reciprocated. Instead, I tried to focus on my dilemma with Craig, the man who openly cared but for whom I wasn't sure I could reciprocate. Was everyone's life this complicated?

I stretched my leg toward the ceiling, grabbing my ankle for stability. I didn't realize I'd been dancing for five hours until Toni poked his bandanna-laden head into the studio and glanced at his wristwatch.

"You still here, girl? I thought you would've been gone by now. It's nearly nine."

I stretched my leg backward and held the pose, working on my balance. "Yep. Still here."

Toni was always good at sensing how a person was feeling. From the first day of the audition, he seemed to read me like a book. His makeup studio was like a revolving chair of sadness and glee. I'd seen him cure people's heartache in his leather swivel chair in mere hours. Toni must've noticed my defeated aura because he slid into the studio, closed the door behind him and leaned on the painted brick wall beside the door.

"What's going on? Spill the beans, little mama." He crossed his arms, ready for my explanation.

I sighed. Who better to share my deepest feelings with than the resident psychologist, right?

"I've had a lot on my mind these past few weeks. Hell, the past few months, actually. It's such a change being here in Atlanta, finally getting to pursue my craft and figuring out what I want out of life. Now I have all this personal stuff taking my mind off what I love." I relaxed my legs and planted my heels together, toes facing outward.

Toni breathed heavily. "Looks like you've been doing more of what you love and less of living life these past few weeks." He wagged his finger at me as I stared at him through the mirrored glass. "There's one thing you have to remember about life, Mali. It is forgiving. No matter what happens, you will always make mistakes, lose friends, gain lovers. But life goes on."

"Can I ask you something?"

"Sure. Anything. Well, not anything…but let's see what you got." He smiled.

"If you had a guy that loved you but you didn't quite feel the same, and a guy that you loved but didn't think he felt the same…which one would you choose?"

Toni rolled his eyes. "I thought you had a hard question." He laughed aloud. "I'd choose both. No, I'm joking. But I'm really not. Seriously, in your case, you should go with your gut. If you think the man that cares about you could help you fall in love with him given more time and less distraction, then he could be a good choice. A man that loves you more than you love him will always be faithful and that's hard to come by." He paused. "But then there's the man that makes your heart flutter like a little honey bee and you're confused about how he feels. Sweetie, the only way to know for sure is to just ask him how he feels about you. Then you'll have your answer. Good or bad."

"But what if he doesn't feel the same about me? That'll be so embarrassing. I don't think I'll be able to show my face on campus again."

"If he turns you down then he's a damn fool. You're beautiful, smart and talented. If he can't see that, then he doesn't deserve a diamond like you." Toni rolled his neck and popped his hand on his imaginary hip.

I smiled. "Thanks for the advice, Toni. Maybe I'll be lucky and Justice will feel the same way."

Toni choked. "Did you say Justice? You mean, Justice Bradford?"

I skipped over to Toni to help him clear his throat but he held out his hand to keep me at a distance. "You okay, Toni?"

"Mmm-hmm, yep. I'm good. You just took me off guard when you said Justice."

"Oh, so you know him?"

Toni wrestled with his answer before saying, "I know of him. I mean, who doesn't, right?"

"Everyone knows him. That's why it's so hard to tell him how I feel. Can you imagine how many women probably feel the same way I do about him?"

Toni finally seemed to settle his breathing. "That doesn't matter, girl. Whether a million women want him or just one, it's up to him to choose the right one. He'll choose on his own. You'll just have to accept it." I nodded at his wisdom. He was absolutely right. Justice would go with his heart and there was nothing I could do about it.

"How'd you get to be so good at relationship advice, anyway?"

"Honey, I've been in love with the same man for over ten years. We fight, we argue and we make sweet, passionate love...but at the end of the day, he's my partner and I don't want to start over with anyone else."

"Will I ever get to meet him?"

"Of course, chile. But stop worrying about my love life and start figuring out which one of those hunks you're going to choose." He swiped his index finger in the air and pulled open the door. With an air kiss, he vanished into the hall and the *click-clack* of his high-fashion shoes faded within seconds.

Toni's words lingered in my mind. As a gay man, he sure as hell knew more about relationships than anyone I'd ever met, male or female. He made it sound so easy. His advice said I should call Justice and ask him how he felt about me. Then I could tell him how I felt about him, right? Oh no. I wasn't quite ready for that letdown. I'd go the route least traveled by talking to Craig first. I needed to know if he could indeed teach me to love him.

After phoning him to meet me at a local restaurant near Centennial Park, I arrived within minutes of our meeting time. Craig looked laid-back in a slightly wrinkled button-down shirt and khaki pants. It was Saturday, date night for many couples, which made the restaurant overcrowded and noisy. He glanced curiously around the packed restaurant and spotted me as I strolled toward him, still in my workout gear. I slid my arms from my puffy jacket, worn to brave the chilly Atlanta wind. His smile spread wide as he stood to help me into my seat. I slid across the red leather and rested in front of his bright, green-eyed gaze.

"I didn't think you were coming," he confessed.

"Sorry I've been so distant these last few weeks. I've had a lot to take in, in a short amount of time."

"I want to apologize about that. I didn't mean to tell you like that in front of a crowd of people. I was shocked that you were coming to my set and I just wanted to get it off my chest. I've wanted to sit down with you for months. So I apologize for rushing it." He looked genuinely pained as he swept back his bangs.

"Thanks for apologizing but it's not really necessary. I thought your poem was really great." I smirked, remembering his words.

"I appreciate that. Glad you liked it. I haven't read a poem onstage in a very long time."

"Why not?"

"I vowed that I wouldn't read another poem until I was spiritually or emotionally inspired. Sounds so serious, right?"

I shrugged. "What made you stop? You just thought up one day that you were going to wait for inspiration?"

"No. Not exactly." He unfolded his napkin and placed it on his lap. "I stopped after my girlfriend passed away."

"Oh my God, I'm sorry."

"No. It's okay. I can talk about it now. For a while there, I couldn't do much of anything...started questioning life, its meaning, whether I wanted to live. I went into a deep depression that only God could bring me out of." He looked saddened at the memory of his darker self.

"I'm so sorry, Craig. My goodness. She must've been young."

"She was young. Only nineteen when she was killed by a drunk driver right outside of campus. It was a huge news ordeal for months. People fighting over whether we should add laws, ban drinking at the school and a bunch of other things. The part they forgot was that the people who really knew her and loved her were hurting beyond measure." The redness leaked into his cheeks as he paused. "The news coverage didn't really help me much, to say the least. It's horrible going through pain with everyone watching like it's a sitcom on prime-time television."

"How'd you get through it?"

"Honestly, I don't know. My family and friends stuck close to me. My roommate pushed me to share some of my journal writings since the crash. I only read one poem at the coffeehouse after her death. It was for her. It was a pretty intense time for everyone, including me." He wiped at the corner of his eye, even though nothing was there. He continued, "Everyone at the coffeehouse was so supportive but I couldn't stand to see anyone smile after what I'd lost. So I turned into a recluse. I was standing on the outskirts of life, watching like a spectator, until you walked into the dorm."

I blushed. "I didn't know I had that effect on anyone."

"And that's the beauty of you. You don't even realize how beautiful you are. It's kind of…refreshing." He chuckled.

"So what made you become my mystery man? Why didn't you just come by the dorm and ask me out? It might've saved you some time." I snickered.

"Trust me, I thought about it. There were many nights when I'd see you walking alone that I wanted to walk with you but I knew it wasn't time. I wasn't ready. Other times you were either walking with Deuce or meeting with Justice Bradford, so I didn't feel the options were in the weird guy's favor." He smiled down at the menu. "I just held tight to our phone conversations until the right moment…which turned out to still be the wrong moment." He laughed.

The mention of Justice's name formed knots in the base of my stomach. There was so much unfinished business, so many things unsaid. Now was not the time to figure out my problems. I was making strides in the right direction. I scanned the menu as the waitress plodded to our table, clearly annoyed with the length of our conversation before ordering. We quickly ordered the chicken-fried steak and potatoes, then settled back into easy conversation.

The night ended well after the couples had filtered out to the local movie theater and pub. Craig and I laughed together easily. There was a closeness between Craig and me from months of talking to each other but I still couldn't quiet my thoughts of Justice. The inevitable conversation was looming larger and becoming more pressing as Craig smiled wantonly across the table. To explore a relationship with Craig, I would need to squelch my desire for Justice once and for all. I silently promised myself to confront Justice sooner rather than later, so I could move into the next chapter of my life, with or without him. A chapter that would finally explain who I was and what I wanted.

Craig dropped me off in front of Cramer Hall and waved as I told him to text me later. Carey sat on her polka-dot comforter as I entered the dorm room. She could hardly contain her curiosity.

"Sooooo….how did it go?" she spilled out before I could kick my shoes into the closet.

"It went well. He's pretty cool. But I already knew that since we've been talking to each other for a while now."

"So did you guys talk about a relationship together?" She was squeezing her comforter between her thighs, trying to contain her interest.

"We didn't talk about a relationship together but he did tell me about his girlfriend that passed away."

"Oh." She fiddled with the covers, loosening them from her thighs and pulling them from underneath her.

"What do you mean, 'oh'? Why didn't you tell me about what happened? You knew at the coffeehouse what he was talking about. You could have told me, ya know." I sat on the bed opposite hers, waiting to hear the answer to the question I had been thinking about since Craig started spilling his secrets hours ago.

"That was a really bad time for him. It wasn't my place to tell you what happened, Mali. I'm your friend…but I'm his sister. There's a code, ya know." She mimicked me.

"A code? Yeah, I know all about the code. It's the same code that says a brother can't date his sister's friends, remember? But somehow that one slipped through the cracks," I said.

"I never said I was totally fine with it. But you guys are grown, you'll figure it out." She waved her hand as if to say she was through with that part of the conversation. "Did you guys kiss?"

"No!" I screeched and tossed my pillow at her head.

Carey breathed a sigh of relief and feigned wiping sweat from her brow. We both giggled at her apparent interest in her mine and her brother's nonexistent love life. It was a good Saturday night as Carey made peanut butter and jelly sandwiches for us between late-night reruns of reality television programs. At one in the morning, Carey and I were nearly comatose as the television created rays of blue light in the darkened room. My phone buzzed loudly against the soft murmur of the television. I smirked, knowing Craig was the only person with insomnia that liked to text this late at night. My body felt heavy as a reached for the phone and tapped the screen, which had gone into sleep mode. It was a message from Justice but it was incoherent.

I want more see you for the game, popped up in my text box. What was he talking about? It didn't make any sense. He was probably coming down from the championship win with Big Deuce and from the sound of it, he was totally wasted. I decided to call, just to make sure he wasn't drunk-texting me from a ditch somewhere. The phone rung twice before a muffled sound erupted into the receiver and a female voice answered.

"Hello?" I greeted cautiously, still confused at a female answering Justice's phone.

"Who is this?" the female said with an edge of attitude.

"Uh, this is Mali. Who is this? Where is Justice?"

She snickered wickedly as I moved my ear from the receiver slightly. Her voice sounded vaguely familiar. "Well isn't this a co-inkee-dink? This is Mali Struthers, right?"

"Where the hell is Justice?" How did she know my name?

"Justice is right here with me. I just put him to sleep, actually." Her sinister laugh echoed on the line. "Mali, you remember that day when you screwed me over and I told you that karma's a bitch?"

I scanned my memory trying to remember any person I had screwed over. No one came to mind.

"I've never screwed over anyone. Who is this?" I urged.

"Well, since you screwed me over...I screwed your man over and over... and over." She giggled at her own joke. "I don't expect your backstabbing ass to remember every person you stepped on to get a small opportunity in your dance career. Because of you, I lost my teacher's-aid position and was held back in my dance studies. I never thought I'd have the opportunity to get you back soooo good. But now that I've peeked at Justice's phone, I've noticed lots of calls and text messages to you. I hate to tell you this but...those lips have been all over this body. And I mean ALL over this body. I guess he has a thing for dancers, huh?" She yawned on the line loudly. "I've grown tired of talking to you, and I have a fine man waiting for me in bed. What about you? Better yet, no need to answer." She huffed in a deep breath and hummed into the line sleepily, "For all the humiliation you put me through, I would tell you to kiss my ass...but you probably already have."

Before I could get a word in, the phone was disconnected. I sat up enraged at Brianna's attempt to get back at me. Little did she know, Justice and I were not together but it didn't make the stinging feeling in my heart less excruciating. Was Justice dating her? Even worse, was he sleeping with her? I dialed Justice's number but the bitch turned off his cell phone, so I could only leave a message. I was sure she didn't have access to his voice mail but a message would probably sound psychotic in my current state of mind. How in the hell did she get his cell phone anyway? Was she telling the truth about sleeping with Justice or was she just trying to get me back for losing her position? I hadn't noticed that Carey was pacing the room with me, begging me to tell her what was going on.

"I need a ride," was all I could muster through the heat rising from my belly. Before Carey could answer, I snatched my coat and stormed from the room toward the stairs. The ride to Justice's apartment was a blur of streetlights, parked cars and nameless buildings. When we finally circled into his parking lot, I breathed deeply.

"Mali, what are we doing here?" Carey said quietly.

"I don't know. Are you coming?" I said through tight eyes. Carey nodded as we exited her tiny car and walked the steps to Justice's apartment. I listened for any sounds coming from the interior of the apartment but it was silent. So I pressed my ear to the wood, just to make sure. Carey looked at me incredulously as I tried the doorknob to find it locked. I sucked in a breath and knocked on the door loudly. No one answered on the first knock, so I repeated it a little harder. It seemed like centuries before the lock clicked back and the wooden door squeezed open an inch to reveal Brianna's pale face and disheveled hair. Before I knew it, I had kicked the door open and Brianna flew back, holding her cheek in awe.

"How dare you!" she screamed, grabbing me as I tried to walk back to Justice's bedroom.

"Let me go!" I grabbed her tiny wrists and pushed her into the wall, knocking down a mirror with the back of her head. It shattered as it hit the carpet like an opening bell to a UFC fight. Brianna rebounded from the wall like a cat springing onto a tree branch. She was covering my body with her weight, snatching and pulling at my hair like she was Edward Scissorhands. I clawed at her face, finally getting enough space to wrestle her to the ground. In the distance, I heard Carey yelling "Stop it!" but I couldn't stop. It felt too good to finally release all the balled-up anger and fear I had carried for years out of my system. Every blow that landed against Brianna's face was like a blow to my dad for his evilness. It felt good as Brianna and I rolled around on the living room carpet, each of us scratching at the other, trying to get the upper hand.

"Get off her!"

The voice boomed so loud that it startled Brianna and stopped her from attacking my face as she straddled me. Justice snatched Brianna by the arm until she was standing next to him, heaving like a dog on a porch with no shade from the summer heat. Justice's eyes were like red, watery slits, struggling to stay open. The stench of liquor filled the room from his heavy breathing. His muscled abdomen rippled as his chest rose and fell quickly. I lay on the floor, breathless, staring at him in his boxer briefs next to Brianna's barely clothed, thin frame. Justice reminded me of my dad with his bloodshot eyes and drunken, unstable balance. I realized he was no different than him after all. My stomach wretched at the thought that I was falling in love with my father. I fought back tears as I struggled to pull myself up from the floor. Justice reached his hand out to help.

"Don't you touch me. Don't you *ever* touch me!" I pointed at him.

A look of confusion furrowed his brow. He followed my stare to Brianna, smirking next to him, his hand still on her arm. I turned to leave as Carey appeared from the corner near the door, looking distressed and anxious.

"Let's go," I told Carey authoritatively. She disappeared from the apartment before I could take another step toward the door.

"Mali, wait. Let me explain," Justice said from behind me.

I whirled on him angrily. "What is there to explain, Justice? You're nothing but a drunk! And to think that I was falling for you while you could give a damn about me! Don't ever call me again. You got what you wanted." I motioned to Brianna, who had nestled herself on the sunken couch like a cat curling into a warm spot.

"Mali, you don't understand…" Justice pleaded as I walked out. I'd seen enough. I sprinted through the tears that flooded my cheeks and crawled into Carey's waiting VW. I sobbed uncontrollably as she sped through downtown Atlanta back toward the safety of Cramer Hall.

Justice

∞

The glass had been ground into the carpet and tiny shards were glistening in the dim light of the living room. I knew I should pick them up but I was drunk. I smelled and looked like I had been living under the Moreland Ave. bypass yet the only thing that burned into my mind was what just went down in my apartment. Brianna was laid out on the couch like a cracked porcelain doll, staring off into nowhere. Her cheek and neck had red welts growing angrier as time passed. Little drops of blood had emerged like tiny freckles on her cheekbones. She seemed to not feel the pain as she fought to hide the sinister smirk that kept flashing across her face. Clearly she was replaying the fight back in her head and it was amusing her to no end.

"You need to get your shit and get out," I half slurred, half whispered.

"Why?" Brianna's face turned serious as she stared at me leaning against the front door, trying to avoid the glass pieces sticking up from the carpet.

"Because you're a messy bitch, that's why."

"I'm the messy bitch? What about the crazy girl storming into your apartment, attacking me? I think you owe me an apology. I was protecting you, for goodness sake!" Her voice thundered in my ears like she was speaking into a bullhorn. My temples thudded loudly at the sound.

"You weren't protecting me. You were happy she was here. I saw how you looked at her." I struggled to talk. My throat was dry and hoarse from dehydration.

"You're talking nonsense. You should thank me for not letting someone rampage through your house while you slept."

"Thank you? Thank you for what? You broke my table, trashed my apartment and ruined my friendship with Mali." I stumbled across the room toward the TV and held its edge until I felt my legs catch up.

She looked pained at the words but then said, "You're drunk. Let's just go lay down for a while and you'll see it all differently in the morning." She stood slowly and put her hand out to me as if I was a child needing help to get into bed.

"Brianna, leave." I crossed my arms across my chest and struggled to focus on her face. The blur of her angry eyes and her defiant body language let me know she wasn't planning on heeding my wishes.

"I'm not leaving you like this. You'll thank me tomorrow." She turned and went into the bedroom without another word.

I didn't have the energy or the balance to fight. So I sank face-first into the couch cushions and faded into the most uncomfortable sleep of my life.

The sun was like a ray of ultrasonic waves peeking through the blinds as my head pounded against my skull. A pool of drool had soaked into the couch cushion where my face was planted all night. As I scanned the room I noted the broken mirror behind the door still laying haphazardly on the carpet, broken into a million tiny pieces, and the coffee table leaning on three legs in the center of the room. The fourth leg was nowhere in sight. The memory of last night came back in a wave of regret. What the hell was Mali doing at my house in the middle of the night? Why were Brianna and Mali fighting? More importantly, was I imagining that Mali confessed her love for me last night? I couldn't make out if it was a drunken hallucination, something my mind made up so I could feel some ounce of happiness with the night's events. I needed to talk to her but I was pretty sure she wasn't going to talk to me after barging in on Brianna and me last night. I swung my legs off the edge of the couch and saw a plate of pancakes with sausages sitting in the adjoining chair with a small note folded beneath the plate. I reached for the note and disregarded the meal entirely.

Sorry for last night. ~Love Brianna

I balled up the note in my fist and hurled it to the corner of the room. It bounced against my gym bag and rolled under the TV stand. It was time to stop being scared and start being a man. I picked up the empty bottles of liquor still sitting on the kitchen counters and threw them into the waste basket. I'd never take another drink again if that's what it took to get Mali back. Before I could finish sliding the pancakes and sausage into the trash bin, a knock on the door interrupted me. I pulled it open to find Big Deuce standing on the landing with a smile spread across his dark face.

"What's up, bro?" Deuce clasped my hand and we bumped chests before I closed the front door behind him.

"Damn, man, what the hell happened up in here?" He scanned the room, taking in the damage.

"You ain't gonna believe me if I told you."

"Shit, try me," he said as his mood shifted.

"Bro, Mali and Brianna was up in here brawling last night."

"What the hell you say?" Deuce stopped walking toward the kitchen and turned around with eyes as big as silver dollars.

"Yeah, man, Mali busted up in here when Brianna opened the door. I guess she just lost it or something. When I woke up, I found both of them scrapping on the living room floor." I pointed to my injured table.

"Daaamn…" Big Deuce wiped his face and plopped down on the couch.

"I've had a long damn night. Mali was pissed when she left here. If I wasn't so drunk I would've went after her." I grabbed the broom to start sweeping the glass out the carpet.

"That don't even sound like something Mali would do, though. How did she know Brianna was over here?" Deuce inquired.

I stood there wondering the same thing. "Good question. I don't know."

Big Deuce pulled his massive body from the couch and grabbed my cell phone perched on the TV stand. Within minutes he said, "Brianna answered your phone."

"You gotta be fuckin' kidding me." He handed me the phone and I scrolled through the call log. I saw exactly what Deuce was talking about. A call from Mali at 1:06 a.m. for four minutes then three missed calls back to my phone. Brianna must've said something bad enough to get her out of her bed and over to my house.

"Looks like you broke the number one rule when letting a girl sleep over at your crib…always lock your phone, dumbass." Deuce shook his head and picked up the broken mirror. "And you have seven years' bad luck."

I stared at Deuce. "I ain't worried about the damn rules, man. I need to get Mali back. She told me she loved me last night."

Deuce's eyes sank to the ground in thought. "You serious? She said that?"

"I know she did. I may have been drunk but she sobered me up when she said that. I can't believe I screwed it up with her."

"You love that girl, don't you?"

I nodded slowly, trying to hide the pain in my eyes. I wasn't sure if I could undo the mess I'd created but I was going to try.

"Hey, man, I'll help you get her back. I know how to get through to her. Just give me twenty-four hours." Deuce sounded confident that he could mend all the broken ties and bandage all the wounds created last night, so I believed him. I hoped he was packing a miraculous idea because I'd need nothing short of a miracle to get her back.

The time it took for Deuce to call me with news was like watching the second hand tick around the clock. When his name popped up on my cell phone, I answered it on the half ring quickly.

"Yo. Any news?" I said eagerly.

"Man, she's pretty pissed off at you."

"Tell me something I don't know, Deuce." I wiped my forehead in frustration.

"Well, I've got some bad news and some good news. What you wanna hear first?"

"I've had enough bad news to last a lifetime."

"The good news is that she still cares about you. I talked with her roommate after Mali left for class. She told me Mali was up crying all night, cussing you out and saying she couldn't believe she let herself go that far."

"Remind me again how that is good news?" I interrupted, annoyed.

"Damn, do I have to teach you everything? If she wasn't crying and cussing, then that means she was really through with you. For her to be so torn up over last night, it shows she still loves you."

"Okay, and the bad news?" I sighed heavily, preparing for the worst.

"She's got a boyfriend, I think." Deuce added quickly, "Or at least someone she's going out with. Her roommate said she was going on a date tonight with some guy."

My heart raced at the sound of someone else being with the woman I loved. The jealous beast within wanted to find this guy and bash him in the head until he forgot she even existed.

"Who's this guy?" I said through clenched teeth.

"That's the part that I couldn't get out of her roommate. But it doesn't matter because I have something even better," Deuce sang into the phone.

"What? What did you get?"

"I know where they will be tonight."

I wanted to leap into action, but I calmed myself. He sensed my anticipation. "You going to be alright with crashing this party?"

"I want to do this alone."

Deuce hesitated. "I don't think you should…"

"Deuce, I know what you're thinking. I'm not going to do anything to jeopardize the school or my future. I just want to let her know how I feel while I still can."

Deuce lamented silently for what seemed like hours until he finally gave in. "She'll be at Gladys Knights Chicken and Waffles downtown at six. Call me if you need me, bro."

When the line went dead, I was still sitting on the chair in front of my battered coffee table feeling like my life was full of misery. I felt a twinge of fear deep down in my gut. What if this didn't work? I would have lost two loves in the same year. I quieted my fears and headed for the shower. I needed to get cleaned up and looking like my old self if I was going to woo Mali back into my life.

It took me only twelve minutes to arrive at Gladys Knights Chicken and Waffles, the home of the famous "midnight train." My mouth watered at the thought of the crispy fried chicken and fluffy golden waffles served just inside those doors. The line outside the small building dissipated as people found their booths inside and laughed over good food. I waited across the street in my Impala with the hazard lights blinking as I stared in the rearview at the cars swerving angrily around my vehicle. I didn't have much more time before someone was bound to bump my rear end in frustration. I tapped the dashboard impatiently waiting for Mali and this mystery man to appear. Finally, in the distance, walking from the rear parking lot, I spotted Mali. She looked amazing in an oversized puffy jacket, tattered jeans and red Chuck Taylors. Sauntering behind her with a weird, gangly gait was a scraggly white boy with long hair flying around his face in the cool night air. The creep gripped her waist and ushered her through the front doors of Gladys Knights. I felt my hair stand at attention seeing him touch her. I wheeled the Impala into traffic, punched off the hazard lights and completed a U-turn in the middle of Peachtree Street. Before parking in the rear of the restaurant, I rode past the front window to see them sitting near the back of the restaurant, almost out of view. The walk from the parking lot to the restaurant was filled with my own thoughts warning me not to go too far. *Don't mess up everything you've worked so hard for.*

I pulled open the door to Gladys Knights and crossed the threshold into the point of no return. I was going to tell Mali how I felt whether it embarrassed or hurt me. Girls at a table near the entrance waved excitedly as I entered.

"Oh my God, that's JB." One girl pointed as the others swiveled in their booth to get a look.

"Justice!" Two girls waved over the edge of the booth and I kindly waved back.

"Girl, he is so damn fine!" someone whispered as I continued my walk to the rear of the restaurant. It's funny how a complete stranger can give a person confidence to do some shit they wouldn't normally do on their own. I puffed out my chest, ready to expose myself to Mali…and undoubtedly the entire restaurant. Luckily, I was looking good in a cream-colored sweater that clung to my muscular frame and light blue jeans. My brown Timberland boots clunked against the tile floors as I saw the scraggly boy stop talking and stare into my eyes. He must've known what I was there for because he nodded in my direction and Mali's head peered around the side of the brown leather booth in amazement.

"What are you doing here?" she said with a bitterness I hadn't heard in her before.

"Mali, I need to talk to you."

"I don't think now is a good time. Don't you see I'm having dinner with someone?" She motioned to the lanky man as he swept his hair out of his face like Justin Bieber. I had to laugh.

"Don't tell me this is your type?" I pointed at the man across the booth as he looked from Mali then back to me.

"Yeah, you know what…he IS my type. He is a good, honest man that doesn't slut off with whatever chick will give it up. So yeah, I guess that makes him my type." She rolled her eyes and faced the man as if I was intruding on their date. I was, but so what? I was on a mission.

"Mali, if you want me to give you a minute…" the mystery man said softly.

"No. I've given him far too many minutes of my time already," Mali said, quietly brooding.

"I'm sorry, man, what's your name?" I pushed my hand in his direction.

"Craig." He didn't take my outstretched hand.

"Justice, what do you want?" Mali interrupted rudely. I had never seen her so upset.

"I want to have a conversation with you, in private. Ask you why you came to my house last night and why you fought with Brianna." I stood my ground.

Mali looked embarrassed as Craig's gaze narrowed on her. He must not have known about last night.

"Just forget about it, Justice. I don't want to talk about it anymore," Mali said forcefully.

"You haven't talked about anything with me yet. You've got me so confused. How are you upset with me when you charged into my house unannounced and fought with my guest? What did I do wrong?" I asked. Her face dropped into her hands as she cried silently. Hearing the words come out of my mouth made the situation sound really crazy. My heart doubled over on itself as her curls bounced every time her shoulders wretched. I didn't want to hurt her. I just wanted to understand.

"Maybe you should leave," Craig said as he slid into the booth next to Mali and wrapped his arm around her shoulder.

"Mali, if you are not going to talk to me, then I will just tell you what I came to tell you." I leaned on the table so she could hear me. "I love you, Mali. I'm in love with you and I have been since the first time I saw you. I don't care why you did what you did. I just want you, with all your crazy ways and corny jokes. I love the way you dance with all your heart and smile when you talk. I like that you don't know what your next move is but you're excited about it." I tried to push down the lump in my throat to stop my heart from beating so fast. I couldn't go on anymore. "Ah shit, I'm probably not making any sense at all to you."

Mali continued crying in Craig's arms as I walked through the crowd of onlookers, staring from me to the table. Some men looked hateful while women looked longingly at me as I barreled to my car in enough time to sit inside and let a rush of air escape. I didn't notice I was holding my breath the entire time.

I pulled out of the parking space just as I heard a knock at the rear of my vehicle. I looked in my rearview mirror and saw Mali standing in the glow of my break lights. I slammed the car into Park and stood in front of her in the parking lot. Her brown eyes were puffy and red from crying.

"Where's Craig?" I asked, looking back toward the restaurant.

"He's inside."

"I'm sorry for ruining your date."

"No you're not," she said easily. I couldn't dispute that.

After a moment she said, "Did you mean everything you said in there?"

Her brown eyes seared into me, searching for something but I couldn't tell what.

"Every word," I said.

"I don't know what to say."

"Why do you seem so sad?" I queried.

"Justice, you have to understand something about me." She gulped. "I don't like living with a secret. There's a lot of things, painful things, you don't know about me."

"What secret? There's nothing you can say that will make me love you any less," I reassured her.

"My dad...he's a horrible man. An abusive, degrading drunk. I'm so scared of becoming like my father." She dropped her head. "When I came by your house...that scared me. I'd never felt rage like that before but I've seen it my whole life. I know what it can do to a person. I don't want to be like him." She wiped her tears away with the back of her hand and struggled to breathe normally. She seemed so tiny to me, like she'd reverted back to her childhood at the mere thought of her father.

"You're nothing like your dad. You don't have a mean bone in your body." I pulled her head up to peer into her eyes. "He can't hurt you anymore because I'm here. I'd never let anyone lay a hand on you. You know that, right?"

She nodded her head and continued, "I don't want to see you drunk again. All I could see was my dad when you were standing there. I can't..." She dropped her head as tears spilled from her eyes.

I wiped the curls that whipped into her eyes from the chilling breeze. The touch of her warm skin ignited me as she caught my hand and rubbed it against her moist cheek, wiping the tears away. Her eyes fluttered closed as I leaned into her soft, pouty lips and tasted the sweetness of her mouth. In her kiss, I felt all the longing, the pain and the desire I'd bottled up for months. I yearned to feel her body pressed to mine.

"I love you," she whispered against my lips as we parted. I held her tiny frame tightly as I felt her body warm against mine. Her shoulders quivered in my bear hug. I wasn't sure if it was the cold or her body vibrating against mine in desire. One thing I knew for sure: I didn't ever want to let her go.

Nicole

∞

"Stop hogging it all, damn!" I spat at Webby as he snorted the second-to-last line. I'd already had three lines but I wasn't feeling the buzz completely. I needed that last line and he was being greedy as hell by trying to take it all. I slapped Webby's shoulder as he leaned his head back and sniffed at the air, moving his nose in circles trying to get every ounce.

"Come on, Nicole! Stop with all the damn whining. I left you the last one, shit."

He snatched his shoulder from my reach just as my hand swatted the air. I didn't care if I was nagging him. If I didn't stop him, he'd snort the whole damn bag. Then there wouldn't be any for either of us later. Webby started taking a few more lines in the past few months because the sex was always amazing when he did, and so I started with just a teensy bit more too…just so I could feel how good the sex really was while we were high. Boy oh boy…there ain't nothing better than hot, sweaty sex with a fine-ass man on some powder. He lasts ALL night long, no lie.

It had been three and a half months since my conversation with Joy after she leaked the single to everyone and anyone who would listen. To her chagrin, the single was still scaling the Billboard charts and becoming an international hit. Webby was already setting up the tour dates across the country and scheduling his listening party for June. So not hearing from Joy was not alarming in the least; in fact, it was the best thing that could've happened to me. Since she was out of my life, Webby and I were inseparable, but it still seemed to me like something was missing. Granted, Webby and I argued a lot more but that was because he loved so hard.

"Did you call Veronica about the event tonight?" Webby asked as he scanned the closet for an outfit.

"Yeah," I said, still annoyed.

"Okay cool. I want to make sure we have a VIP section lined up. I ain't trying to have any problems at the door." I rolled my eyes. This was mainly my club promotion but he'd found a way to get his name in the mix. It pissed me off that I couldn't have anything on my own anymore. Didn't he know who I was?

"You know this is *my* promo. So everything is taken care of," I retorted.

He chuckled in the closet before saying, "They want to see a superstar and, of course, that luscious ass of yours."

I was fuming. One minute, he didn't want me to be a video model and then the next, he wanted to be a part of all my club promotions. I was tired of sharing the little bit of spotlight I had.

"Oh, so you think they are only paying me because you're going to be there?!" I spun on the bed to face the closet. Webby stopped pulling hangers from the rod and looked at me.

"Babe, let's be serious. I have a hot single and you have, well...me." He smiled brightly, oblivious to my growing rage.

"You must've forgotten where you met me. Remember, you were the one quoting my accomplishments...not me."

"How could I not tell you what you wanted to hear? Look at you! You're sexy as hell." He motioned toward my body since I had moved into the doorway of the massive closet.

"So all you ever wanted was my body. It's always been about sex, huh?" I crossed my arms, upset.

"Of course not, baby." He wrapped his arms around my waist. "But that always helps a man know what he wants for the future. I mean, look at it this way…you don't cook, you don't clean and you don't have any little Webbys running around this house…so your only job is looking good and being my girl. Got it?"

I felt my jaw drop at his apparent lack of tact. He was right. I didn't do much of anything other than spend his money and travel but I still wanted some respect. I demanded respect.

"I think I'm going to do the gig solo tonight," I said defiantly.

"Aww, babe. Don't be like that." Webby kissed me on the cheek and walked into the bathroom.

"I'm serious. I need to do this on my own. I need to."

He poked his head out the bathroom and said, "Fine. I'm sure I can find something else to do. I just hope they aren't disappointed when you show up without me."

I feigned a crooked smile and rolled my eyes as he continued primping in the bathroom. It took me only an hour to get dressed and into my red BMW. I had the option of Webby's Escalade, Porsche or Mercedes but after the conversation I'd had with Webby, going back to my old red BMW seemed like the proper place for me. The weather in Atlanta had finally given a sneak peek at the upcoming spring season with a whopping seventy-five degrees during the day and chilly sixty-three degrees tonight. It was just chilly enough to crack the window on the BMW and let the wind blow through the car. It took me thirty-five minutes to reach Club Sanction in Midtown, not great time as I replayed the conversation with Webby and didn't focus on the road. Our talk made me wonder what I was doing with my life. Then I remembered my greatest feat yet—the movie. Will had already scheduled the viewing party in conjunction with another party so it could pull in more people. I was only half listening when he explained the logistics of the event because I was so excited to hear that everything was finalized and ready to go. Instantly, I wanted to call Joy and congratulate her but thought better of it. I wasn't going to rock that cradle.

Luckily, when I pulled into Club Sanction, I had a special parking area and was able to pull the BMW right outside the rear door of the club. I was led in by the promotion manager, Becka, a white girl with long blond hair and pudgy cheeks. She led me through the back entryway, weaved through the crowd of men and women swaying to the music up to the VIP section and assured me my drink was coming. The VIP section had handsome men and beautiful women lingering along the couches and standing up dancing to the music. Having people around I didn't know was not unusual for promotional events. The promotion team usually hired models from various agencies and sent them here to make me look like I hung with the best of the best and nothing less. So I welcomed them with open arms, kissing each model on the cheek and hugging like old friends. Sometimes being as fake as a Louis Vuitton bag sold on a street corner was a part of the job. Anyone sent here to make me look better was well worth it in my book, so I played the game. Becka waddled to the VIP section, bumping through the crowd, holding steady to my amaretto sour. She handed me the drink as she finally made it through the VIP ropes.

"Is Webby on his way?" she yelled over the music.

I shook my head as she nodded in response, speaking into her earpiece. She waited a few minutes, listening closely with her finger pressed to her ear at the person speaking on the other end.

"Everything good?" I said, agitated that she was still standing in the VIP. Her fat ass was messing up the ambiance.

"Yes. We just need to talk to the owner about the new rate without Webby. People were coming tonight thinking they'd get to see both you and Webby." She held her hand flat over the earpiece as she spoke.

"So what's the new rate?"

"We will have to work it out later."

"No. Let's work it out now." I grabbed her arm and started leading her from the VIP section. When it came to my money, I wasn't playing any games.

Becka looked surprised as I opened the rope and motioned her to lead the way. She spoke into her earpiece under the music and started walking past the bar. Toni spotted me before I could see him dart out into the crowd and hug my neck. I was happy to see my friend but I had money on my mind. He'd have to wait.

"Bitch, you haven't returned my calls!" he said playfully. I kept my eye trained on Becka as she weaved through the crowded club.

"Hey, Toni! I'll be right back. I gotta take care of this money first." I stood on my tippy toes and looked across the crowd for a short blond head. I spotted her going into a black door near the bathrooms.

"Okay, love. Handle your business!"

I weaved through the crowd trying to stay close to the outskirts as not to get sucked in by the men who lurked around

looking for a female to dance with. I ducked and dodged until the
door was only feet away. I felt a pinch on my behind so hard it
made me almost topple in my heels. I whirled around to see Joy
standing in the shadows of the crowd, smiling.

"I couldn't pass up an opportunity to see you!" she yelled
over the music.

"I'll talk to you in just a second. I've gotta handle this." I
pointed a thumb behind me at the black door Becka had escaped
inside. Three months had changed her. She looked even *better* than
before. The movie money must have helped her out. I opened the
black door and closed Joy out on the other side, with a look of
defeat spread across her face. My heart was beating way too fast for
a walk across the club. I knew people would come out to this event
but I wasn't expecting to see Joy after not talking to her for
months. Maybe she had found some peace and calmed down. If so,
maybe we could rekindle some things… I did miss her. But only a
little.

Inside the black door was a long hallway with doors
alternating on each side. The music was muted and I could hear
talking in an office toward the end. I found the door and knocked
softly.

"Come in!" a male voice sang, so I opened the door and
stepped in.

An obese, sweaty-faced man sat behind a table that looked
too small to hide his overlapping gut. His cheeks were rosy and
inflamed, which made me check the temperature in the room. He
looked like he was about to overheat even though the room was
cool enough to make my skin prickle.

"Nicole Bunn! How ya doin', girl?" He held his hands up
from behind the desk as if he was getting arrested. Someone
needed to arrest him for those nasty pit stains.

"In the flesh," I said easily. Becka was standing in the corner, back turned, speaking softly into her earpiece. She didn't acknowledge my entrance like Big Bubba had.

"Oh, I'm so rude. I'm Egg. This is my club." He held out his hand but didn't attempt to stand. I didn't want to wait to see that happen anyway. I shook his hand firmly.

"Nice to meet you…Egg?"

He smiled. "They used to call me Egghead back in the day, on account of me being so smart. Now they just call me Egg…because, well, you can see why." He widened his arms and looked down at his layers of fat, unashamed.

"Well, Egg, I was under the impression that there was a problem with the money." I glanced at Becka, who turned for only a second to smirk at Egg then continued her conversation.

"Ohh, it's no problem, Miss Bunn. We just have to subtract what we were paying to see Webby."

"And how much is that?"

"Well, hell, almost all of it!" He chuckled. "But I left you a little extra on there because you are just…a little peach," he said in his Southern drawl. His face beaded with sweat as he looked up and down my body.

"Well, how much does that leave…exactly? I'm not here to play games, Egg."

"Aren't you a feisty one? I like that." His gap-toothed smile looked like he was missing a few teeth.

Egg wrestled into his desk drawer and pulled out a stack of hundreds. I smiled at the sight of the stack. That'd be more than enough! But before I could start counting the money in my mind, Egg slid out two bills and put them on the desk.

"There you go, sweetie."

"I thought you said you gave me a little extra? That ain't enough to buy a bottle of Moët in VIP. We agreed to $1,500 for the night. I should at least get half," I reasoned.

Egg looked over to Becka and jutted his double chin toward the door. She rolled her eyes at me before exiting the office. Egg jiggled as he scooted his chair back to replace the money in his top drawer.

"That rate was for you and Webby. People want to see Webby, darlin'. Now don't get me wrong, you are quite a sight for sore eyes…but people are going to be pissed with me if I don't deliver Webby tonight." He strained to keep his eyes on my face. If I wasn't in a full bodysuit, I'd think his laser vision would burn my skin to a crispy black.

I couldn't go back home and admit to Webby that I'd made only a fraction of the money because he wasn't there.

"How can we work this out? I want that $1,500."

Egg licked his lips and dug into the top drawer. He pulled off six more bills and placed them on the desk.

"Whatcha feel about showing me a little friendliness for half the money?" He laid his pudgy hand on the bills before saying, "I'd like to see what you got under that nice little bodysuit. Mmm-hmm…I bet it's as clean as the driven snow."

My stomach lurched at the sight of Egg but I wanted the money. I didn't care about getting naked for this old-ass nasty pervert for $800. Hell, some strippers didn't make that in a night and I didn't even have to dance. I unzipped the bodysuit and pulled my arms from the top as I peeled it down past my torso.

"Go slow," he commanded. His eyes never left my perky nipples.

I wiggled my hips from the spandex-like material and slid it down past my thighs to my knees. What a bright idea not to wear panties, I thought to myself. I kept my eyes on the floor as I heard small, guttural moans from Egg. I kicked off my black heels and stepped out of the bodysuit without effort. I stood stark naked in front of Egg as he worked his hand below the table, face sweating profusely.

"Turn around and bend over," he said with a gurgle in his rushed breathing.

"That wasn't part of the deal…"

"Just do it! Or you get nothing," he said desperately.

I turned to the black door, wondering why I was in this situation. Why was I letting this pig of a man visually rape me? Then I remembered the money under his sweaty palm and the feeling I'd have when I told Webby that I'd done something without him, that I, too, was wanted by people. With that in mind, I touched my toes and spread open my goodness for Egg to enjoy. It took only five minutes for his guttural moans to grow louder and the sound of his spasms to fill the silent room. I dressed in enough time to see that Egg had expended all his energy and fallen into an exhausted state, nearly asleep. I grabbed the $800 and looked behind the desk for any bills I may have missed. Unfortunately, the mess he'd made beneath the desk was not what I planned to see but the desk drawer was slightly ajar against his heaving belly. I stuck a finger into the drawer and felt for any additional bills, grabbing three on the first try. I stuck them into my bra for safekeeping. Egg snorted loudly, startling me back toward the door. I wasn't going to be greedy—$1,000 was good enough. I hightailed it out of Egg's office and back into the crowded club. The music thumped against my head as I made my way toward the back parking lot. I'd earned my money for the night, so I wasn't staying a second longer.

"Hey, stranger!" Joy must've been waiting by the door because she caught me in midstride.

"Oh. Hey, Joy. I really can't talk right now."

"So you're blowing me off again? Is that it?" She squinted her eyes in the darkness of the club.

"I'm not blowing you off. It's just a bad time. I need to get outta here." I glanced back toward the black door, hoping I wouldn't see Egg pointing security in my direction.

"What happened? You need me to do anything?" Joy seemed concerned.

"No. I'll handle it. I don't need your help."

"You needed me before," Joy said smartly.

"I'm not going into this with you. I don't have the time or the patience to hear your damn mouth." I was truly getting sick of this chick. She was like a damn gnat that wouldn't go away, no matter how many times you swatted at it.

"You're going to get enough of using people one day. I promise you that!" Joy stormed off toward the exit.

I placed a palm to my head and felt beads of sweat. I needed to do a line to deal with this shit. I backtracked to the bathroom and sat in an empty stall. I searched in my bra for the small packet of powder next to the wad of cash from Egg. I dipped a pinky nail into the sack and snorted a dip in each nostril. When I opened my eyes, Toni was standing there, mouth agape.

"What the fuck are you doing?!" Toni snapped.

"What the fuck are you doing in the women's bathroom? You got your shit nipped and tucked already?" I giggled. I was feeling a whole lot better already.

"Real funny, Nicole. What are you doing with that shit?"

"I thought my momma and daddy died a long time ago," I said sarcastically.

"Don't give me that. You're fucked up. You need someone to look after you when you doing cocaine, Nicole. This ain't you. Did Webby get you on this shit?"

"Webby, Webby, Webby. Everyone wants to know about motherfuckin' Webby," I whined. "Toni, give me some damn space…puh-leeze!" I shoved past Toni, headed toward the door. "I'm getting out of here. I'm going home."

"No you don't. You ain't driving like that. Give me your keys." He pushed his arm across the door, blocking my path. If he wasn't so angry I would've pushed past his scrawny ass.

I felt up and down my sides and shrugged my shoulders. "Left them in the car."

"I can't believe this, Nicole. Come on. Let's go." He laced his arm with mine and led me through the crowd until we reached the VIP exit. My car was sitting on four flat tires when the club door slammed shut behind us. Glass from the floodlight above my car was sprinkled on the ground near the deflated tires. Someone had knifed my wheels while I was inside the club.

"Oh shit!" Toni said at the sight of the tires.

"What the hell…" I ran around the car and found a long scratch mark on the passenger side of my cherry-red BMW that only stopped at the rear wheel well. It was clearly scratched out of sheer anger because white powder plunged from the deep, thin scratch.

"Who would do this?" Toni questioned.

I choked back the urge to scream the answer. My insides raged as I stared at the damage to my beautiful BMW. I already knew whose name was written all over this because it was easy to read in the passenger-side door...Joy.

∞

The Crash

∞

Mali

∞

April was a whirlwind of interviews with the media, photo shoots and radio station appointments for Justice. Being drafted to the Minnesota Vikings at the top of the second round was an amazing feat, yet I hadn't been able to see my boyfriend in nearly ten days since the news hit. Atlanta was buzzing with the new draft players on the radio, on television and at nightclubs. Big Deuce had also managed to get picked up by the New England Patriots, so he was MIA for the past week with Justice. Since my breakdown in the Gladys Knights parking lot, my relationship with Justice had certainly picked up. I finally felt like I was a part of a positive, healthy relationship. I was still working on quieting my father's demeaning voice in my head every time I attempted something new but I could feel myself getting stronger with Justice's help.

The dorm felt cluttered with mine and Carey's ball gowns, shoes and piles of makeup kits on the beds. Tonight was a black-tie gala at Dunkin Studios celebrating a new movie release. So we were lucky to have Carey's mother, Marney, in town to help pick beautiful gowns since neither of us had gone to the prom in high school and had absolutely horrible taste in formal wear. Marney and Carey were rifling through the closets, bickering back and forth about the mess as I lounged on my bed picking through the makeup bag Marney had brought with her. Having Marney in the room was comforting but the look on Carey's face told a very different story about her mom's visit. I grabbed my cell phone and walked out into the floor's study area since the bickering was rising steadily. I didn't feel like refereeing a fight.

Seeing Marney made me miss my mother. I hadn't spoken to her in nearly a month. I'd tried my best to not spoil the good things happening for me in the present by living in the past with her. Even though she could suck the life out of an angel with her solemn attitude, she was my mother and I missed her. I dialed home and waited for her to pick up.

"Hello." It was my father.

"Hey, Dad." I tried to sound lighthearted but it just came off sounding scared.

"Mali?"

"Yes, sir. It's me."

"Oh…guess you wanna speak with your mother," he said matter-of-factly.

"How are you doing, Dad?" I blurted before he could hand the phone to my mother. The phone line was silent for far too long. I was beginning to think he'd left the phone on the kitchen table and walked off.

"I'm doing better. Going to some classes. They helping me stop drinking so much." He actually sounded more sober than I'd heard in years.

"That's good news." I tried to sound enthusiastic but I'd heard it before, "How's Mom doing?"

"She's doing okay. Got the garden growing better than I seen in months. She's pulling some tomatoes right now, as we speak." I smiled absently. I'd never talked to my dad this long before, in person or otherwise.

"Well, I just wanted to call and tell Mom…and you," I tried to force the words, "that I miss you and I love you guys…no matter what's happened in the past."

I could hear a deep hum in my dad's throat. It was his way of trying to find the right words to say back. Words I'd never heard from his lips.

"Well, okay. I'll tell her. You take care of yourself," he said quickly.

The dial tone rang in my ear as a reminder that sometimes a big triumph is worth a little setback. I was proud of my dad for trying, even though he had a long way to go—but change was in the air. I smiled to myself as I tapped the End button on my cell and walked back into the dorm to brave Hurricane Marney.

"Mali, there you are!" Marney clapped her hands together as if in prayer.

"Uggghhh," Carey groaned in response.

"Oh stop it, Carey. Jeez-us Lawd ole' Mighty, we don't have much time to get you all dressed up and ready to go! Justice will be here in…" she eyed her wristwatch, "…two hours and twelve minutes. That's not enough time to transform you and Carey both. We gotta get scootin', ladies!"

Marney whipped around the room for the next two hours juggling between flawlessly sweeping on my makeup and tucking and pulling Carey's hind parts into a fitted, beaded gown. Ten minutes before we were scheduled to meet Justice downstairs, we stood in the middle of our room like statues, staring at each other's transformations from college freshmen to beautiful women. After all the sass we took from Marney, there was no doubt in my mind that we'd called the right one to help us. Carey looked gorgeous in an emerald gown that clung to the floor even with her wearing four-inch strappy gold sandals. She teetered a bit in the high heels as she stared at herself in the full-length mirror with a smile on her red lips. Carey had opted to wear contacts for the first time this year and I could see that she was a classic beauty behind those clunky black glasses all along. She swept a tear from her eye and dove over her mother's shoulder for a hug.

"Thank you, Momma," she murmured into her neck.

"You're welcome, my sweet baby. You girls go have fun tonight," Marney said, a tear forcing its way down her rosy, plump cheeks.

I picked up the bottom edge to my long red dress and kissed Marney on the cheek in thanks. She nodded as we closed the door behind us and *click-clacked* all the way to the elevator and out into the parking lot.

Justice and Big Deuce were standing outside a glossy black limousine in debonair tuxedos that were tailored to perfection. Big Deuce was the first to give a reaction to Carey's transformation.

"Are you Carey?" he said incredulously.

"Yes. I was the one you spoke with on the phone, remember?"

"Yeah. I remember. I saw you at the welcome party too! I thought you wore glasses, though." Big Deuce strained to remember, then gave up. "If I would have known you were this beautiful, I would have stopped by a long time ago!" Justice elbowed Big Deuce as we all laughed at his apparent amazement that a bookworm could turn into a beautiful butterfly.

"You look absolutely gorgeous, baby." Justice hugged me tightly and planted a quick kiss on my lips. I wished it would have lasted longer but I squeezed his hand in mine to let him know I'd missed seeing him the past week. We packed into the limousine and started the trip to Dunkin Studios. Carey and Big Deuce talked softly at the other end of the limousine. Their laughter rang out across the limo as they joked together.

Justice broke the silence. "I want to congratulate you on your first video. I saw it while I was waiting for the Hot 107.9 interview. It looked amazing! Keep pushing even higher, baby." He leaned in and kissed me so sweetly. Webby's video had been released almost three weeks ago for his single and it was the number two rated video on MTV and number one on BET.

"It's been a long process getting here but you know that. I would have never guessed when I moved to Atlanta that I'd meet you and have all these great things happen for me."

"You earned everything yourself. I didn't do anything but distract you."

"If you call making me the happiest woman alive, then yeah, you're a major distraction." I giggled.

"You do realize that I can't tell anyone I met my girlfriend in dance class, right?" Justice laughed. "But seriously, I'm proud of you."

"And that's coming from an NFL superstar. I feel so…so…privileged," I joked.

"I'm not a superstar until I actually play a game in the NFL…but until then, you can just call me 'The King.'" We laughed loudly.

"You know what I never understood?" Big Deuce said once the car grew silent from our laughter.

"I'm sure there's a lot you don't understand, Deuce. Try to narrow it down for us, bro." Justice smirked.

Big Deuce turned to Carey. "When I called you that night to ask you about Mali. Why did you tell me where she was going on the date? You didn't have to tell me anything."

Carey blushed. "I wanted you to go after her. I knew how she felt about Justice."

"I'm sure that's not the only reason," I blurted before I could stop myself.

Carey rolled her eyes. "And I didn't want her dating my brother, either. It was a win-win situation for me."

"Your brother? You gotta be joking! That was *your* brother?" Justice pointed.

"Yes. It was her brother. Why is that so hard to believe?" I questioned.

"Because he was so...so...strange. You know, with the hair and the silence. It was kinda creepy," Justice said.

"Trust me, I'm a little strange too." Carey wiggled her fingers at Justice like she was going to tickle him.

We all laughed at her silly antics until Big Deuce interrupted again.

"So how's your brother doing after everything? I mean, he did lose Mali to Justice."

"You know, I don't think he ever thought Mali was going to be with him anyway," Carey offered.

"We're still friends," I said as we pulled into the crammed parking lot outside Dunkin Studios. We all peered at the chaos out the tinted windows.

"Here we go!" Deuce said as he eyed the paparazzi lining the red carpet, snapping pictures at the actors.

We filed out of the limo, one by one, and headed down the red carpet. The paparazzi yelled Justice's name as we posed. Big Deuce had his turn as he gripped Carey's small frame next to him. The black-tie gala was actually a viewing party for Will Dunkin's feature film *Crazy Dirty Love*. It was set to air on Lifetime network next week. During the event, he'd promised to play Webby's new single and video on the big screen since he'd be at the gala tonight. That would give me an opportunity to network with some of the bigwigs in the building. We finished our photo ops on the red carpet just in time to catch Will shaking hands with his lead actor. I tapped Will on his shoulder to get his attention.

"Mali! I'm so glad you could make it!" He clapped his heavy hand on my back in a stiff hug. Justice shook his hand firmly.

"This is my boyfriend, Justice Bradford."

"How could I not know who this is? Every man that watches football and loves the state of Georgia knows this guy like he was their own son!" Justice smiled at his appraisal.

"I also brought some friends with me." I turned to introduce Deuce and Carey but they had already walked off, mingling in the crowd together.

"No worries. I want you guys to relax, have a good time and enjoy the movie," Will stated. "Oh! Mali, I have a bit of good news for you but maybe I should let Webby tell you himself?"

I felt Justice's hand clench tightly on mine but I loosened his grasp and answered, "Well, you can tell me now and I'll act surprised later."

Will glanced at Justice for a few seconds too long and then said, "Webby wants to take the choreography team and dancers on tour with him in June. He just signed the contract this morning. Congratulations!"

The excitement suffocated me. I was going to travel with one of the leading rap artists, choreograph his entire tour and get paid to do it? My skin was tingling with the thought of doing something so big. I couldn't help but hug Will. Before I could release Will from the hug, Justice walked off with a sigh.

"You might want to go talk to him. I think he's upset," Will said.

"No. He's not upset," I told Will while searching for Justice in the crowd. "I'll talk with you later. Thanks again."

I bobbed and weaved through the crowd of moviegoers, hoping to catch sight of Justice. I spotted Big Deuce and Carey near the middle row of chairs facing the screen.

"You guys seen Justice?"

"Yeah, I think he's over at the bar." Carey pointed toward the brightly lit bar with rows upon rows of liquor lined up in front of a mirrored tile wall. I scanned the bar and found Justice sitting on a stool near the corner.

"Why'd you leave like that?" I said as I pulled out a seat next to Justice.

"He said you were going on tour with Webby. I don't think that's a good idea."

"What do you mean it's not a good idea? You were the one who told me to keep pushing higher. This is higher!" I whispered loudly. I didn't want to cause a scene.

"A tour can take months, Mali. Don't you get that? I will be in Minnesota training. Then when the season starts, I'll be traveling nonstop. And what about school? You've worked too hard to throw away your education."

The realization hit me. If I went on tour, I wouldn't see Justice or work with Mrs. Della-Rose. There had to be a way to make it work.

"Maybe I could fly to see you between tours? Or you could fly to see me? I can take online classes for school. I won't drop out. We can make it work if we both try."

"This is how it starts. You give up everything for stardom." Justice's face showed his concern.

"It's not for stardom. It's for my dream of being a dancer. And I'm living my dream right now with you," I assured him.

"Do you even know this guy Webby? Do you know what kind of guy he is?"

"I've worked with him on the video shoots. He seems alright. Why does that matter, anyway?"

Justice rested his chin on his clasped hands and stared across the bar at nothing in particular.

"Justice, tell me what's going on. You're acting weird all of a sudden. No secrets, remember?"

He closed his eyes briefly, then said, "My ex-girlfriend cheated on me with Webby. She was a dancer in one of his videos. He stole her from me. He bought her gifts, wined and dined her. He did the things I couldn't do for her."

The pain in his voice was evident. I couldn't believe all this time he'd hid the fact that she'd cheated on him.

"Why didn't you tell me that before?"

"It hurts to think about, let alone talk about. She was the only girl I'd ever loved and I trusted her. It took me a while to get over it." His eyes were intense as he stared into mine. "So can you understand why I don't want you going away with that guy?"

"Justice, I'm not your ex-girlfriend. I'd never betray you like that." I wanted to make the hurt go away but I could see that it was deeply embedded in him. Only time could heal his wound.

"I know. But it doesn't make trusting him any easier. What's stopping him from setting his sights on you? Making you fall in love with him?"

"You don't have to trust him as long as you trust me. I would never..." I grabbed his hands, "...never do that to you. I love you too much."

Justice leaned across the bar and kissed me until my legs felt like limp noodles hanging from the bar stool. He looked at me deeply, searching my soul for the truth. I begged him with my eyes to believe me, trust me. When he'd looked long and hard enough, he kissed my forehead and helped me from the stool.

"You're an angel," he whispered in my ear as we joined Deuce and Carey at our seats for appetizers and refreshments.

The movie, *Crazy Dirty Love*, was set to start in less than thirty minutes. Well-dressed guests shuffled about hurriedly trying to secure food and drink before the lights went dark. As we chatted with Deuce and Carey over miniature chicken wraps, the big screen sprang to life with a large white print on a black background, introducing Webby's new single and the video we'd worked for weeks to choreograph. I looked at Justice, smiling slightly, as he watched the video. I could tell the sight of Webby was nagging him but he plastered a weak smile across his lips and left it there for the remainder of the music video.

Justice

∞

In life, a person comes to a point when they have to face their own ugly truths. Sitting here, at this viewing party full of snobbish industry women strutting around in fur wraps, and men flashing their German car fobs, I glanced to my left and saw Mali sitting next to me. I realized she is not jaded by their shiny lives in the least. Her eyes don't shimmer against their rose-gold watches and diamond necklaces. In fact, she is more interested in Deuce and Carey's newfound friendship than anything else going on in the party.

My truth was realizing that I'd found a way to love again after Nicole. I was living reckless, trying to hide my broken heart between the legs of women who only cared whether they could have sex with a ball player. Luckily, Mali helped pull me from the self-destruction that was bound to make me lose it all. Even a month ago, I wouldn't have guessed that I'd be in another relationship—definitely not a healthy relationship. I'd grown used to the fighting, the arguing and the emotional control with Nicole. So much so, that I began to believe that was the way it was supposed to be. But being with Mali was different. She talks to me about what bothers her, doesn't berate me about my shortcomings and accepts my decisions without confrontation. I smiled at Mali as she threw back her curly hair and laughed loudly at Deuce's joke. She was an incredible young woman.

"You alright, man?" Big Deuce questioned. I was the only one who didn't laugh at his joke.

"Yeah, I'm great." I smiled sincerely at Mali.

"Got something on ya mind?" As Deuce asked, Carey and Mali stopped giggling and looked in my direction.

"I always have a lot on my mind…unlike you, bro." With that, the mood was light again and we laughed together effortlessly.

I couldn't admit that I was still struggling with Mali's news. I swallowed the uneasy feeling of Mali going on tour with Webby, of all people, and smiled at my group of friends, some old and some new. Carey had her arm clasped around Deuce's big bicep as she leaned into him like a schoolgirl who'd found a new best friend. Mali was cross-legged and radiant in the amber glow of the room.

"Mali Struthers! Congratulations!" a voice boomed behind us. The hair stood up on the back of my neck as Webby swooped down to plant a kiss on Mali's cheek.

"Hey, man." I stood up as my full height made me look more menacing.

"JB? Oh damn, it's Justice-motherfuckin'- Bradford!" Webby grabbed my hand and pulled me in for a hug. "I can't believe you're here, man. I watched you in the Hawai'i Bowl. You were killing the game!"

I hadn't realized that Big Deuce had moved in close behind me until I could feel his breath on my neck as he said, "Yo. You can't be kissing up on my boy's girlfriend like that. I don't care who you are." Big Deuce inched up closer until I could hear his heightened breathing.

"Mali Struthers is your girlfriend? My bad, I didn't even know. No harm, no foul. I ain't trying to disrespect the greatest to come out of Georgia." Webby raised his hands mockingly in defense.

"Alright then." Deuce turned away slowly toward Carey and whispered, "Punk-ass motherfucker."

"Justice, you got a good catch right there." Webby pointed down at Mali, who had shifted uncomfortably in her seat. "She's one of the hardest-working women that I've seen in the industry. She is all work and no play."

"I know how she is. That's why I'm with her," I said with more edge than I intended.

"Look, JB, let me tell you something. I've been arguing with all my boys about the draft. I told them you are one of the greatest players to come from Atlanta University. I think Philadelphia should have picked you up, though, since they need a good receiver. They lost Simeon to an injury last season. Minnesota is cool but their coach is still trying to figure out his offensive strategy. It doesn't matter, though, because you're pretty much the best the league has to offer for wide receivers."

"You watch my games, huh?" I couldn't believe this motherfucker had the audacity to talk to me right now. Was he trying to be funny or something?

"Of course, dog. I went to AU for two years before my music took off. So AU is kinda close to my heart, know what I'm saying?"

"I feel the same way. Sad to leave AU but I gotta go make this money." I couldn't help but gloat. I was entitled to a minor amount of gloating since the guy stole my damn girlfriend.

"Look, I have some really lucrative projects with my label right now. Plus, I own an advertising firm that could really help you make some money in these streets. I ain't make all these millions from music alone. I like to skim my money off the front and back end, know what I'm saying?" His dark face exposed bright white teeth as he grinned. "It's called diversifying, my friend. I want to make sure you diversify too…one AU classmate helping out another."

"I think my management team has some stuff in the works already but good looking out. I'm all about my money." I glanced at Mali, who looked confused. "And my family."

"Oh, for sure. I'm all about people who down for me. You know you have to keep your house clean if you expect not to find roaches and rodents dwelling with you. I've been in this game for a long time so I've seen them all. See, you're just starting out but I can assure you that you will run into some trifling-ass people who act like they got your back, then flip it on you." Webby looked around the studio, searching for something or someone.

"Preach!" Big Deuce said loudly as Carey tried to shush him.

"Oh, there she is. Baby!" Webby yelled across the crowd and raised his glass to catch the attention of someone. I glanced down at Mali as she shrugged her shoulders at my unsaid question. Why was Webby acting like he didn't know what he did to me?

Before I could think of the answer, Nicole weaved through the crowd and planted a kiss on Webby's lips so juicy, everyone heard the *smack* of their lips. I buried the urge to grab both of their necks and head-butt them into each other. Nicole had on a skintight black cocktail dress and tall heels. She'd lost a bit of weight and her face had grown gaunt over the past few months. She didn't look as good as she used to. Thank God for small favors.

"Justice Bradford, right?" Nicole said easily and stuck her hand out. I didn't take it. Instead, I reached down and helped Mali from her seat.

"I'm Mali, Justice's girlfriend. This is Deuce and Carey. Nice to meet you…"

"Nicole," she said. "Nicole Bunn. I'm sure you've heard of me since you know Will, apparently."

"Actually, I haven't. Did you used to work here?" Mali retorted with poise.

Nicole rolled her eyes, trying to feign exhaustion. "Yes. I worked for Will as a dancer. I was the lead chick on most videos for the last three years." She smiled smartly, obviously proud of her accomplishment.

"Oh! You know what, I do remember you. I didn't recognize your face since all your shots were mostly from the back." Mali flashed a sarcastic smile.

"What the hell did she say to me?" Nicole fumed but Webby put a hand across her chest as if to hold her back.

"If you ever want to try out for a dancing spot again, look me up. I'm sure I could teach you my choreography in a few hours," Mali offered.

"Your choreography?"

"Babe, she's the new lead choreographer for Will and she's working on my tour. I told you that already," Webby interjected.

"Well, you need to keep the help in line," Nicole spat, rolling her neck with attitude. Her eyes looked dazed as her focus shifted from me to Mali and back again.

"Don't be disrespectful to my business associates." Webby pointed in Nicole's face like she was a child being scolded by a parent. "I won't keep telling you to play your role. I make the money and you spend the money, right? So stand there and look pretty while I get this money. Better yet, go get me another drink."

"You ain't gotta…" Nicole was irate as Mali winked at her before she turned to walk away. Nicole stormed off toward the bar, heels clacking loudly against the concrete flooring. Mali scooted over to talk with Deuce and Carey, most likely about the reunion that was transpiring right before their very eyes.

"I'm sorry about her behavior." Webby chuckled as he leaned toward me to whisper, "Women. They ain't good for nothing but some pussy and spending all my damn money."

I shook my head. I guess Nicole got exactly what she wanted…a man with money.

"The movie is about to start soon. Let me go check on my friends. It was…interesting…talking with you," I said, feeling light as a feather. Justice had been served…no pun intended.

"No problem. Hey, here's my card. I'm serious about those endorsements. We can get this money together. Remember that." He pushed the card into my hand and sauntered off into the crowd, shaking hands as he moved through without difficulty.

After meeting Webby for the first time, my mind was swimming with confusion. Clearly, Nicole had never told him I was her ex, which meant she probably never told him she was even in a relationship. All this time, I was blaming Webby for going after Nicole and stealing her from me while unbeknownst to both Webby and me, it was all part of Nicole's plan to get rich quick. I erased the thought from my mind. Nicole was old news now. I was going to enjoy tonight and support Mali's opportunities. I saw Deuce, Carey and Mali laughing at the cocktail table near our seating section and made my way over.

"Can you believe what just happened?" I said, kissing Mali on her neck.

"That was ridiculous!" Carey said quickly.

"No. That was worse than ridiculous…that was downright ludicrous!" Deuce added.

"How could you date someone like that? She is so different than what I expected," Mali offered.

"Trust me, she's different than what I expected too." I laughed as everyone joined in.

"Why did she act like she didn't even know you?" Carey asked through furrowed brows.

"Isn't it obvious why she did that? She's been lying to Webby the same way she was lying to Justice. Dude, if she wasn't the female that hurt my best friend…I'd have to give her props for running game like a pro," Deuce proclaimed.

"Don't admire her. She looks like she's on something…" Carey mused.

"That poor guy doesn't even know what he's in for with her. I would warn him if he wasn't such a dick." I shook my head.

"He'll get what he deserves. He wasn't exactly a knight in shining armor. You saw how he talked to her?" Mali pointed out to Carey.

"I know! I would have popped him in his lip if he would've talked to me like that!" Carey admitted.

"Oh really? You must think you're a pint-sized gladiator or something?" Deuce smiled and pinched Carey's side to make her giggle.

"How could someone be in a relationship like that?" Mali said.

The group fell silent as everyone stared at me, waiting for an answer because I was, indeed, the only one who had been in a relationship *like that*. The question stung me. I didn't really know why I'd been in a relationship with Nicole for so long. I realized after being with Mali that I wasn't really happy at all. I was just keeping the peace, working double time to make someone love me, who wasn't capable of loving anyone but herself. So why did I stay? Was it selfishness? Maybe I didn't want anyone else to have Nicole even though I really didn't want to be with her? Was it status? Maybe I was exactly like Webby. Maybe I only wanted her as a trophy, an object to conquer. Or was it the comfort and stability that kept me there? I struggled to answer Mali's question. I couldn't definitively say exactly why I had stayed with Nicole's crazy ass for so long. Hell, maybe I was a little crazy too.

After much thought, the truth was the only thing I could say. "I don't know. I don't know why I stayed in a relationship like that."

"I know why you stayed, bro." Deuce hugged Carey under his arm and rocked her gently. "You stayed because you are a loyal type of guy. Plain and simple. You told me numerous times you were going to make sure you took care of her because she sacrificed her dream for you. In all the years I've known you, you never once told me that you were in love with her. You just always stick to your word."

Deuce was right. I had felt obligated to stay with Nicole because she squandered her chance to be at NYU to be with me. I'd made it my duty to never let her regret that decision.

"You know, you're right, Deuce. He is extremely loyal," Mali said. "But Nicole is manipulative. She probably knew you were that way and used it to her advantage."

"Oh yeah! Look at it from her perspective…she can go to NYU and work hard to achieve her own goals. Or she can follow you to AU, guilt-trip you until you get to the NFL and be taken care of for the rest of her life! You see, she never wanted to work.

She saw the JB meal ticket a long time ago. I'm just surprised she's not pregnant yet," Carey explained.

"Damn, that would mean she was plotting all this since high school. That's a long damn time to keep up a charade." Deuce's face looked serious as he pondered the possible extent of Nicole's manipulation.

"When a woman has a plan…" Carey pointed across the table to Mali, who nodded her head in agreement.

The conversation had my mind running in circles, remembering talks Nicole and I had in high school. Remembering how she told me that night in the shed that she was coming with me. Remembered how she always made up with me so conveniently after arguments. The realization of her lack of attending classes at AU as the draft drew nearer. She had been keeping me on a leash like a puppy, guiding me toward the future she wanted for herself. I felt embarrassed at the thought of being used and discarded like a pair of her old stilettos.

But there was still something I didn't understand, just didn't make any sense.

"So after all that work, why would she abandon it? Why wouldn't she just keep playing the game until after the draft? She would have gotten everything in a couple months," I said hurriedly. My confusion was turning to anger at being so damn stupid for Nicole.

Carey and Mali looked around the studio, noticing a crowd of onlookers that had stopped sipping their drinks to stare at us. The viewing party was quieting down, preparing for the start of the movie, and more than a few people were taking notice of our conversation.

"Let's go sit down. We're causing a scene." Mali gripped my hand and led me to our seats. Deuce saddled into the seat next to me with Carey on his right.

"I know you don't want to hear this. But maybe she found someone with more money, more opportunity…an easier mark, so to speak," Mali whispered.

My voice caught in my throat. I had realized a lot of things about Nicole since we broke up but never had I imagined that I was a *mark*, someone to use and abuse at will. All the love she had confessed to me was a lie, a way to keep her plan in motion. Wiping the pain from my face, I stared into the crowded studio, not focusing on anything but the aching feeling pitted in the core of my chest. Seeing things a little clearer, everyone was right about her. My mother, Big Deuce and even Mali had figured out something that took me years to see. My pride was doing backflips in my chest, trying to kick its way out. I may not have known much but I knew that karma was a bitch and so was Nicole.

Nicole

∞

Who the hell did that nappy-headed girl think she was? How dare she come at me, flipping her curls and rolling her eyes like I wasn't the one that paved the way for dumb bitches like her. No damn respect in this industry! I couldn't put my finger on it but I felt like I'd seen her somewhere before. Oh well, who cares? I crashed back another vodka tonic to take the edge off and slid the glass back onto the bar top. The bartender nodded his approval and poured a second one without asking. I flashed him an appreciative smile and tossed back the second glass, just as quick as the first. I was starting to feel a little buzz now. My high was wearing off from earlier and meeting with Justice and his new skinny-ass girlfriend got me all worked up. I patted the sweat from my armpits with a bar napkin and scanned the room for Webby. Was it me or was it like a sauna up in this warehouse? Where did Webby slither off to? I had a bone to pick with him after treating me like some throwaway ho in front of Justice and his snobby-ass girlfriend. Yeah, I definitely needed to tell him a thing or two.

Will patted my shoulder and leaned in to my ear. "You okay, Nicole? You don't look so good."

"I'm doing fine. Just looking for Webby. I need to talk to him." I tried to hide my agitation. I knew I was looking good in my tight black dress. What the hell was he talking about? He had eyes, didn't he?

"Last I saw, Webby was talking to Bobby and Toni over there." He pointed across the crowd but I couldn't see Webby in the distance.

"You know what? I'm glad you came over." I tapped the bar for another drink. "Who is this girl, Mali? Why didn't you tell me you were hiring for lead choreographer?"

Will straightened his shirt and fiddled with his bow tie. "We had auditions like we always do. You didn't show up, remember? You were traveling with Webby and not answering my phone calls."

I blushed. "Oh. That's right."

"Anyway, she's doing an excellent job. Did you meet her yet?"

"Mmm-hmm…I met her." I rolled my eyes.

"Well, if you ever feel like dancing again, you know you can call me and I'll get you back on line."

"I ain't working for that girl. That's Justice's new girlfriend! You know that, right?"

"So you found out, huh? I didn't know until tonight but I figured you'd handle it alright if you didn't know already." He paused, then said quietly, "Are you handling it alright?"

"Look at me." I stretched out my arms and spun on my heels, almost tripping on the bar stool but catching myself on the edge of bar. "See? I'm doing just grrrreat!"

Will looked past my fake smile and said, "Nicole, I'm your friend, so take my advice. Get your act together. You look like you're losing weight. You're not looking like you used to."

"Fuck you, Will." I didn't have time for him to lecture me because I lost a little weight. The same actress he hired for the movie was as thin as a light pole, yet he wasn't pulling on her shoulder trying to have a damn intervention.

"Nicole…" Will grabbed my arm and I pulled away. I reached for the drink that had been sitting on the bar throughout our little talk, raised it high as I saluted Will with a wave and walked off in the direction he'd pointed out earlier. I was through with Will but I still had business with Webby to take care of.

I eyed Justice whispering to his girlfriend near the large screen showing Webby's video shoot as the announcer stated, "The show will begin in fifteen minutes. Please find your seats. Thank you."

Droves of people puttered around trying to find their reserved seats without spilling their liquor. I stumbled amongst them, finding it difficult to sip from my glass while walking. Before I could cross the studio toward Webby, Joy stepped in front of me, blocking my path.

"Hello, Nicole."

If she didn't look stunning in her white silk gown that showed her bare nipples through the thin fabric, I would have pushed her out of my way. Instead, I stopped cold in my tracks. Her face was made to look like a '40s starlet with red lips and smoky eyes while her hair flowed around her face in deep waves. Suddenly, I felt really underdressed in my black cocktail dress.

"Joy." I composed myself coolly.

"Can I talk to you for a second?"

"Well, I'm in the middle of…" I looked over her shoulder and spotted Webby talking to Toni and Bobby as Will had told me moments ago.

"It'll just take a minute. It's very important." Her face was like stone as a smile forced through.

"Fine. Let's go," I forced through gritted teeth. I was tired of everyone running me down to talk to me.

We walked through the crowded room and into a corridor leading to the studio's control room. As Joy pushed open the door, heat from the tall servers pushed out into the hallway. Lights blinked on six-feet-tall towers of equipment as six television screens showed the main room in the studio at different angles. The screens zoomed in on guests as they sat down for the presentation and, seconds later, blinked to a picture of the bar as the bartender poured drinks quickly and darted from spout to spout filling glasses at top speed. The control room was dark and stuffy yet two rolling chairs were slid neatly under the desk that held the security monitors. Joy grabbed my shoulder quickly and spun me to her face. She kissed me hard against the lips as if trying to suck the life from my body. Her lips felt safe and full of passion but I had to get out this hole I'd dug with her.

"What the hell are you doing?" I said as I pushed her backward into the large tower behind her. She bumped her elbow and rubbed it without tearing her eyes from mine.

"I'm doing what I've been trying to do since you pushed me away for…that lowlife out there. You think he's going to be hot forever? I know you, Nicole. I know what you want. The time we shared together, making love in Webby's shower, his bed, all over his house. You can't deny what we felt."

It was so hard to lie to her and I wanted to so badly but I said, "I won't stand here and lie to you and say I didn't feel something but I can't keep cheating on Webby with you. I've got to get this money."

"You're a lot like me in so many ways." She wiped her brow. "Hell, you are exactly like me, actually. You love your money. You get confused about where you want to be. You don't want to be abandoned. Hell, neither do I." A tear slid down her pale cheek. "You know you never once asked me about my parents or why I was stripping to go to college. You didn't care that my dad raped me for five years as my mother stood by and let it happen."

"I'm sorry. I didn't know." My heart ached for her.

"Can't you see? We were supposed to meet like we did. We both had horrible beginnings and followed similar paths to be exactly in this moment, right now…close enough to taste the success. Can't you see that I love you more than anyone I've ever known? We could conquer the world together. With my skills and your connections, we could start our own empire. You don't need Webby. Please, just give us a chance again." She reached for my hands and gripped them tightly. Her eyes glossed over with affection.

I held her soft hands, trying to swallow my feelings for the person who'd finally understood the depths of me.

"I believe we met for a reason, Joy. You know me better than anyone in this world, I think." My throat felt tight, my mouth dry, but I pressed on to the truth. "I love you too…but I can't give you what you want. I can't be with you."

"Why?" Her eyes begged for an answer that would make sense. Unfortunately, there wouldn't be one.

"I'm with Webby and I'm not gay."

Joy wiped the wetness from her face with her fingertips. "Webby is not the right one for you. He doesn't even care about you! He treats you like shit. Why would you settle for that when I'm offering you something real?"

Joy didn't want to hear what I was telling her as she hugged herself in the blue glow of the television screens. It wasn't based on my feelings for her because I did love her in my own way but I couldn't pass up a lavish life with Webby to start over struggling alongside her in this industry. It wasn't economically smart.

"He provides the lifestyle I want and I give him what he wants. It's a great deal. It's my choice and that's it."

"It's not supposed to be a deal, Nicole. It's love. Do you even love him? I know you don't."

"I don't need love to keep a roof over my head and clothes on my back," I reminded her.

"I could give you those same things! How can you use me like this? You tell me you care about me then toss me aside when you get money from MY movie deal? The same thing you're doing to Webby, you did to me!" Joy was steaming under her pretty facade.

"*Your* movie deal? You wouldn't have a movie deal without my contacts. So technically, I could say *you* used *me*!" I countered.

"I see you like to play hardball." Joy nodded to herself. "You think the world revolves around you. It's all about Nicole and Webby, huh? I wonder what Webby will think when he hears about your affair with me. Or even better, the fact that you lied about having a boyfriend just to get closer to Webby's money. You're lucky Justice is as mature as he is. He could've put your gold-digging ass on blast tonight. But guess what? I won't give you the same courtesy! I'm putting your dirty, coked-out ass on blast tonight. Nobody is going to want you after tonight." Joy inched close enough for me to feel her breath. "When Webby realizes you cut him out the movie deal so you could get all the money, you think he's going to stay with you? You'll be begging to be back with me then, won't you? Maybe he'd like a blow-by-blow account of how good you fucked me on his sheets and on his countertops before dinner?" Joy was raging as she pointed her finger to the tip of my nose.

Before I could stop myself, I smacked her cheek so hard it whipped her head back against the equipment tower. She gripped the back of her head in pain as she steadied herself from the blow.

"You can tell him what you want. He won't believe your lying ass anyway after I tell him you leaked his song! Just remember this…you don't want to fuck with me!"

I stormed from the control room, leaving Joy clutching her head in the dark. I breezed down the dim corridor, fixing my dress before turning the corner to the main room. I stood as still as a statue upon entering the viewing party. The entire room was staring at my entrance. A few people whispered to one another but no one tore their angry eyes from me. Some people looked sad, others shook their heads slowly. What was going on?

Will was the first person to step out of the crowd of gawking celebrities, models and random partygoers. His face was painted red as he grabbed both my shoulders and looked seriously into my eyes.

"We heard everything through the speaker system. You must've hit the button in the control room," he whispered.

"Oh God no…"

My heart dropped from my chest to my feet and heat rose from my tummy, making me feel queasy. If Will wasn't holding me up, I would have fainted in a heap on the floor. I scanned the faces of the surrounding judges and jury members disguised as industry execs and saw no friendly faces in the scowls looking back at me. I straightened against Will's grip and pulled my head high. I needed to maintain some semblance of dignity. Why did they care about Joy and me anyway? It's my life.

"Where's Webby?" I croaked to Will, who had pushed me into the corner near the hallway in an attempt to shield me.

"He left after hearing your conversation. I don't think he's in the talking mood to say the least. How could you do all those things, Nicole? You're on cocaine?" Will pressed.

"I don't know. I screwed up. I got caught up." My eyes glazed over. *Don't cry, dammit.*

I turned to see Joy ambling down the hall, fixing her hair over her shoulder, looking as if the fight never occurred. I couldn't believe I thought I loved her psychotic ass. Will followed my gaze and scowled.

"And you, how could you leak music from my studio? You're finished in this business. You can't be trusted!" Will's voice rose as he pointed at Joy, who had just stepped into the main room and into the glaring crowd.

"What the hell are you talking about? I didn't leak Webby's music." Joy flipped her head easily and scanned the crowd to find a face that believed her. There was none.

"You are a liar! We heard everything you said back there!" Will was furious at finally seeing the culprit who had put his company's security and integrity in jeopardy.

Joy giggled under her breath. "Don't be silly, Will."

"I will never do business with you and I recommend my colleagues here tonight take heed and erase you from their memories."

"So you're calling me a liar? Will, you've been lying to everyone for *decades*!" Joy's calm had dissolved and her eyes were wild and crazed as she stepped toward Will defiantly. "How about you tell everyone who your real girlfriend is? Or should I say…boyfriend! While all of y'all are judging me and Nicole…you working with the biggest homo in the business! Just ask Toni, who he spends his nights with! You like to keep your fuck buddy close, huh? Come on, tell us, are you throwing or catching?"

The crowd rumbled to life. I grabbed Will, holding him back as he struggled to get hold of Joy.

"Shut your damn mouth!" Will demanded, never turning to face his guests. "Get her out of my face!" Will pointed toward the door as security personnel slid between guests who had closed in around the spectacle.

"You're kicking *me* out? Have you lost your damn mind? This is my movie you're playing here tonight. You remember that!" Joy spat through gritted teeth as security grabbed her arms and escorted her through the crowd.

The murmur from the crowd grew loud as it breathed life into a building that, until a few moments ago, felt cold and dead. People whispered amongst each other about whether Will Dunkin was actually gay and was he fucking the flamboyantly gay, Toni. The murmurs continued. Did Webby get played again, this time by his new gold-digging girlfriend, Nicole? Some were heard whispering about Justice being lucky to have gotten me out of his life while he had the chance. That he was lucky to have a beautiful girlfriend that seemed to love him. Toni had escaped the scene and was probably locked in his makeup studio as patrons questioned his relationship with the famous millionaire media tycoon. Will immediately went to handle damage control with his guests, denying all Joy's accounts, which were probably truer than we wanted to believe. The night was a disaster. Voices jumbled in my head as I tried to make sense of everything. The urge to throw up panged the pit of my stomach, so I ran full speed toward the exit, past the crowds of haters and judges and out the side door to the VIP parking lot. It was filled with luxury cars and trucks but it was quiet and isolated, exactly what I needed. I heaved against the building, only bringing up liquid that burned my throat on its way to the concrete. After wiping my lips with the back of my hand, I heard a car honk its horn in the distance. It was the limousine that Webby and I arrived in. I knew if there was one thing that I could do well, it was get a man to stay with me. I prepared for some serious begging but the important thing was that Webby waited for me. I rejoiced internally that Joy's plan hadn't worked like she thought it would as I walked to the black limo and pulled open the door.

"Get in." Webby's voice sounded deeper than usual, low and eerie. I wasn't going to walk home, so I cast my fear aside and did as I was told.

I slid into the limo and shut the door behind me. It took a minute for my eyes to settle with the darkness of the cabin and the LED lights that clung to the side panels and drink bar. The lights left a creepy glow against Webby's upset face. He looked possessed by demons as his dark skin faded into the background and the coldness of his eyes were the only flicker of light. He sat sprawled across the black leather. I could tell he was trying to seem calm and cool but his fidgeting said otherwise. How was I going to talk my way out of this one?

"Webby, let me apologize," I offered.

He lifted his hand quickly and waved my apology to the wind like he knew it was coming and didn't want to waste time on it. Without a word, he tapped the window dividing the driver from the back cabin and in seconds the driver exited the limo and walked around the building and out of sight.

"You think I'm a fool, Nicole?" Webby's voice was controlled but his face was filled with hatred.

"N-n-no. Of course not. I love…"

Before I could finish my sentence, his shoe connected with the front of my face and my head swung backward against the leather. I held my face in my hands, stunned by the blow. What just happened?

"You think I'm going to let you make a fool of me in front of my colleagues, huh?"

He kicked me three times, all landing in my chest and abdomen as I grunted with each blow. I tasted the blood in my mouth from biting my tongue. I spit it out onto the dark carpet of the limo.

"Wait, please!" I shielded myself with my hands as Webby lurched across the cabin and pounded me with his fists until I lay crumpled against the door, heaving and spitting blood with each breath.

"I'll kill yo' ass if you EVER disrespect me again! You understand me?!" he yelled against my face, which had lodged between the door and seat. I nodded in answer and he grabbed a fistful of my hair to turn my mangled, battered face to his. "You lucky I love you or I'd kill you right here, right now. Now tell me you love me."

"I l-l-love y-y-you," I sputtered, swallowing my bloody spit.

"I should leave your ass on the street after what you did but I'm not that type of guy. You see what you make me do? I won't let you bring the worst out of me, Nicole." He jabbed his finger into my forehead. "I thought I was past all this shit with my ex. I took it easy on her but you…you ain't gonna leave me for nobody else, especially not a woman." Webby settled back on his seat, chuckling to his cell phone.

"I'm sorry, baby," I whispered, trying to pull myself up on the seat but my ribs grated inside me, so I slumped back on the floor.

"I know you're sorry. A sorry excuse for a woman, but I blame that on your parents for raising you like that. I'm going to make you a good woman one way or another. Or I'm going to give your ass the boot."

"Don't leave me," I begged as I held my side that raged with a burning heat that was almost unbearable.

"That's not the boot I was talking about..." Webby corrected as he texted quietly until the driver returned. The engine rumbled as the limo came to life and pulled from the rear parking lot, past the front entrance that raged with paparazzi still clawing to get the latest story. Little did they know, some secrets were better left stored deep in the closet, never to see the light of day. I looked out the window at the paparazzi and hoped that I'd finally made it in the industry. The story was going to surface first thing in the morning and my name would be in all the headlines. The movie was bound to surge up the charts from all the publicity and I had a rich man that wouldn't abandon me even when he saw all the skeletons in my closet. I dabbed the blood from the corner of my mouth with my tongue and smiled. What was success without a little bloodshed?

Note from the Author

First, I want to thank you for reading my work. I know we all have busy lives and sharing my imaginary characters with you hopefully felt like a vacation from the madness. As you may already know, this is my first novel. I've poured a lot of love and time into this project, creating characters I thought you'd fall in love with or despise with a passion. I've learned so much about myself as an author and I'm sure I will continue to grow with time. If you find it in your heart to follow my work, look for my future novel, *Girl Soldier*, releasing late 2014 and link to my novellas, short stories, flash fiction and poetry on my website (www.trhorne.com). Thanks again!

Book Clubs or those wondering about the characters and background work on this novel, view my website for reader's discussion topics.

Acknowledgements

First, let me thank God for all the blessings he's shown me throughout my life. I've been blessed with a great family, good health and supportive friends. What more could I ask for, right? Well, I was going to ask for this debut to be a national bestseller but then that's just being greedy, right? ;0)

I would like to thank my closest friends who have given me the courage to do something I always dreamed of but second guessed in myself. Kim Fambro, Rahsheda Stamps, Joel Robertson (for your ideas and encouragement to finish), Tiffany Stevenson (for listening to me rant about the book non-stop), Teesha and Jherrod (good friends and good times), Ted Hackney (for reading an unedited excerpt…brave soul), Brother Juan and family (for the gumbo when I needed it most) and even friends I haven't spoken to that gave me material to pull from, Mary "Shay" Smith, Asya "Beanie" Beyah-Salaam-Washum and Tyesha "Tiki" Walker. Even though time and circumstance may push us apart, the foundation is too strong to crumble even when the house itself may blow away due to the storms in our lives. I love you ladies!

Special thanks go to my cover designers Jelena and Mr. Cedic – You have a great ability to design straight from the heart. Also, my copyeditor, Michael Mandarano, for his keen eyes, thoughtful emails and encouraging comments.

Now, I want to thank my friends in Japan for their constant understanding of my typing away on the keyboard like a madwoman or being sidetracked in the middle of our conversations. Mike (for your wild stories), Charles (for my spiritual enlightenment) and Kameek, (the girl whose laugh can be heard 'round the world). Thanks for making me realize the world was still moving without me being fully engaged in it. Thank you to Byrd Elementary staff who allowed me to spread my love of writing to the youth.

Last but certainly not least, I thank my family across the nation. Through your positivity and guidance I was able to fulfill a lifelong goal. So, to my mother, Renee Brunson for believing I could accomplish anything; my Dad, Terrance Horne, for reminding me that I'm his little girl, no matter how hard I try to be a grown up; my sister and brothers, Jessica, Nikko, Tee and Brian for being competitive with me, pushing me to be better and loving me no matter what; my stepmother, Leslie, for telling me I was smart and beautiful until I wouldn't accept hearing otherwise; my aunts, Debra (for your strength in the face of cancer) and Robin, for keeping me laughing and reminding me of "choking on cuteness" at every reunion; my cousin, Darry, for being my first business partner (remember our candy stand on John Ave.?); my Mema, for sharing our family history with me; my Grandma, for sneaking hot pickles, spicy lemons and hot candy to me as a child when my mom said "oh no, not my kids"…oh yes, your kids did…and I've passed my love of hot food to your grandson…so we win. And lastly, for those I lost and miss dearly, Popo and Grandma Sydelle…I know you are watching over me, especially on those bumpy plane rides to the states.

This acknowledgement wouldn't be complete if I didn't include my "Sweetie Pie" Caden. From the moment you were born, I changed. Thank you for making me a better person than I was. I can't remember my life without you, it's pretty hazy but in my heart, I don't think it was as exciting as it is with you here. I just pray that as you age, you remember why we named you 'Soldier of Justice'. Next is Yoshi, my black lab/Rottweiler mix that always found a way to remind me to go outside and play every once in a while. Most importantly, I give thanks to my husband, Bijai. Thank you for encouraging me to follow my dreams, no matter how outlandish they sound (I'm going to start my doctorate program while writing a novel and opening my own business). You always said, "How can I help?" and that's the mark of a truly great husband. You were my first audience when talking about the storyline and you kept me on task, giving great ideas that are incorporated in the story. Thank you for taking up the slack with the dirty dishes and late night meals. I think if it's a national bestseller, you might forgive me for all my shortcomings this year…(*hint, hint readers*)

Only time will tell! Thanks to all the old and new fans that keep reading alive and give an old indie writer like myself a chance to be heard. I hope you all enjoyed the product of my imagination. Remember to share your feelings about the book to help me get the word out a bit. Money is tight in this economy and word of mouth is the best free marketing. If you're interested in more about me, future books and reader's guides, make sure to join the fan club at www.trhorne.com .

55879891R00175

Madė in the USA
Charleston, SC
08 May 2016